PENGUIN BOOKS

BLONDE ROOTS

'Who would have thought it possible? A dazzling, hilarious, funky and utterly contemporary novel about the transatlantic slave trade. I can think of no other

Glasgow libraries

Elderpark Library
228a Langlands Road
Glasgow G51 3TZ
Phone: 0141 276 1540

This book is due for return on or before the last date s ʌ. It may be renewed by telephone, personal application, fax or p this date, author, title and the book number.

WITHDRAWN

KT-382-038

Glasgow Life and its service brands, including Glasgow Libraries, (found at www.glasgowlife.org.uk) are operating names for Culture and Sport Glasgow.

Glasgow
CITY COUNCIL

slavery – with white Europeans as the slaves – and is incredibly inventive and funny' Kira Cochrane, *Guardian*

'A clever, turn-the-world-on-its-head novel, a book about slavery that provides a wonderfully opposite slant on what terms such as "black" and "white" might mean' Kate Mosse, *The Times*

'A brilliant satire whose flashes of comedy make the underlying tragedy all the more poignant' *Scotland on Sunday*

'Bernardine Evaristo rises to a new challenge with every book. Her reimagining of history is by turns provocative, illuminating, moving and entertaining – what more can one ask for?' Margaret Busby, editor of *Daughters of Africa*

'Sharp, witty, funny, unflinching and at times painful, *Blonde Roots* raises deep questions, challenges received wisdoms and plumbs new depths of compassion and empathy' Chris Abani, author of *Graceland*

'One of the remarkable achievements of the book is its ability to take on a horrendous subject such as transatlantic slavery, in which millions of Africans perished, and, while never losing sight of the seriousness of the subject, the writer still manages to make us laugh' *Calabash Magazine*

'A pleasingly subversive, well-crafted novel of slavery and deliverance that turns conventions – and the world – upside down' *Kirkus*

'It is an education in the history that was stripped from a proud people, told in perhaps the only way that would compel the public to pay attention. It is a marvellous achievement, as both a fiction and an argument, and is certainly a book for our times' *Halftribe*

'How on earth do we help an ethnic majority understand the realities of racism? . . . *Blonde Roots* is the daring and shocking result . . . Evaristo's writing is vibrant, but interspersed with a biting wit. Hers is an alien universe that bears enough echoes of our own for the book to be deliberately unsettling' *Culture Watch*

'An astonishing, uncomfortable and beautiful alternative history that goes back several centuries to flip the slave trade . . . Evaristo's intellectually rigorous narrative constantly surprises. This difficult and provocative book is a conversation sparker' *Publishers Weekly*

ABOUT THE AUTHOR

Bernardine Evaristo is the award-winning Anglo-Nigerian author of several books of fiction and verse fiction that explore aspects of the African diaspora: past, present, real, imagined. Her novel *Girl, Woman, Other* won the Booker Prize in 2019. Her writing also spans short fiction, reviews, essays, drama and writing for radio. She is Professor of Creative Writing at Brunel University, London, and Vice Chair of the Royal Society of Literature. She was made an MBE in 2009.

As a literary activist for inclusion, Bernardine has founded a number of successful initiatives, including Spread the Word writer development agency (1995–ongoing), the Complete Works mentoring scheme for poets of colour (2007–2017) and the Brunel International African Poetry Prize (2012–ongoing).

www.bevaristo.com

Blonde Roots

BERNARDINE EVARISTO

PENGUIN BOOKS

PENGUIN BOOKS

UK | USA | Canada | Ireland | Australia
India | New Zealand | South Africa

Penguin Books is part of the Penguin Random House group of companies
whose addresses can be found at global.penguinrandomhouse.com.

Penguin
Random House
UK

First published by Hamish Hamilton 2008
Published in Penguin Books 2009
Reissued 2020

019

Copyright © Bernardine Evaristo, 2008

The moral right of the author has been asserted

Printed and bound in Great Britain by Clays Ltd, Elcograf S.p.A.

A CIP catalogue record for this book is available from the British Library

ISBN: 978–0–141–03152–1

www.greenpenguin.co.uk

MIX
Paper from
responsible sources
FSC
www.fsc.org FSC® C018179

Penguin Random House is committed to a
sustainable future for our business, our readers
and our planet. This book is made from Forest
Stewardship Council® certified paper.

Remembering the 10 to 12 million Africans
taken to Europe and the Americas as slaves
. . . and their descendants
1444–1888

Contents

Book Three

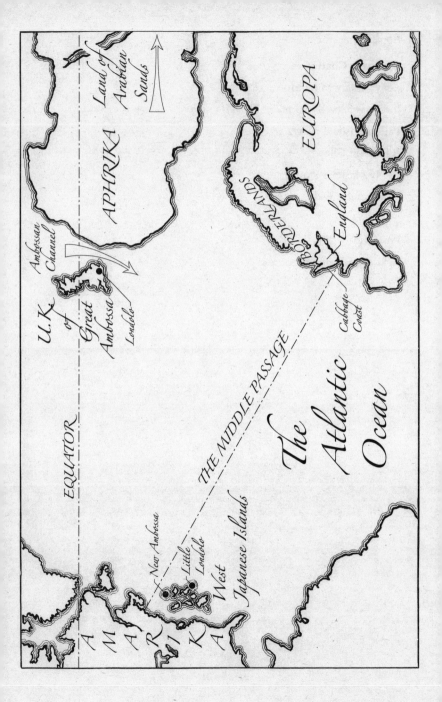

All things are subject to interpretation: whichever interpretation prevails at a given time is a function of power and not truth

Nietzsche

Book One

Oh Lord Take Me Home

So while my boss Bwana and his family are out clinking rum-and-coke glasses and shaking their wobbly backsides at fancy parties down the road, I've been assigned duties in his office to sort through his ledgers. I used to hope that the celebration of Voodoomass would be the one day off in the year for us slaves – but oh no, it's business as usual.

Outside the window the palm trees which line the avenues are decorated with gold and silver streamers. They are tall, sleek, snooty with the deportment of those who grow up balancing the precious milk of coconuts on their heads; and dangling from their glossy green fronds are flickering oil lamps sitting in red-painted cassava gourds.

The cobblestone pavement has been swept smooth of yesterday's sandstorm and the hawkers selling takeaways have been sent packing.

Frogs and crickets provide a drunken night-time chorus while camel-drawn carriages deliver stoosh party guests to our neighbouring compounds. The men wear flamboyant kaftans and their glamorously fat women try to outdo each other with peacock-print headscarves tied up into the most extravagant girlie bows.

All the houses are freshly whitewashed, with stained-glass windows depicting the gods: Oshan, Shangira, Yemonja. Stone sphinxes guard porches and stationed by doorways are torch lamps on tall marble plinths – their flames are slippery blue fingers grasping out at the sticky night-time air.

From the upper rooms of the houses blast the hectic

electronic beats of the young, and from downstairs comes the mellow music of the marimba, amid the laughter and bantering of people who have every reason to celebrate this season of goodwill, because they are free men and free women in the heart of the most expensive piece of real estate in the known world: Mayfah.

Chief Kaga Konata Katamba I is the Bwana in question. He made his fortune in the import-export game, the notorious transatlantic slave run, before settling down to life in polite society as an absentee sugar baron, part-time husband, freelance father, retired decent human being and, it goes without saying, sacked soul.

My boss is also a full-time anti-abolitionist, publishing his pro-slavery rants in his mouthpiece *The Flame* – a pamphlet distributed far and wide – as a freebie.

In spite of myself, I'd just begun to flick through the latest godawful issue, feeling my stomach constrict and my throat tighten, when a hand shoved a folded note through the open office window and vanished before I could see who it was attached to.

I opened the note, read the magic words and felt my head suddenly drowning.

Waves crashed and thundered inside my skull.

I let out the most almighty, silent howl.

Then I passed out.

How long for, I've no idea, maybe a few minutes, but when I came to I was slumped in my seat, my head dropped forwards, the note still in my hand.

I read it again through a film of water.

It was real and it was true – I was being given the chance to escape.

Oh Lord.

After so many years on the waiting list the thing I most desired was in the palm of my hand. Yet it was all too quick. I sat there frozen. A thousand *what ifs* ran through my mind. In returning my life to its rightful owner – me – I would also be putting my life at stake. If I wasn't careful or lucky I'd end up at the local whipping post or chopping block.

Then my survival instincts kicked in.

My head cleared.

I was back again.

I ripped the note to shreds.

I stood up and looked at the wooden mask of Bwana's face on the wall.

And I gave it the right, royal one finger salute.

The note told me that the Underground Railroad was operating again after service had been suspended owing to derailment. It was often the case when energy couldn't be filched from the city's power station or the train broke down due to the overload of escaping slaves wanting to cadge a safe ride out of the city, to begin the long journey back to the Motherland.

I hoped I could trust the message because the Resistance was often infiltrated by sleepers who eventually went operational to betray whole rebel cells.

Deep down I knew that the slave traders were never going to give up their cash cow. It was, after all, one of the most lucrative international businesses *ever*, involving the large-scale transport of whytes, shipped in our millions from the continent of Europa to the West Japanese Islands, so called because when the 'great' explorer and adventurer, Chinua Chikwuemeka, was trying to find a new route to Asia, he mistook those islands for the legendary isles of Japan, and the name stuck.

So here I am in the United Kingdom of Great Ambossa (UK or GA for short), which is part of the continent of Aphrika. The mainland lies just over the Ambossan Channel. It's also known as the Sunny Continent, of course, on account of it being so flaming hot here.

Great Ambossa is actually a very small island with a growing population to feed and so it stretches its greedy little fingers all over the globe, stealing countries and stealing people.

Me included. I'm one of the Stolen Ones.

That's why I'm here.

The note gave me only one hour to get to the disused Paddinto Station and directions on how to find the manhole hidden behind some bushes through which I could slip down into the subway. There I would be met by a member of the Resistance who would lead me through its dank subterranean tunnels. That was the promise, anyway, and if it wasn't the practice I'd be done for.

Slavery had taught me that promises never came with a money-back guarantee and if you complained to customer services they'd report you to management and then you'd really get it in the neck.

But I am a firm believer in hope. I am still alive, after all.

The city of Londolo's Tube trains had officially stopped burrowing many years ago when the tunnels started collapsing under the weight of the buildings above them. The city returned to the slower but more reliable modes of transport: carriages, horses, carts, camels, elephants, stagecoaches and, for the really nutty fitness fanatics, velocipedes. The only vehicle we slaves owned was called Shanks's Pony.

But here's the thing: at some point, a bright spark in the Resistance had a brainwave and the disused subway was put to use, enabling many to make their way out of the heavily guarded city of Londolo as far as the docks, where they began the long, hazardous trip back to Europa.

For the first time since I had been taken away, I could seriously consider that I might be returning home. Was it possible? I still had such vivid memories of my parents, my three sisters, our little flint cottage on the estate, and my beloved cocker spaniel, Rory. My family were probably all dead now, if they had survived the raids by the Border Lander men who had been my first captors.

The Ambossans called us tribes but we were many nations, each with our own language and funny old customs, like the Border Landers, whose men wore tartan skirts with no knickers underneath.

The Ambossans also called Europa the Grey Continent, on account of the skies always being overcast.

But oh, how I longed for those cloudy grey skies.

How I longed for the incessant drizzle and harsh wind slapping my ears.

How I longed for my snug winter woollies and sturdy wooden clogs.

How I longed for Mam's warm dripping sandwiches and thick pumpkin broth.

How I longed for the fire crackling in the hearth and our family sing-song around it.

How I longed for the far northern district from whence I was taken.

How I longed for England.

How I longed for home.

I am proud to declare that I come from a long line of cabbage farmers.

My people were honest peasants who worked the land and never turned to theft even when it snowed in summer or rained all winter so that the crops miscarried in their pods and turned to mulch.

We weren't landowners, oh no, we were *serfs*, the bottom link in the agricultural food chain, although no actual chains clinked on the ground when we walked around. Nor were we property, exactly, but our roots went deep into the soil because when the land changed hands through death, marriage or even war, so did we, and so tied we remained, for generation upon generation.

The deal was that we were leased some fields by our master, Lord Perceval Montague (Percy, behind his back), the umpteenth eldest son in the family to whom my family had an umbilical bond. In return all male serfs were conscripted to be foot soldiers in his battles, and believe you me it was a lawless society back then. It was pretty wild in the far north in those days. If someone wanted to raid your land or steal your flock, they did it through brute force, unless you were able to meet fire with gunpowder, or rally a private army to defend yourself, even if it was just a motley crew of shambolic farmhands.

So we worked our patch of land, as well as Percy's.

Whatever we harvested, we had to give half to him.

He was supposed to offer poor relief, but rarely did.

We were charged for extras such as taking his cart to go to market or using his grain mill or bread oven, which, if we had poor harvests, meant a debt carried over on our annual accounts for several years.

Montague Manor was an imposing pile of granite, tomb-like slabs framed against skies which shuddered beneath the chain mail of the north's daily bout of rain.

It proved an irresistible attraction to us kids yet I was the only one of my sisters with enough derring-do to risk succumbing to the lure of the big house.

Once, when everyone was at the annual summer fayre on the estate, my sisters peeping through some bushes as cowardly witnesses, I sneaked in through the manor's heavy wooden door into the cavernous Grand Hall. I tried to tiptoe, but my clogs echoed around the high ceiling.

The walls were hung with tapestries of fair maidens stroking the horns of unicorns, reindeer antlers spread out like the branches of trees, and a massive bear's head with salivating gnashers was stuck up directly opposite the front door. Its wet, limpid eyes followed my every move.

When I heard moans coming from deep underneath the ground, I panicked, about-turned and charged out, bumping into a stuffed wolf by the front door, which looked ready to lurch and take a bite. The moans must have come from Percy's legendary dungeons where he imprisoned poachers and captives from the Border skirmishes. Eventually they'd be packed off for the long trek through the forests to the next ship docked on the coast bound for the New World – or so we'd heard.

To us peasants the New World was a distant land far across the seas about which we knew nothing, except that no one wanted to go there, because those that did never came back.

Home was Apple Tree Cottage on the edge of the estate. A hotchpotch of timber beams and earth-packed walls. It was infested with rustling insects. Indeed the whole house was alive with vermin – from the wasps nesting in the straw-thatched roof to the body-hopping fleas for whom our blood was the elixir of life. A front door opened onto a tiny parlour with an earthen floor and a peat fire. Two sleeping spaces were separated by heavy green woollen drapes either side of the corridor which served as the kitchen. We couldn't afford window glass because of the tax, and so with the shutters closed it was always winter inside.

Me, Madge, Sharon and Alice shared a straw mattress. We slept under a multicoloured quilt made out of cast-offs stitched by two great-aunts who'd died before we were born. I bagsyed the middle, kept warm by my sisters during those freezing north-easterly nights.

Then there was Rory the dog who was always bounding around knocking things over even though he wasn't 'a puppy no more', as Mam'd shout. Her foot would send him on an impromptu long jump from which he'd land with a squeal, legs comically splayed flat.

Our Pa and our Mam were Mr Jack and Eliza Scagglethorpe.

Pa's muscles clung to him in hard sinews because there was little fat to shelter his bones. He had a bushy scrag-end of a beard which he 'couldn't be arsed' to trim and his cheeks were blistered from where the bitter winds had rubbed them raw. He had the stoop of a thin tree blown forwards by a gale, because he'd been planting and digging up cabbages since he was a tiny kid.

Pa's hair was the dark ginger of the folk from the Border Lands. It fell to his shoulders in spirals beneath the wide-brimmed farmer's hat he always wore when outdoors.

Before I was old enough to know better he'd roll up his smock, instruct me to put a finger to the throbbing pulse of the veins on his arms and tell me centipedes lived inside them. I'd run away shrieking with him chasing me, both of us knocking over stools, pails and my sisters in the process.

Pa was passionate about his cabbages, said they had to be treated lovingly, like children. What didn't I know about flaming cabbages! January King was 'crispy and full of flavour', the Autumn Queen was dark green and the Savoy King was 'a tough little bugger'. What didn't I know about the Cabbage Wars of old, when the Scagglethorpes had fought victoriously for the Montagues against the Paldergraves?

I hated eating cabbage in those BS (Before Slavery) days.

What I'd give for one now.

Pa never once complained about not having a son but we all knew what was on his mind, because sometimes when he looked at us, his disappointment was undisguised.

Who was going to carry on the Scagglethorpe cabbage farming tradition?

He'd always shake it off, though.

'Go on,' he'd urge us girls. 'Tell me I have one wish.'

'What wish?'

'Don't be so stupid. Tell me I have a wish. That you can grant me.'

'But we don't have special powers, we're not fairy godmothers.'

'It's a game, you silly lot, give me one wish or I'll throw a cabbage at your thick skulls.'

'All right then, Pa, you have one wish.'

'Well, now, let's see. What would I want? Oh, I know what I'd wish for,' he'd say, scratching his chin like the thought was just coming to him.

'To see my girls in those crinolines with expensive whale-bones that those ladies up there wear, pretty paste on your cheeks, pearls around your swan-like necks; to see you swirling around at dances with kindly gentlemen on your arms, winning smiles on your lips and glass slippers on your feet.'

'Oooh, don't be so soppy,' I'd say, before going to fetch the looking glass to see if my neck really was 'swan-like'.

That night I dreamed of a lacy, yellow crinoline with puffed-up sleeves. My gown was so *exquisite*, my glass slippers so dainty, that when I ran across the meadows, hair flowing in the wind, everyone gasped at how elegant I'd turned out.

Then I ruined it by getting bunions because the slippers were too tight and one of them cracked and the glass cut into my foot, waking me up with the pain of it.

Pa rose before daylight had kicked night-time into touch. He'd return after dark when he'd be mardy until he'd eaten.

He liked a tankard of ale (only ever admitted the one) of a Friday night after dinner when he'd go to Johnny Johnson's barn over at None-Go-By Farm for a 'wee session' with 'the lads' – all old men pushing forty. He'd come home reeking of the barley and herbs in his ale, singing a bawdy song which we could hear from fields off, then catching his breath as he leaned against the opened door frame blasting cold air into our parlour, ranting on about how 'the working man will have his day', before staggering inside in his manure-caked boots and collapsing into his chair, legs sprawled open, head thrown back so that his bristly Adam's apple stuck out and quivered.

'How are the *lads*?' Mam would say out loud once he was snoring, not looking up from her knitting needles which clacked like warring swords.

I'll never forget the first time it was my turn to take Pa hot bread and dripping for lunch.

The clouds had sunk so low from the heavens I couldn't find him for ages, until there he was, looming out of the fog, one hand rested on his pitchfork, looking for all the world like a scarecrow, and I suddenly saw how all the back-breaking work had drained him.

He was singing, but not one of his usual smutty songs which made us girls giggle and our Mam scowl. Instead he sounded like one of the choir boys at church whose voices hadn't become coarse and mud-filled and angry from years of breaking up icy ground with shovels, slopping out donkey shit or chopping wood for hours in freezing winter dressed in rough sackcloth, with their bare feet shod only in clogs.

It was the voice of the boy inside the man. The child inside my father.

His heart was full of yearning, for something he'd lost or wanted to have.

My heart crumbled like stale bread.

Are you going to Scarborough Fayre?
Parsley, sage, rosemary and thyme,
Remember me to one who lives there,
She once was a true love of mine.

On my tenth birthday it was my turn to go out onto the fields blindfold to pull up the first cabbage of the season. Aged ten you'd already survived the pox, the sweat and just about every other disease that spirited children away early, so it was likely you might grow to adulthood. If the cabbage came up with a lot of earth attached it meant you'd be rich, if not then you'd be poor.

That spring dawn we all trekked across the damp grass and past trees beginning to unfurl the tiny lavender-coloured petals of blossom.

I'd already decided on my career path. I was going to become one of those rare silk-trading women, like that young Margaret Roper from the village at Duddingley who went off on the back of a cart and came back in her own carriage. Like her I'd be apprenticed for seven years, then I'd run my own business. First I had to persuade Pa to persuade Percy to let me go. I knew Pa would scoff at the idea of one of his silly daughters becoming a proper businesswoman.

It didn't put me off.

The debt would take many years to pay off but eventually I'd be rich enough to settle it myself.

I had it all sorted.

As you do, when you're ten.

The cabbage came up with a huge clump of sod attached.

I did a cartwheel, singing out, 'Wey, hey, hey, the cat and fiddle and the cow jumped over the moon.'

Oh, so it really sodding worked then, didn't it?

Memories would not get me to the station on time.

I flew out of Bwana's office like a leopard on cola nuts and rushed across the compound, the largest in the city. Across the freshly sprinkled, squeaky-green lawn, past the rockery studded with cacti, past the wide-hipped, big-mama palms of the pineapple grove, past the orange and pink slides and round-abouts of the adventure playground, past the saccharine scent of the mangosteen, pawpaw and vanilla trees, past the open-air swimming pool with mosquitoes buzzing over its stagnant surface, past the camel paddocks, and behind all that, finally, to the secreted slave quarters, which had been considerately built next to the sewage dump and pigs' pen.

There I entered the tiny hut I shared with my room-mates: Yomisi and Sitembile.

Yomisi was in her thirties, like me. Only she'd been born Gertraude Shultz on a wheat farm in Bavaria. Aged eighteen she was kidnapped by slave-catchers as she made her way back from church one chilly Sunday morning, foolishly taking the short cut across the graveyard. She eventually ended up in Londolo, sleeping side by side with yours truly. It was an unlikely bonding: I was the optimist, she the pessimist. I clutched my return ticket to my chest, always dreaming of escape; she'd ripped hers to shreds the very first time she was gang-raped by her three kidnappers shortly after capture.

She'd been hell-bent on revenge ever since.

Yomisi was Bwana's cook. Steel-thin, green-eyed, heavy-lidded, she was forced to wear an iron muzzle in the kitchen to prevent her eating on the job. It encaged her face in metal bands which clamped a perforated plate over her mouth. A lock secured this contraption at the back.

Her lips cracked. Her mouth dehydrated. Her tongue swelled. Her gums bled.

Even when the muzzle was removed at night she spoke through gritted teeth.

Sometimes Bwana vomited the night away or one of his children ran a fever. The runs were commonplace. Bwana's regular hallucinations bordered on insanity, and the entire family frequently broke out in rashes so unbearable they could be seen clawing off layers of skin in a communal frenzy.

All fingers pointed to the juju of Bwana's business enemies, none at the passive, stick-like cook.

Crushed glass.

Rotten meat disguised by strong herbs and spices.

Fungi.

Plants she would not name.

It was the only thing that gave her pleasure.

My second room-mate was the cheery young Sitembile, who was in her early twenties. She liked to remind we lesser mortals that she was born Princess Olivia de Champfleur-Saxe-Coburg-Grimaldi-Bourbon-Orleans-Hapsburg in a palace in the ancient land of Monaco. Taken hostage in a war with the French, she was sold into captivity when her father the King wouldn't pay for the release of a girl child when he already had five sons in line to inherit the crown.

Sitembile held the honoured position of household toilet

cleaner, emptying approximately fifty toilet pots each morning, before spending the rest of the day scooping out the bog holes and hosing them down with lime disinfectant to deter bugs and flies.

When time allowed, and it rarely did, she sat on our stoop, chattering away, embarking on a conversation in her head, letting the listener in halfway through and then being surprised when we complained we didn't have a clue what she was going on about.

She'd sit there twisting her hair into pigtails mixed with clay, rubbing ochre into her skin to darken its pigment in the hope that she might be spotted by one of Bwana's nicer, younger, more handsome business associates and be whisked away to a new life as a favoured mistress. With substantial curves either side of a naturally tiny waist, it was just possible.

Yomisi tried to dampen Sitembile's enthusiasm with her oft-declared dictum that dreams and disappointment were inseparable bedfellows.

I helped rub ochre into Sitembile's smooth, undamaged back, countering that dreams kept our spirits buoyant.

We three women had slipped into each other's lives and found a way to be together.

Now I was slipping out.

Without saying a word.

Our shack was constructed out of corrugated iron which was boiling on summer nights. Not for us the fancy, cool, white-washed wattle-and-daub residences spread out at the top end of the compound with palm-thatched roofs and mangrove posts and windows and wraparound verandas. No, we either roasted or we froze in our grubby tin boxes, and our neighbour next door was a twelve-foot-high termite mound, which we daren't disturb as it would most likely rebuild itself inside our dwelling.

As I entered our hut I knew that the others would be occupied elsewhere in the compound because we never stopped working. Even when it seemed that every job was completed, Madama Blessing, Bwana's imperious Number One wife, kept everyone busy. The story goes that she was once the sweetest young virgin in town, but that after years of marriage to Bwana, and his accumulation of more and more wives for her to control, the power had gone to her head and she had turned into the gargoyle we all knew and hated.

That day she had been wearing a chunky gold chain which hung from the folds of her neck, with a ruby and diamond-studded Akua'ba fertility doll as pendant. It was quite ridiculous when she was obviously post-menopausal. A gold ring in the shape of a snarling lion's head leapt from her manicured hands so that even when she was trying to be nice you were reminded that she wasn't. A beautiful glazed-ivory bone shot through her nose and a lip plug pierced through her bottom lip showed she was a woman with a husband (like anyone needed reminding).

On this most festive of days she had woken up in one of her charming early-morning moods and ordered every available slave to get down on their hands and knees and scrub the immeasurable lengths of her cherished beige flagstone floors – with soap and a nailbrush. To get deep into the grooves, she explained, sweeping her eyes at the assembled bare feet of her staff before propelling her bulk from the hips and shoulders down the hallway with all the grace of a three-legged, half-blind, three-thousand-pound hippo.

As the eyes are the window of the soul, if she had bothered to look into ours, she would have seen an axe murderer in each and every one of them.

Madama Blessing herself had large startled eyes which dominated her face and when they swooped and swerved you prayed they would not rest on you, because if they did it would be with shocked outrage at a crime for which you had to be punished, even though you had not committed it yet. At the same time she had bucket-loads of self-pity, which was often the case with our masters – *they* were the injured ones, not us. She wore her favourite outfit made out of Adinkra cloth. It was stamped with the design known as *Atamfo Atwameho*, which means 'Enemies Surround Me'.

I gathered up a bundle of my clothing and threw it into a basket, grabbed a wrappa and whipped it over my shoulders. It would hide the nice personalised tattoos which ran across my shoulders. As was the fashion with slave society, the name of my first mistress, Panyin Ige Ghika – P.I.G. – was inscribed.

I was once the companion of P.I.G.'s daughter – Little Miracle.

Oh Little Miracle – more about her later.

When Bwana bought me he had me tattooed with his initials too – K.K.K.

Can you imagine having a red-hot poker searing into your skin? Twice? The delayed shock reaction as it sizzles and smokes, then the warm bloody tears streaming down your arms and spine?

I didn't have much to take with me. We didn't wear much because of the heat, which I never did get used to, nor to the Ambossan dress code – the wraparound wrappas – or having to go barefoot, which felt so uncomfortable, especially when I had such fond memories of wearing clogs. How I longed for their cool moulded insoles; to feel a mild shudder when the wood impacted on hard ground. And going topless is no joke when you've had three children and your breasts swing like soggy butternut squash. And don't get me started on the hairstyle Madama Blessing insisted I adopt as the household's most high-status slave. My long straight blonde hair was threaded through with wire and put into plaited hoops all over my head. I wanted to protest that we whytes just didn't have the bone structure to carry it off. But she expected me to look respectable when I opened the door to her distinguished guests and not like some uncouth wretch from Europa. The guests were usually Members of the House of Governors, the UK's ruling body, many of them fellow plantation owners who had purchased a seat in the House.

All these thoughts were whirring around in my brain as I raked through the sandy ground beneath my sleeping pallet and brought up an old goatskin pouch filled with forty-six cowrie-pounds. I had managed to pilfer a shell here and there over the long years while out shopping for Bwana and his family. I always hoped I would need them one day.

I quietly shut the door, checking the coast was clear. I put my basket on my head and crept through a gap in the bushes. It led to a back alley which was the means by which we slaves sneaked in and out of the compound to engage in romantic trysts with our lovers, myself included, although I had been single a long time. I was a very monogamous person, holding onto the one-man, one-woman practice of my own culture, no matter how much the polygamous Ambossans ridiculed it as uneconomical, selfish, typically hypocritical and just plain backwards.

The love of my life had been Frank. His slave name was Ndumbo, but I never called him that in private. A maker and mender of things, he was a renowned carpenter. He said he never felt more alive than when facing the silent congregation of the severed limbs of the forest at their mortuary – the logging camp at Golda's Green. There they underwent seasoning by the elements until ready to be reincarnated into functional or decorative artefacts by their High Priest – my Frank.

Frank was over six feet tall, broad-shouldered, dark haired – a gentleman.

He never once spoke sharply to me, or bossed me around, and whenever he smiled at me, it was with an appreciation which took a while for me to accept. I was so used to being taken for granted.

We spent what free time we could together and our pleasures were, by necessity, simple:

Sharing a slice of coconut rum cake Yomisi had pilfered from the kitchen.

Lying in the grass and counting the stars in the night sky.

The wooden bangles and anklets he made for me, engraved on the inside with my name and his.

I secretly taught him to write his name on a slate: Frank Adam Merryweather, son of Frank William Merryweather, of Hull, England.

The look on his face when it was first accomplished without any spelling mistakes. How he beamed like an elated child.

At night Frank's dexterous carpenter's hands roamed so expertly over the contours of my back and limbs that my deadened body was resensitised and reshaped into a work of art.

The next day I'd go about my duties with softened bones and looser joints and weightless muscles and a wandering mind that could settle on nothing and no one but him.

Frank was such a harmless man, but his mistress, that five-foot-nothing Madama Subria, accused him of sexually assaulting her and reported him to her husband. He sold Frank on to one of the islands of West Japan but not before he'd endured fifty lashes of the cat-o'-nine-tails at the whipping post at Cumburlasgar Gateway up the road. Every slave in the neighbourhood was forced to attend.

Imagine how I felt watching that? Poor Frank's shredded back. His stubborn silence, then pitiful mewls, until he let rip such terrible screams they tore open the fabric of the skies.

The irony was that Madama Subria was always trying to seduce him with her petulant pouts and hip-hugging lappas, flouncing about, rolling her ample Ambossan bottom (so that each cheek moved independently of the other – quite a feat) whenever he walked behind her in the corridor. He ignored her advances until one day she got him to repair the hinges on the gold and ivory chest in the master bedroom. She suddenly stripped off her clothes and stood there completely starkers.

What you have to understand is that Madama Subria was as spoilt as every other mistress of means. When you have an army of slaves at your beck and call you expect to get what you want when you want it.

Lesson Number One – slaves do not reject their masters' advances.

My man learned that the hard way.

She was livid. She took her revenge.

We slaves don't end relationships. Other people do it for us. Often we don't start them either, other people do it for us. We're encouraged to breed merely to increase the workforce.

My three were sold on.

Each time they promised I could keep the child. A bold-faced lie, because some expectant mothers would rather kill themselves if they knew their child was going to be taken away at birth.

As I went into labour, crouched on a tattered raffia mat, the midwife, Ma Ramla (Sigfrieda, from Germany), mopped my brow with a damp cloth, burned sandalwood joss sticks, held me from behind and encouraged me to push.

Each child was placed into the guardianship of a wet nurse, until they were sold. Another strategy, I discovered, because it had been known for mothers to become uncontrollably violent when told to hand over the infant they had breastfed for months.

Two girls and a boy.

I never saw my children again.

Sometimes, when I place my hand over my stomach, I can still feel their little kicks.

I remember how carrying the extra weight of a child filled me up.

How I'd sing nursery rhymes to them in the womb:

Little Bow Peep has lost her sheep
And doesn't know where to find them.
Leave them alone and they will come home
Bringing their tails behind them.

I remember Frank was there at the birth of the first child, squeezing my hand.

His silence for months afterwards.

How we never spoke of our loss.

How he never attended the second or third births.

Just as well.

*

I still dream that my children will come searching for me.

Somehow – they will find their mother.

Oh Lord.

I miss Frank every day.

When he was my lover, I never felt alone.

The back alley was deserted. Thank God it was dark. I had to exit onto our avenue before crossing down a side street and heading towards Edgwa District and then into Paddinto District. I put my head around the entrance. Gleaming gilt and chrome carriages were still arriving for the Voodoomass parties but it was otherwise deserted.

I would have to walk with the slow confidence of one allowed out at night. If a neighbour saw me the alarm would be raised. Freedom was within my grasp but my knee caps were being tapped by a sledgehammer. I struggled to stay upright. It would be so easy to slip back inside the compound.

Madama Blessing would be outraged at my escape, and having witnessed her response to imaginary crimes I dreaded to think how she'd behave if her anger could stand up in court, accuse me of the crimes of Ungratefulness and Dishonesty, and prove my guilt beyond Reasonable Doubt by presenting the Evidence (Caught Escaping) to a jury of her peers, all of whom were, like her, Ambossan slave owners.

As for Bwana, unlike his wife, he didn't waste his emotions, such as they were, on his slaves. He took disciplinary action when required with all the passion of a hard-headed businessman for whom slaves fell into either the profit or loss column. Take my children, for example. Bwana had no need for any more four-legged gurglers crawling around his compound who didn't carry his DNA in their genes, so it made sound business sense to enter them under the profit column.

As far as I could tell the only flame that set him alight was when he howled out at night from some woman's bed with such unbridled ferocity, we in the slaves' quarters felt our spines run cold.

Yet Bwana and his family were the known and here was I venturing into the dangerous unknown. I had become so much more than your non-achieving, low-flying slave. I had been elevated to the position of Bwana's personal secretary because I was articulate and bright (but not too clever, or so they thought).

The terms of my engagement stipulated that it was a job for life, that my hours should run from Monday to Sunday, 12 a.m. to 11.55 p.m. daily, although I needed to be available to do overtime when required. I would receive an annual wage of nothing with an added bonus of nothing for good behaviour but to expect forfeits in the form of beatings for any insolence, tardiness or absences.

Luckily, I was only knocked about a bit in the early days as part of my in-service training when my work report read: Attendance 100%. Punctuality 100%. Motivation 10%. *Could work harder and prone to distraction, i.e. daydreaming.* After that I met all my performance targets. I was also expected to look presentable at all times and I learned how to affect a pleasant smile devoid of any personal satisfaction. Our 'contentment' must never exceed theirs.

It was pretty standard for a domestic slave, and I have to say Bwana had no cause for complaint with me.

I was the perfect house wigger.

I peered down the avenue, hidden behind an enormous bread-fruit tree full of bulbous green fruit which was about to fall right down on my soft human head and splatter my brains about.

My heart rattled like dried peas in a gourd.

Another carriage clattered past with a laughing couple inside, its wheels and hooves kicking sand up into my face. I caught sight of the woman; it was that coquette Madama Subria.

I had watched her with tears pouring over my heart as she had observed Frank being tied up to a tree and whipped. She had been blinking, rapidly. At first I thought she was sorry for him, then it dawned on me that she was brimming with tears for herself. I read these people so well. It's very easy when you're invisible.

I could see how the Ambossans had hardened their hearts to our humanity. They convinced themselves that we do not feel as they do, so that they do not have to feel anything for us. It's very convenient and lucrative for them.

Madama Subria, I realised, had lost the hope of someone special to keep her entertained when she was bored. Mr Subria must have forced her to attend the whipping. These Ambossan women were usually much too 'faint-hearted' for that. He had a prestigious position as a senior executive with Baringso Bank plc.

Tall, funereal, he stood next to his attractive little wife with an uncharacteristic smile playing on his lips.

The carriage passed and I darted out of the alley.

Once I reached Edgwa District I felt safer. I walked underneath its famous entrance: two elephant-shaped tusks, which met in the middle as a grand arch, sixty magnificent feet high.

Edgwa, after the genteel refinement of Mayfah, was an assault on my senses, buzzing with crowds and booming with the bone-rattling thud of Aphro-beats from the music booths. It was famous for its bazaar which ran all day, all night, and for several miles down the litter-strewn thoroughfare of m'Aiduru Valley, another rich enclave of chiefs and their sprawling compounds. The Valley had a canal running through it which the residents used for an elite form of energy-efficient transport: slave-powered dug-out canoes. In this way they avoided the crowds and the red laterite soil of the market, which sprayed dust onto their clothes when dry and sank their feet into its mucky gunk when wet.

I feigned a mild interest in the stalls as I passed, to appear as if I was out running an errand for my master, my head held high, basket on top, hands dangling. Yet to walk too upright and proud was deemed a sign of uppityness. It was a fine balance to tread: inner dignity versus survival instincts. I needn't have worried because the only thing on the traders' minds was whether you were likely to buy, and if so how much they could unreasonably charge, at which point you were expected to haggle, to endure a battle of wits and willpower.

I passed overripe melons on stalls, their heads cleaved open, putridly sweet, cerise juice oozing out. They lolled like the heads of runaways who hadn't made it, black seed eyes staring spookily up at me.

I passed a gunsmith at work, an anvil placed between legs spread out on the ground.

Salesmen from the Cotton Marketing Board sold baskets of raw white cotton so seductive I resisted the urge to plunge my hands into the thick foamy softness.

I looked up just as a street seller thrust a fistful of four squirming, dying rats into my face. In his other hand were sachets of rat poison.

A tall, wiry young man was speed-walking towards me, balancing a plank of wood on his head some four feet long. I ducked under just in time.

Puffed-up matrons, walking off their feasts before resuming festivities later, pushed past me, their haughty faces marked with chalk and camwood, their thighs rubbing together like smacking lips.

Spiced chicken roasting on a spit almost made me faint with hunger as my revved-up adrenaline had by now burned up every ounce of carbohydrate from my last meal.

There were pyramids of red coffee beans, bowls of pink grapefruits, bolts of multicoloured waxed cloth, decorated bed-boards, carved tip-stools.

Hard green bananas, still on the stem, looked like bunches of upturned fingers.

Desert-salt looked like cakes of packed mud.

Many of the market traders were immigrants from North Aphrika and the Lands of the Arabian Sands, some of whom had been instrumental in the slave trade – the Business. They came to Slavery HQ with the most impressive CVs detailing their brilliant horsemanship and exemplary skills at raiding villages and kidnapping Europane women and children into slavery. Some had been pirates, enslaving those Europane fishermen or seamen unlucky enough to be sailing the high seas at the wrong time. Unfortunately these Arabian immigrants soon found that their well-honed skills were pretty redundant in the UK, where the task of slavery was somewhat more *managerial*.

Among the crowds were also the regular impoverished masses of the city, the Ambossan working classes who found work when they could and wore scraps of material so flimsy they came apart as easily as spiders' webs. Such poverty had surprised me when I first arrived. Poor blaks in Great Ambossa? But it was true.

I was even more astonished to discover that in earlier times Ambossans themselves had been sent to labour in the sugar-cane fields on the islands, alongside we whytes. Some were indentured servants, others had been kidnapped as slaves.

The Europane was considered better suited to the job in hand, though.

Weren't we the lucky ones?

The Ambossan poor wandered the streets on feast days, had little reason to celebrate and needed no excuse to escape from their cardboard shacks in the shantytowns of Harlesdene in the north, Poplarare in the east, Pe Khama in the south, or Goatsherd Bush in the west.

Their gamine children were bug-eyed with chiselled cheekbones, slack lips, sunken chests, bony hips and spindly heron's legs.

They wouldn't bother me. Indeed it was a little-known fact that some of the Ambossan working class were active in the Resistance, united with us in the fight against the ruling class.

Yet others were less sympathetic, shouting out 'Wigger, go home! You're taking our jobs!' from the other side of the road, even pelting us with rocks.

The thoroughfare was littered with discarded pecan-nut shells, coconut kernels, bacon rind, tobacco butts, mongoose and antelope droppings, used condoms made of pig-gut and the rest of the ordinary debris of city life.

I tried to walk quickly without appearing to. I had twenty minutes left to get to Paddinto Station and it was going well until I came upon five or six whyte men with raggedy beards and scabrous chests. As they were playing dominoes underneath a baobab tree at night they were obviously free men and I could see that they had the feral awareness of most free whytes, alert to their surroundings, ready to slip out of view down a passage or get lost in a crowd to avoid confrontation or danger. As I suspected they would, they all looked up. (Whytes always clocked one another when out and about. It was a minority-awareness thing.) I tried hard not to panic but the parameters of my life were suddenly changing. I was in no-man's-land: I was escaping slavery and walking towards freedom, but I had not yet arrived. Of one thing I was now sure: when I left my master's compound I had lost his protection, which meant I couldn't pretend I hadn't seen the men, as usual. For those of us who were still enslaved the small communities of free ones were either objects of pity (many were desperate scavengers) or envy.

This surprised me too when I had first arrived in Great Ambossa. That those slaves who were freed, for one reason or another, could remain in the country, although many Ambossans lobbied to get them kicked out.

The free whytes were mainly consigned to living in squalor in communal tents in tumbledown ghettos on the outskirts of the large cities, derisively referred to by the rich Ambossans as the 'Vanilla Suburbs', quite distinct from the far superior coco-palmed avenues of their own 'Chocolate Cities'.

We heard that in the Burbs you could buy the traditional costume of many nations such as sporrans, knickerbockers, leather jerkins, peasant skirts, metal helmets with horns, chain-mail tunics, boleros, trailing gowns with fur collars, bodices which reduced your waist to eighteen inches and bustles which expanded your hips to a hefty size eighty.

In the Burbs there were hooch and grog dens, madrigal boy bands, recorder recitals and even civil rights protest singers. And there were also tambourine-bashing, tongue-speaking underground temples which syncretised Christianity with Voodoo.

There were also whyte hairdressers who sold thin-toothed

combs for our unmanageable, flyaway fine hair. In the Burbs you rarely saw a free whyte with natural hair. They wore the perms, twists and braids of Ambossan women, although Aphros were most in demand. The hairdressers used kinky Aphrikan hair on the Burbite women, who had their own fine hair chopped off and these bushy pieces sewn onto them so that the effect was (un)naturally Aphrikan. It took up to ten hours and when the blonde, red, brown or straight roots came through it looked just plain tacky, apparently.

Our men used to joke that if you ran your fingers through a whyte woman's hair, chance was it would come off in your hands. You'd see clumps of kinky hair littering the streets like black sheep's wool.

In the Burbs tanning was all the rage too, and you could get a nose flattening job done quite cheaply, we heard, although I always thought that flat, fat nostrils on whyte faces looked ridiculous. The very thought of a mallet smashing down on my nose was just too scary for words.

Most importantly the Burbs sold exotic Europane food unobtainable elsewhere. You could get Brussels sprouts, cucumber, lettuce, peas, tapioca pudding, lemonade, processed white bread, even cabbage.

My mouth used to water at the very thought of all that lovely plain food without any horrid peppers and spices.

The Burbs were out of bounds to the likes of me, of course, but I used to dream of wandering around the legendary Brixtane in the south of the city or To Ten Ha Ma in the east, which had been originally settled by Chinese seamen.

Some of these free whytes earned a paltry living as porters or watermen down at the docks, while the women took in laundry, or more often were hawkers – of all kinds of wares.

To the Ambossans the Vanilla Suburbs were generally a

no-go area except for the feared sheriffs who trawled the dunes most days looking for runaways. Naturally it was the last destination for an escaping slave. More recently I'd heard that the more adventurous Aphrikan holidaymakers from the mainland of the continent had taken to visiting the Burbs on tourist trips to Great Ambossa. From the safety of their carriages and with an escort of Masai or Zulu warriors, they would gawk at the ghetto natives with anthropological fascination.

The free whytes all stuck together in a city where sheriffs roamed the thoroughfares and stopped and searched young males under the dreaded SUS Laws – which meant detainment on suspicion of being either runaways or common-or-garden criminals. Naturally, having a whyte skin was all the evidence the sheriffs needed to accost a young man and strip-search him. Most carriage drivers were always being stopped and searched by the sheriffs when they were out on the road without passengers, especially those owned by the wealthy who indulged in custom-made fittings such as gold-plated spokes.

Adding to the danger were the opportunistic press gangs who roamed the backstreets and would happily tear up a Freedom Certificate and cart a hapless free man or woman off to a waiting slave ship at the docks of West Japan Quays on the Isle of Wild Dogs.

I prayed those whyte men wouldn't follow me. As a single whyte female I was often sought after by my own men, who found my bony size-4 figure attractive. A prominent clavicle, corrugated chest bones, concave stomach and thin blonde hair were considered the embodiment of beauty in Europa, even though the Ambossans considered me ugly as sin. And as it was their world I was living in, I had image issues, of course.

Every morning I'd repeat an uplifting mantra to myself

while looking in the mirror. I'd try not to see the 'pinched nostrils, pasty skin, greasy hair, pale shifty eyes and flat bottom' which the Ambossans labelled inferior. Instead I tried to say with confidence:

'I may be *fair* and *flaxen*. I may have *slim* nostrils and *slender* lips. I may have *oil-rich* hair and a *non-rotund* bottom. I may blush easily, go *rubicund* in the sun and have *covert yet mentally alert* blue eyes. Yes, I may be whyte. But I am whyte and I am beautiful!'

Our guys would call women who looked like me Barbee, named after the popular rag dolls of the Motherland, those floppy little female figures with one-inch waists, blue-button eyes and four-inch blonde tresses which every little girl loved over there.

Not here, though. Find a little slave girl on this continent and you'll discover she's hankering after one of the Aphrikan Queens, a rag doll with a big butt, big lips, lots of bangles and woolly hair.

It was so bad for our self-esteem.

In private the more voluptuous whyte women were sometimes highly desired by the Ambossan male. In any case, all whyte women were labelled sexually insatiable. A sick joke, of course, because how could we refuse their advances?

The Ambossan male liked his women large and juicy: a fat woman was a well-fed one and when he strolled out with her it was as good as flashing his cheque book. Some women ate chicken hormones to pump up their breasts and behinds. Bwana had always left me alone, and if his latest bride-to-be was anything less than a perfect size 20, she was sent to the fattening farm out in Onga to be beefed up for him. She'd sit there all day forced to do nothing but sit around eating yam dumplings, doughnuts, eba, fried plantain, greasy chips, starchy rice, sorghum, hunks of beef and lamb, fried pork fat, cashew nuts, bread rolls, cheese, chocolate cake, avocados and whole chickens with their skins on.

I walked on through the market, relieved not to be followed, then turned off into Paddinto District. In a few minutes I would be at the station. The sun had gone down hours ago but I could still feel its hot, rancid tongue scratching my neck.

I held my breath as I walked past the mud tower blocks which housed the city's offices, in between the proliferation of trendy coffee houses which were springing up to meet the twin demands for coffee and business.

The coffee houses in Paddinto were legendary – some even had auction blocks. Stupidly I'd thought they'd be closed on this most sanctified of days but to the traders, I guess, wealth was more important than worship. Several were doing business. Damn!

I slunk past the Cocoa Tree, Coasta Coffee, Hut Tropicana, Cafe Shaka, Demerara's Den, Starbright and then the highly fashionable Shuga, part of a trendy chain store of cafes which stretched from the West Japan Quays all the way to Amersha, a distant north-western outpost of the city.

Shuga specialised in the novelty of cappuccino with rum, known as rumpaccino, the gimmick of the daily news relayed via talking drum 'On the Hour every Hour' (even though this antiquated postal service went out of fashion moons ago), homemade star-apple pie with peanut ice cream, and, advertised in chalk on a black signboard, 'Fresh Slaves'.

The men inside Shuga could sniff out a slave a mile away. Hounds to a fox one and all. Some were agents for Amarikan or West Japanese planters, there to buy new Europanes, others were middle-class householders seeking new staff.

I had always tried to console myself with the fact that while they were destroying us they were also destroying themselves.

Such was the demand for sugar, the price of a sweet tooth was a toothless smile. Such was the demand for coffee, the price of caffeine was addiction, heart palpitations, osteoporosis and general irritability. The price of rum was chronic liver disease, alcoholism and permanent memory loss. The cost of tobacco was cancer, stained teeth and emphysema.

I had stopped directly outside Shuga while my mind took off on yet another sprint of its own. Years of suppressed rage were rising to the surface because freedom was so close. I had done the very thing I should not. I had looked inside its 'rustic' spit-and-sawdust room with the mandatory portrait of President-for-Life Sanni Abasta in prime position above the counter.

I found myself staring at a male on the auction block.

The air was charged with tobacco smoke and pungent with steaming coffee beans.

Men were bidding for him.

He was about fifteen, I reckoned. A prize buck, then. He had his back to me but his pimpled, fisted face was turned towards the door, away from the men.

It was flushed with adolescent shame rather than the teeth-grinding rage of a fully-fledged male.

He was completely naked and his pallid back and buttocks were crawling with what looked like cockroaches, but which were lumps of congealed blood. Maybe he'd tried to run away, or spoken his native language, or committed some similar crime.

My eyes roamed over the crowd of men with their animated, perspiring faces, hand-printed robes draped over a shoulder or knotted at the waist, puffing on pipes, sitting with their legs akimbo so that they took up twice their body width. Their hoarse, booming Ambossan voices batted back and forth as they bid for the boy. I suddenly locked eyes with a very young man sitting apart and looking bored, head tilted, twizzling a pigeon feather in his ear. He was staring straight at me through the haze and the bartering with a surprise that was rapidly working itself up to a realisation.

He knew me.

It was Bamwoze.

Bwana's second but most favoured son.

Of all people.

Bamwoze.

I had wet-nursed the little bastard. I had wiped his scuzzy little arse and rocked him to sleep. I had breastfed him when my first newborn had been taken away and I was still heavy with milk.

All the while I was in mourning for my lost child.

I swaddled Bamwoze with all the love meant for my own.

I even kidded myself, at times, that he was indeed my own.

He took to me like a leech and wouldn't let go.

Then he grew up and was sent off to the forest to be initiated into manhood. When he returned from being buried up to his head in dirt for days to prove his endurance and killing a crocodile with his bare hands to prove his strength, he began strutting around the compound like a mini-Bwana and I, whose teats had produced full-fat milk which had formed his bone, brain, skin and muscle, ceased to exist for him.

Nanny no more.

Invisible, see.

Some time afterwards, Bwana discovered Bamwoze had got a local slave girl pregnant, a rite of passage for the sons of masters, but he had tried to elope with her to Europa of all places, which was taking the piss. What were they planning? A Grand Tour?

Bwana disinherited Bamwoze and kicked him out of the house. I don't know what happened to the girl – dead or in the New World, probably. We were all filled with a newfound respect for Bamwoze when we discovered he had forfeited his inheritance for a mulatto. Some time later we heard he'd become a trader in slaves himself, in order to continue living in the comfort to which he was born. The girl had been an aberration, we all realised; just a pretty mulatto trophy or simply part of his teenage rebellion against Bwana. What I knew for sure was that he couldn't give a damn about the rest of us.

And here he was after all these years, locking eyes with me, knowing full well that I was where I shouldn't be and that there could be only one reason for it. He'd been a big lad and was a big man now, typical of the Ambossans. But I recognised the familiar expression of self-pity sweep across the plump face of the child before he became the man; before bones started pushing through his cheeks and shaping his face into something fierce and arrogant.

Here was the spoiled boy who got everything he wanted – more giraffe-burgers, more vanilla drops, yet another baby camel to take him riding around the compound. He had never been denied anything as a child, and so, as is the way with the blessed of this world, nothing was ever enough for him.

The wretch still felt sorry for himself.

I didn't move and neither did he. I could see the indecision in his eyes, weighing up the options, which one would benefit *him* the most. If I moved, I would make up his mind for him and he would raise the alarm. Seconds passed. The sensory overload of the smoke and smell and shouts of the bidding faded away. I knew better than to plead with my eyes because he would feel manipulated and resist. If I looked afraid, he would despise me. So I just went blank – the slaves' default position. Then I sensed a thought take shape in his mind. To let me go would be a way to get back at his father.

We both knew that I had read him.

He smiled to himself, then gestured at me with a magnanimous roll-of-the-eyes *Oh, go on then* nod to be on my way.

Seconds later I was running.

I didn't care any more. I had no time left.

If someone stopped me, so be it.

I found the dusty bushes with little effort, using all my strength to open the round iron manhole. I levered myself down and felt strong hands catch my slim hips with such warm, solid strength it was like being caught by my father after he'd thrown me into the air when I was a kid. Would they be a safe pair? Turning round, I saw an elderly Ambossan holding a pottery lamp reeking of kerosene. His head was as bald, hard and uneven as a gourd, and a band of antelope teeth was draped over it. His welcoming lopsided grin reassured me that he was not out to ensnare me.

'Greetings, Omorenomwara, from your friends at the Resistance. I am your Conductor. We are glad you made it.'

Omorenomwara was the slave name P.I.G. gave me when I was first enslaved. It meant *This child will not suffer*.

I paused.

I could finally give my real name to an Ambossan. It was like reclaiming my identity. I trembled, stuttering.

'Please, call me Doris. I am Doris. My name is Doris.'

He grinned and tried to repeat my real appellation, slowly, looking embarrassed, breaking it down into three elongated syllables, his tongue stumbling over the strange phonetics. He looked so pleased when he managed to pronounce it.

Honestly, it was truly endearing.

'Dooo-raaa-sha,' he said.

Bless.

I smiled encouragingly nonetheless. At least he'd tried.

'We must make haste,' he added. 'I will lead you to the Bakalo Line, where your train awaits you.'

The Gospel Train

It was silent down there except for the scurrying of rodents and lizards and the muted echo of our footsteps. The floor gave way in places and it took an age to descend the escalator as I eased my way down, gripping the rubber banister, my fingernails scraping up mushy dirt. Who knows when I'd be able to wash again? I was a fastidious person and liked a hearty wash-down at least once every two weeks.

When we reached the bottom my anonymous guide turned right into a corridor reeking of must and so clotted with dust that I gagged. But my guide didn't turn around. I was supposed to be a brave escapee, not a wimp. I was a mature woman, not a child. Yet something was stirring deep inside of me. When had I last been in such a dark, enclosed, claustrophobic space?

Cobwebs stretched before us like veins of forest foliage. He brushed them away with his swaying lantern, step by step. I could sense the surge of all those Ambossans who for years had filled those brightly lit tunnels during what they called the Rushing Hour. All those scurrying feet and harried minds. All those sugar-loving, coffee-drinking, baccy-smoking, rum-sipping commuters, most of whom hadn't a thought about who provided their little pleasures, their little dependencies.

Like the caves deep in the hills of my homeland which the sun could never penetrate, these were catacombs running underneath a landmass which weighed down upon it, and it was chilled to its abandoned bone. In time the soil of the land and underground rivers would complete nature's reclamation.

My guide shuffled ahead, his lantern creating spooky patterns of light and shadow which looked like ghouls looming towards us.

He carefully stepped over little craters in the ground and piles of powdery plaster from the caved-in ceilings, glancing behind to check that I did the same. He needn't have worried; I was at his mercy. The Tube was strange territory and I had no bearings. When I looked behind, the tunnel had closed in on us.

When something wet, hairy and slithery crawled onto my foot, I merely bit my lip and managed to kick it off. There were probably more small beasts in that subterranean jungle than I could bear to contemplate, families of tarantulas and scorpions for whom my ankles would be a once-in-a-lifetime delicacy. What had happened to the farm girl I used to be? The girl who could wring a chicken's neck, gut a rabbit, deliver a calf, who had kept a dog as a pet.

The Ambossans regarded the keeping of animals as domestic pets as downright primitive. The very idea of sleeping with a flea-ridden, moulting cat or dog in the same bed, or kissing a canine or feline mouth which licked its own anus, was disgusting.

I turned my attention to my guide. He wore a bleached-orange wrappa and nothing else. He was short for an Ambossan, and tubby, although his fat had the hard substance of a man who has known a lifetime's manual labour rather than the slack softness of one who has not. I was used to reading people from behind, an emotional state emanating from someone's posture, a state of mind indicated by the tilt of the head. There were those who carried a self-combusting anger in their backs. Others had the defeated trundle of a loser, the imploded chest and listless arms that asked *Why should I bother?*

I longed to possess the confident thrust of a person with the freedom to pursue her own course of action.

My guide's body language was that of someone battling a storm. His shoulders were set in a permanent hunch. His forehead was ready to head-butt any opponents. Doubtless he came from one of the slums. No way had he been born with a silver spoon feeding his mouth, yet he had chosen compassion over resentment.

I liked him. Of course I did.

I could always tell whether Bwana or Madama Blessing were in a good mood, or, more likely, ready to crack the proverbial whip, and I was usually prepared when they did. It is the skill of a great slave to predict the master's moods and needs before he himself knows what they are. I relied on knowledge of Bwana's daily schedule (forewarned is forearmed), eavesdropping – which is the advantage of those who blend into the decor until called upon to carry out an errand – and I was expert at reading his facial expressions, body language and intonation. Peripheral vision was also essential, as well as an ability, after so many years, to sense his deeper yearnings.

When Bwana ambled into his den after a dinner of, say, egusi stew, pounded yam, cow-leg and a flagon of palm wine, burping and flatulent, reeking of musk oil, chewing a cola nut and aiming its juice into a spittoon, or stopping to piss into a chamber pot which a slave boy held in the right position for him, I usually knew whether to pour him rum-on-the-rocks, a banana daiquiri or a pina colada, or whether to leave him alone or order in some takeaway sex from one of the high-class agencies like Ladies of the Night, recruited from one of the poorer Aphrikan countries like the Congo or Malawi.

As intimately as I knew him, he barely registered me. My job was to make sure his office was run efficiently.

The Ambossans were generally a proud, stalwart people. A commonly held joke was that the Gambians knocked on a door, the Ghanaians pushed it open but what did the Ambossans do? Why, they just kicked the door down, man!

Bwana was indeed a true Ambossan chief. He had the moist, spongy lips of a man used to having them gratified, a broad porous nose which puckered when irked and oozed perspiration when enraged, the intractable shoulders of a muscle-man and an expansive girth which gave him the gravitas of an ageing military dictator.

The rich Ambossan male was often whippet-thin when young but built up an armour of fat as he aged. A big man was supposed to take up a lot of physical space too. This one also walked with the unhurried sway of someone whose authority was without question. A slight gesture of a hand, a raised eyebrow or a stern look sent his minions scurrying. Needless to say, women adored him. The wives of friends and acquaintances who came to visit dissolved into girly titters when he turned his charms onto each one in turn. The number of surreptitious, passionate glances – I could not begin to count.

Naturally, Bwana was foremost in my mind as we burrowed underneath the city of soil and sand. When he discovered my escape, his nostrils would emit flames so hot his lips would melt.

I turned my attention to the posters on the tunnel walls: stained, crinkled, slumping in their cracked glass cases like people with humped backs, sloppy bellies and weak knees. They were advertising dramas of yore, the classic: *Guess Who's Not Coming To Dinner*, *To Sir with Hate*, *Little Whyte Sambo Esq.*, and the famous tragedies *The Tragic Mulatto*, *The Tragic Quadroon* and *The Tragic Octoroon*. One poster made me do a double-take. It was for *The Whyte and Blak Minstrel Show*.

The Ambossans still flocked in their thousands to see it at

the Palladia Arena during the rainy season. It featured Ambossan performers as whyteface minstrels, faces smeared with chalk, lips thinned down to a red slit. They sang out of tune in reedy voices, their upper lips stiff as they danced with idiotic, jerky movements while attempting the hop, skip and jump of Morris dancing. They wore clogs on their feet, bells on their ankles, waved hankies in the air and rubbed their bottoms up against each other. All the while singing music hall songs about being lazy, lying, conniving, cowardly, ignorant, sexually repressed buffoons.

Bwana and his huge extended family went to the Palladia every year. They took up the entire stalls and returned singing the minstrel songs very loudly thinking they were being so damned funny. It was a kind of madness, because the performing caricatures they mimicked bore no relation to the whytes in their service. Still, credit where it's due, it was the only time they tried to entertain the staff.

Suddenly my guide did a sharp right, jolting me back. He led me down a short set of stairs which opened onto tunnels on either side.

One dusty sign on the wall read BAKALO LINE – Southbound via Baka Street, Marbone, Ox Fordah Crossroads, Embankere, Wata Lo, Londolo Bridge, Kanada Wadi.

The other sign read BAKALO LINE – Northbound via Pharoah's Plains, m'Aiduru Valley, Kenshala Dunes, Harlesdene, Kentouni, Harro Wa.

We did a right turn onto a platform with rail tracks and standing before us was my gift from the Resistance – a one-carriage train. Another man was sitting in the driver's seat in a little cabin at the front. Perhaps Tuareg, he wore an indigo turban which was wrapped around his mouth and jaw, hiding most of his face. Only his eyes and nose peeked out, deep creases running down either side.

He nodded, once, clearly a man of few gestures and, as I discovered, even fewer words.

This was it, then, one of the famous Tube trains which had shunted back and forth for an age underneath the city. It was a wreck – no windows, no doors, no seats.

We had not spoken for the entire journey.

My guide gripped my shoulders and I surprised myself by wanting to cry. He was risking his life for me.

Captured Resistance members were tortured but I sensed this man would never spill the beans. If caught, his fate was inevitable.

'Take care, Doris,' he said. (This time it came out as Duo-ro-sisi.)

'The driver will take you to Doklanda. My task is done but I pray that you will reach your homeland. When you do, you must send word to the Co-op. I want to hear you are safe.'

His gaze held mine. This really was it.

'Do not drop your guard until you reach home safely.'

He clasped my shivering hands in his warm, stubby ones.

'Trust only those who earn it.'

Before I could reply he had vanished from whence we came. Now I couldn't disappear back into the labyrinth of tunnels and return to Mayfah even if fear got the better of me, and it had been tugging my arm like a child.

The driver stared ahead and started the engine. I walked into the shell of a carriage, found a spot in the middle of the floor where I could hold onto a metal pole.

The Tube started to move with the quiet stealth of a cobra.

I had visions of hundreds of angry Ambossan men descending the tunnels in loincloths, torch-lights searching, the cracking of muskets, bloodhounds braying.

Bwana was a major mover and shaker in this city. News of

my escape would spread like bush fire. He'd suffer public humiliation if I wasn't captured. Slave and master alike would gloat. As his PA I wasn't your common-or-garden house wigger. I'd be the talking point around every communal eating bowl in the city. I was probably at that very minute going down in recent history.

C£250
FOR THE RETURN
OF THE
SCRAWNY BLONDE SLAVE WOMAN
OMORENOMWARA
– PREFERABLY MORE DEAD THAN ALIVE

To the Ambossans we 'scrawny blondes' all looked alike. It would be in my favour for once.

We were moving deep into the bowels of the earth, slowly. No one above would detect a tremor or sound. I leaned against the rusty pole. I needed to conserve my energy. During my lengthy sojourn at Bwana's, life had become so predictable my senses had gone into a coma. Now the hairs on the back of my neck pricked up, my ears pinned back, my spine arched.

Hours passed. I had no way of telling other than my stomach pangs felt like the sharp kicks of an unborn child and a heaviness swept down from my crown to my toes like molten lead. But every time my head flopped over and my eyes closed, I jolted myself upright again. Adrenaline had got me thus far. My guide had told me to trust no one.

As the train crawled through the black underground tunnel, its chugging rhythms began to lull.

I slid down to the floor and curled my body around the pole.

Maybe I would wake up back in Mayfah as if this night had never happened.

I had lived with fear ever since the man from the Border Lands had grabbed me when I was playing hide-and-seek in the potato fields behind our cottage with my sisters.

Madge. Sharon. Alice.

Beloved. Beloved. Beloved.

Slave or dead? Slave or dead? Dead or slave?

Not knowing their fate put my sleep on the torture rack for years.

Alice was the youngest and prettiest – coming two years after me, that *wasn't* funny. She didn't say a word until she was seven, which made her just so adorable, as did her spider eyelashes and blonde ringlets. (She was the only one of us to inherit Pa's curls.) He once told her at dinner that she was such a pretty little thing she need never open her mouth to speak. Unfortunately she didn't take his advice. During her mute years she learned how to get what she wanted through a branch of sign language known as 'lash-fluttering'.

When we were alone I'd mimic her: grunt like an imbecile, roll my eyes into the back of my head, throw myself onto the floor and dribble. She'd fling her surprisingly mighty little monkey-self onto me, sink her teeth into whichever part of my anatomy was within easy reach, then screech her head off for everyone to hear. Guess who always got it in the neck, and 'should have known better', even though I had her teeth marks as evidence?

Because we were closest in age we were supposed to pair up, but even when she could speak, I refused to. I played with my dolls alone, except when the older two let me partake of their friendship.

Sharon was two years above me and thick as thieves with Madge. You couldn't split them up or wedge yourself in between, no matter how hard you tried: backstabbing, sucking up to one and not the other, planting stolen objects, innuendo.

Sharon was like a mini-Mam, thinner than the rest of us although we were all thin enough to snap in two at the waist like gingerbread men. We all had dark blue eyes, but Sharon insisted hers were *azure*. She imitated our Mam's elegant movements perfectly in the hope that people would comment (which they did), her arms dancing mid-air even when she was doing something as down-to-earth as picking apples off a tree in Percy's orchard or combing her hair.

Sharon hated what she called 'menial tasks', which was a pity because her fingernails got as crusty and jagged as mine when we had to help Pa in the fields or dig ditches up to our waists, and as raw as mine what with scrubbing the laundry on the big stone down by the stream, and bleaching the linen with a mixture of lye and stinking human urine which had been collected in a tub specially for the purpose.

In the summer Sharon wore a garland of buttercups as a crown on her head and in winter, snowdrops. It was the princess look, apparently. One time she changed her name to Sabine but had to drop it when we refused to take it up. I guess Princess Sabine had a better ring to it than Princess Sharon. She expected her prince to arrive one day on a white stallion and star in her very own once-upon-a-time.

She was often to be found standing in the doorway looking out for him.

'Shall I pack your bags?' I'd say in passing, and then, once out of reach, I'd sing,

> Lavender blue, diddle daddle
> Lavender green,
> When he is King, diddle daddle
> You shan't be queen.

Like the nearest she'd get to royalty would be as maid-of-all-work to Percy.

Our Madge looked out for all of us, even Pa. One time at table, after he'd thrown up in the parlour after another of his 'just the one pint' Friday nights out with 'the lads', she told him sharply, 'You and I are going to have words – in private.'

Such talk from a child to an adult was unheard of, as it was from a woman to a man. I couldn't believe her cheek and neither could he because he just nodded meekly. That was the day we realised she'd soon be an adult, a formidable one at that. As first-born Madge had no competition for four years, which should have turned her into a monster when baby Sharon came along, but she worshipped her little sister.

She was known for the twinkle in her eyes, which never dulled even when she was exhausted from shearing sheep, or when I told her she'd likely end up an old spinster spending her days at a spinning wheel if she didn't go to the summer fayre on the estate and find herself a young fellow. Mam and Pa said they couldn't afford a dowry, but the truth was they'd never let *her* go.

I tried to get Madge's twinkle into my own eyes, spending hours practising in front of the looking glass, but it only worked if I slapped my cheek so hard it made me cry.

No one had to tell Madge she'd have to take over running the house if Mam passed on. She never looked wistfully at the horizon or wore garlands in her hair, but spoke of 'duty' and 'responsibility' and being part of 'God's greater plan'.

When I ranked them on a scale of one to ten for perfection, Madge was a nine and a half. I gave myself an eight. Sharon was a four and Alice got a one and three-quarters.

Now, me Mam was tall for a woman but she'd had the pox as a kid which explained why she was often 'a bit under the weather'. Her skin was pale and clung softly to her like the crêpe de Chine Mrs Katharine Holme, the seamstress at Duddingley, made into gowns for the ladies 'up there'. Mam wafted around slowly so that her movements flowed into each other with no beginning and no end – like a dance. I'd try to imitate her too but my movements always ended abruptly.

Everyone said the word for it was 'clumsy'.

Her hair was dead straight and hung to her waist like mine. It was what they called strawberry blonde (Strawberry? Blonde? Never did work that one out) and going prematurely grey underneath her starched linen bonnet.

When Pa was out we'd be sitting around embroidering a tablecloth for market and Mam'd tell us how one summer's evening after a day's harvesting when she was marching impatiently towards womanhood, Lord Perceval Montague (she always used his full name) came up behind her on Lower Lane. The meadows were 'bathed in summer's golden glow' and as he drew aside she felt him rest a palm in the scoop of her back and his steamy breath whispered onto her neck that she'd become 'a winsome lass' and had 'a natural grace'.

Our Mam said she felt 'the butterflies' for the first and last time in her life, that her 'spine tingled', that she could have stayed and swum in his 'come-hither eyes' for ever, except that her grumpy, widowed father, Bob Woulbarowe, tugging their cow up ahead and cursing it, suddenly turned around and called her to heel, even though it could have got him into serious trouble with His Lordship.

Granpa Woulbarowe kept her hidden inside their peat hovel in the wind-blown wilds for three months solid after that, then forced her to wear shapeless black woollens like an old maid thereafter. That's when she began to have 'the turns', her 'humours went out of balance' and she 'got a hunch' her days were 'numbered'. Within the year she was wed off to Pa, although she'd only met him the once before marriage.

Our Mam held up a needle, squinted, pursed her thin lips to a slit and threaded it carefully, all the while saying that in this life there were 'fairy-tale castles' and 'peasant shit-houses', and wasn't it a pity not to have a choice.

That night in bed we girls debated the pros and cons of being Percy's kids.

Lady Madge. Lady Sharon. Lady Doris. Lady Alice.

We thought there might be possibilities.

Our Mam was always showing us what to do because she 'wouldn't be around for ever'. She kept a tiny skull pendant in a box to remind her and said she was surprised she'd 'been given such a long run by the good Lord above but it won't last long, I expect.'

'When I die,' she'd whisper when Pa wasn't around, because he'd soon tell her to hush her nonsense, 'make sure my ashes are scattered on the seven seas.'

'What ashes? What seas?' we'd reply, blinking back tears, thinking of our Mam going up in flames.

'Oh, you know, the seven seas,' she'd add, knowingly. 'And I want that hymn *When the Saints Go Marching In*, sung so it's a joyous occasion, do you hear? Not a wet eye in the house.'

A day didn't go by without her raising the issue of her death. It made me want to curl up in a ball on the floor and sob my heart out, but if you did that after the age of four Mam would give you a good kick in the bum and tell you to put a stocking in it.

When I got older I'd retort, 'Mam, will you make sure you die *after* you've baked the rhubarb crumble?'

We were to be wives and mothers – so we were taught how to cook: cabbage soup, cabbage pie, fried cabbage, pickled cabbage, skillet cabbage, scalloped cabbage, cabbage and turnip bake, cabbage and potato casserole, cabbage and spinach cake. How to separate milk to make butter and cheese. How to bake horse bread from dried peas when the household budget wasn't balancing, and when it was – scones, muffins, gingerbread. How to make milk pudding with barley, and jam from gooseberries and strawberries. How to candy fruit. Occasionally we ate salted stockfish which could last four years but had to be beaten with a wooden hammer for a full hour and then soaked in warm water for four more hours before it was ready. The priest said we had to eat fish twice a week but who could afford that?

Mam taught us how to sew our dresses and blouses from material bought in bulk from the spinners and weavers at the market, which made us girls all look alike, which we hated; how to crochet blankets, knit woollies and scarves, darn socks; how to clean the house, the laundry, the yard; how to store vegetables in the outhouse, potatoes in the soil for the winter; how to distil rosewater, how to smear bread with glue and put a lighted candle in the middle to attract and kill fleas and how to use rags for our menses when the time came, egg whites for our hair, soda, lime and potash to make soap.

Thank God we had the freshwater stream running down from Haven Banks less than a hundred yards from our cottage. Most folk drank watered-down ale.

Pa built our furniture: chairs, tables, cabinets, beds – all of which were lopsided, not that he noticed.

We teased him about it.

'You know full well I can't afford a carpenter,' he'd shout, before storming out of the house.

Entering our cottage used to make me feel a bit wonky.

Mam said to imagine we were on a ship, but I protested I'd never been on one.

Some evenings one of my sisters would get at our Mam's back with the backscratcher Pa made specially for her, a wooden hand on a stick – only it had four fingers cos he'd forgotten the fifth. Two of us massaged a hand each and I'd massage her bony feet, if I could get there first. She'd sit there issuing instructions:

To the right, Madge! Don't forget my fingers, Alice!

We'd be a flurry of skinny elbows stuck up at right angles, white moths fluttering around her as we each tried to make her love us more than she did the others.

The most important outing of our week was to Duddingley with Mam on a Monday morning to sell our handiwork of tablecloths and bonnets. The journey took ages and only one of us got to go along on the back of the cart as there was so much work to do at home. I cherished that time on the road, pretending I was Mam's only child, cuddling up to her as the cart jolted along lanes and dirt tracks strewn with fallen rocks and dangerous potholes which could delay a journey by several hours if the wheels got trapped.

In the market our Mam indulged in gossip because rumour was the lifeblood of conversation. Gossip was our theatre and our fiction.

I'd be hanging onto her arm watching her eyes flash, her face flush and her mouth excitedly emitting 'Nevers' and 'Who'd have thought its'.

As farming folk we generally targeted one person above all others, the only one who wouldn't hear: Percy.

Short, pot-bellied and with a penchant for brocaded doublets and wide-brimmed hats with feathers sticking up, Percy was a huntin'-an'-fishin' man like his deceased father, Lord Peregrine, and like his father he was always entertaining important guests en route to the Border Lands. There were many grand dinners and parties up at Montague Manor. We heard he had a preference for fine white bread, boar's skin filled with jellied meat, baked chewetts, spiced custard pies and syllabub, and that his cellar contained hundreds of barrels of sweet wines.

Then there was the wife, Priscilla, who looked suspiciously foreign, went mad (likely connected), and was locked up in the attic.

The son and heir, Harold, who everyone suspected was really the result of the gardener's dalliance with Priscilla, only no one dared tell Percy.

The illegitimate son, Tom, who was the offspring of Percy's dalliance with the scullery maid Lizzie.

The legitimate daughter, Phoebe, who died in mysterious circumstances on a boat on Larksong Lake with her ladies' companion, Elinor, who was really her secret sister (raised by an elderly aunt of Percy's) because she was the daughter of Percy's dalliance with the governess, Miss Felliplace, who ended up dying of asphyxiation caused by her scarf getting caught in the wheels of Percy's carriage, and who was suspiciously buried in Mad Bess Woods the very next day.

The Montagues gave our lives drama by association, glamour by proximity, status through acquaintance. Without them we would have been your wretched run-of-the-mill peasant family eking out a living on the land. Instead, we were part of an *estate*. We were of the *Montagues*.

One icy morning Percy trotted by on his mare as we were walking through Coppice Forest. He doffed his cap and almost smiled.

Well, Pa jumped up and punched the air silently as if he'd just won himself a chest full of doubloons.

Another stormy morning Pa acted like a spurned lover when Percy nearly ran into us, shouting 'Get out of my way!' when we were sloshing down the donkey track in waterlogged clogs after mass at St Michael's.

Once out of earshot Pa spat out that 'One day the working man will be Percy's comeuppance.'

For all the talk of the 'common man having his day', no one seriously wanted Percy gone. He represented stability, he was the devil we knew, and in any case, if there really was an attempted 'revolution' by Pa and the lads, Percy and his ilk would have all the perpetrators hung, drawn and quartered to a man.

It was at the market that we heard that slave raiders had entered our country from the faraway sea, although none had been sighted in our neighbourhood, as yet. The story went that the Border Landers were involved and so were men called Aphrikans, who were coloured blak.

The slave raiders, it seemed, were in cahoots with aristocrats like Percy and the middlemen who supplied them with slaves for shipment overseas. Criminals and prisoners of war were hot favourites, but when they weren't available it was anyone who could be captured, so long as they weren't too old or, in Percy's case, his own serfs. Children were taken too.

Some said that the guns the greedy aristocrats received in exchange for slaves encouraged them to start more wars just to meet the demand of the slave traders who wanted a yearly increase in exports.

The Aphrikans built heavily fortified castles to hold their

cargo until ships arrived to collect them. It was rumoured that there was one on the coast which could accommodate a thousand slaves at a time.

But all that was happening somewhere far away. None of us knew what happened when the prisoners got on those boats, but it was rumoured to be a bit crowded below decks, and seasickness was rife.

To be honest, it felt so distant from us, we didn't give it much thought. Our world was made up of our immediate neighbours and foreign meant the people of the midlands or fenlands.

We were just simple, country folk, who tried our best to live with ourselves and understand each other.

Our nights were spent singing songs. What else was there to do after work was done and food eaten and we were exhausted but not quite ready for bed? Pa's snoring provided a sonorous bass. We'd be inside in front of the fire in winter with the tallow rush-lights flickering, woollen blankets wrapped around us for extra warmth. Or outside in summer, sitting on stools under a sky bigger than our brains could ever imagine (we could just about manage acres, not planets), surrounded by the silence of the countryside which was really quite noisy what with crickets and owls, small scurrying beasts in the undergrowth, the close buzzing of mosquitoes, the pig snortling, the fowl doing their night-time chicken-pen shuffle, and the stream running nearby.

We'd stamp our feet, bang clay pots, rub sticks up and down a washboard, click wooden cutlery, clap our hands and slip into familiar harmonies. We'd raise a cheer after a song if it was rendered perfectly, or point the finger when someone's harmony didn't slide smoothly into place.

When my mind does a back flip into my BS days, at some

point it goes on past what I remember myself and into what I'd been told. There it goes, legs, hands, the supple spine of a child, flicking back the years to when my mother was in labour and Old Sarah, the local midwife, saved my life.

Our Mam went into the throes with me early one evening a month before I was due to arrive while Pa, as luck would have it, was at work. She lay in a puddle of broken waters and just knew I was going to come out all twisted. I was her seventh child – four had already died. She kept rattling some stones in the cup of her hand which was supposed to prevent a miscarriage.

Mam had to send little Madge off to Old Sarah who lived all the way over at Sheepwash. Somehow she made it and Old Sarah came rushing in through our door, sending Madge to heat up some water, while I was safely disentangled.

Then I was swaddled from head to toe in linen bands so that I didn't grow up deformed and she made a caudle of spiced wine for Mam, to keep her health and spirits up.

Old Sarah lived alone, had never married, had no kids, owned a cat, Tibbles, and was over fifty – all of which should have been enough to see her tied up in a sack and drowned in the river for witchcraft. She also practised the herbs and was known for her healing powers, which could have got her burned alive at the stake outside the church at Duddingley. She was lucky not to have been stripped naked in search of extra teats (from which her imps suckled), inspected for a tell-tale mole (a sign she was 'consorting' with a demon), pricked by a witch-pricker to see if she could bleed, had her shack searched for a pile of stolen, moving penises which fed on oats or corn (as they do); and, failing all of that, a few days of good old-fashioned torture would have seen her confessing to flying on poles, changing into an animal, taking part in witches' Sabbaths and having sexual intercourse with the Devil.

But so many of us owed our lives to Old Sarah that when malice-laced gossip began the rounds – that she was the reason for the Copplestones' mysteriously diseased cow, or the latest Durridge child's freakish sixth toe, or the surprise storm which struck young Jennet Briggs down stone dead in the middle of summer – there were many to defend her.

She died in her sleep long before I could get to thank her.

They searched her body after her death, but no unusual markings or extra breasts were found, to the disappointment of some.

When Pa came home after my birth, he gathered me up and took me outside, and, as was the Scagglethorpe family tradition, held his latest swaddled bundle up to the heavens with outstretched arms.

It was dark but there was a full moon which shone directly onto me, providing a luminous, otherworldly glow, apparently.

'I name you, my dearest, treasured new daughter, Doris Scagglethorpe,' he said, his voice throaty with emotion.

'Doris Scagglethorpe – behold the only thing greater than yourself.'

It

Ten years later I was 'it' in a game of hide-and-seek and Madge, Sharon and Alice were singing out that my days were numbered.

I'd given them the slip and was hiding behind some bushes at the end of the field. I remember peeping from behind the bush to see if they were making their way up to me when an arm hooked itself around my waist and carried me into the fringes of Coppice Forest, which bordered the fields.

It was so unexpected that before I had time to struggle or scream I was in the forest and a sack was slammed down over my head. I felt myself being lifted up again and flung over a brawny shoulder so that my head hung down over his back and the sackcloth grazed my cheeks.

Then he was running. I'd not seen my assailant and no one had seen me leave. I couldn't breathe properly, my hip bones dug into his shoulder, my head filled with blood that began to stream out of my nose. I remember that I wet myself.

It was as fast and shocking as that.

Daylight Robbery

When I had gone some distance slung over my kidnapper's shoulder, bouncing like a ball against the hard muscles of his back, my woollen dress and petticoats ridden up, his coarse hands clasping my knees so firmly the blood stopped flowing, he suddenly stopped and dumped me on the ground like a sack of beets.

I lay there crumpled in a heap, not knowing my arse from my elbow, quite literally, while he untied the sack and dragged it off my head.

I rubbed my giddy eyes and adjusted to my head sitting back on top of my neck, where it belonged, and clutched a stomach which had not, miraculously, turned itself inside out. My kidnapper started unravelling a chain from a leather pouch. I heard the grating of the links as they scraped against each other, and snuck a look at his face. A rusty old iron helmet was pulled down over his eyes and his beard was busy with grey streaks. His face was vivid with crimson blotches, his nose covered with the red veins and blackened pores of the old drunkards who lolled about on the village green while their wizened wives begged for alms outside the church. I could see he needed a drink now because he kept twitching, the same way they did, as if flies were landing on different parts of his anatomy which he tried to shrug off.

He appeared like a giant to me. Surely he wasn't man at all but one of those evil ogres in the legends Pa loved telling us around the hearth on winters nights.

I recognised the muddy green-and-yellow checked kilt worn

by the Border Landers. When he finally spoke, it was in the thick brogue of that foreign tongue. He barked some kind of warning at me, using body language that required no interpreter.

If only I'd not been in shock. If only I'd been older, wiser, more quick-witted, braver, I might have taken that one chance to run away. I was a fast runner. He was too cumbersome to be agile. I was unshackled. I still recognised that part of the forest. It would soon be dark. I would have found my way home.

If only I'd known then that I had already lost my family and neighbourhood, that I would soon lose my name, my language and my country, then my stupid legs might have taken the risk – I'd have dashed into the undergrowth without a backward glance.

Then it was too late, the man cocked his head, turned and lumbered towards me, grabbing my legs so that I fell onto my back and my skirts once more rode indecently up my legs. He bound my mouth with a rag, fastened my hands with rope, and placed an iron collar around my neck to which he attached a chain with workaday expertise.

He began to lead me deeper into the forest following the track cleared by Gervase the beekeeper.

It was a Sunday. Gervase would be at church all day.

We continued on our way: me following the swish of his muddy kilt, the ingrained dirt in the creases at the back of his knees, the contraction of his wide shot-putter's calves, his scuffed, chipped clogs.

He gained momentum with each stride, holding a stake in one hand with which he stabbed the ground. His clogs crushed and crunched the branches and leaves beneath them.

He walked so quickly I choked against the iron collar like a billy goat being dragged up a hill.

I wanted to tap him on the shoulder and tell him that I wasn't one of the local poachers and I wasn't a prisoner of war, either, and that I'd never stolen anything in my life, except for skimming off cream when I was sent to collect milk in the morning but all my sisters did that so please let me go, sir.

If only I'd known then what I know now; that I was a prisoner of someone whose conscience had signed a contract with the Devil long ago.

I belonged to him now.

The weak sun started its weary descent towards the east. I could tell we had walked many hours. I also knew from the position of the sun which direction would take me home, even though I was now in a part of the forest I no longer recognised. My first hours of bondage had an almost instant maturing effect. Once the initial shock had passed, my mind began to plot with the cunning of an adult's. If he ever let go of the chain, I'd beat it into the thicket and follow the stars and moon home.

I kept looking behind me.

At first I fully expected my father to creep out of the undergrowth with 'the lads', all wielding cutlasses and making such a din that my kidnapper would drop the chain and flee into the forest.

Pa released me from the chain, wrapped me in his arms, stroked my hair backwards with the soft pad of his thumbs. He wiped my eyes dry and, with gentle admonition, chided, 'Look at the pickle you've gone and got yourself into this time.'

Expectation turned into prayer.

When that didn't work, fury set in.

Where the bloody hell was my dad, my creator, my protector?

*

As daylight finally began to succumb to darkness we came upon a clearing in the forest. It was a camp. Fires were burning. A boar was roasting on a spit. There were barrels of alcohol. I could hear laughter. Was it a fayre?

But before my elation could bubble its way up to the surface, I saw something which filled me with alarm.

In the middle of the clearing was a roped-off corral. Surrounding it were guards with swords, muskets and truncheons. There must have been hundreds of people inside, all chained to one another, lolling about, looking filthy and exhausted.

I was no longer alone but the community I was about to join was a wretched one.

There were big working men in there, rendered as helpless as children. Some of them would have fought in wars, could carry a cow on their backs and brag about it in the local inn, could shoot an apple from the top of a boy's head and leave him standing.

The women sat with their backs to the guards.

I would soon understand why.

I would also soon learn to tell the difference between exhaustion and defeat. To recognise the point at which a person's spirit is extinguished. After which death is the inevitable consequence. And how some chose death as the only route to freedom.

I later learned that some of those people came from as far away as Spain, France, Belgium, Portugal, Denmark and Germany.

I never knew then that we came from every walk of life too. Regardless of social status, profession, political or religious persuasion, we were all going to the final frontier of Europa – the end of civilisation as we knew it.

In time I came across people who had been farmers, blacksmiths, bakers, pastry makers, medicine men, preacher men, musicians, fishmongers, poulterers, watermen, fishermen, woolmen, silk women, wrestlers, paviers, cooks, cock fighters, girdlers, carpenters, haberdashers and housewives, as well as lords and ladies, even those of royal blood. Among our number were the king and queen of the Royal House of Portugal – and all their children.

To the right of the corral slave traders were sizing up new arrivals like myself, exchanging goods which were loaded up on to carts; or they were sitting cross-legged on the ground, a day's work done, toasting their good health and good fortune, knocking back grog which a serving boy poured into pewter tankards from a barrel.

They looked as if they'd discovered one of the great secrets of life – that money really did grow on trees.

My kidnapper tugged me towards the traders. I had lost control of my body. It was no longer I who decided whether I walked to my right, to my left, backwards or forwards, and at what speed.

He approached two men with big-feathered hats and black hair cascading to their shoulders – in the style of the pirates I'd heard about in Pa's stories. They had neatly trimmed black beards which tapered to a point, like the description of the Devil I'd listened to in sermons at church. They wore velvet-green frock coats with toggles, silk knee breeches and over-the-knee tan leather boots with little heels. It was the attire of gentlemen. They looked like identical twin brothers. Rich twin brothers. My kidnapper's demeanour changed as he approached them. He bowed deeply, helmet in hand. They remained upright and nodded, curtly.

They made an offer. It was accepted. I was sold.

I wasn't worth haggling over.

A guard prodded me with his musket into the corral, where I was introduced to an iron coffle – a rod to which collars were attached either end. Attached to the collar behind me was a boy who wore hessian knickerbockers and a labourer's smock. His face was smeared with freckles and his hair stuck out haphazardly like thick sheaves of corn. He smiled, I stared blankly back. He went cross-eyed.

I had found a friend.

His name was Garanwyn and he came from a farm on the Welsh border with England. He and his younger brother Dafyyd had been sold by a rival farmer who wanted to increase his stock of sheep.

Dafyyd was curled up asleep in front of me, sucking the fingers of his right hand into his little mouth. Blue veins mapped out his blood supply beneath translucent skin which showed the ribs of the carcass he would soon become.

Looking up, I caught sight of my kidnapper heading back into the forest, an invigorated spring in his step, even as he tried to keep steady two caskets of grog which were balanced on his shoulders.

A shiny new kettle was tied around his waist.

When I turned my attention over to where the traders gathered, I unexpectedly caught sight of someone I recognised. His cart had just rolled in loaded up with sheep's wool, cow hide, a couple of live bullocks. Stumbling and chained behind it were two bruised and furious young men with thighs like shanks of oxen.

It was none other than Gideon – the eldest son of Old John Hopkins, the master tanner at Duddingley. Gideon sold his father's leather in the wealthy faraway spa town of Upper Whiddon. He fancied himself a ladies' man although his prominent overbite meant women recoiled at the thought of clinking teeth with him. We girls avoided him because if we didn't, he'd find a way to touch us when Mam wasn't looking.

Now I stared at him with such an intensity he turned around with the force of it. Gideon knew me. He'd rescue me, surely, even if it meant clinking my teeth with his.

His face flushed when he saw me – one of the young Scagglethorpe girls. Was it embarrassment? Guilt? Pity? Had he led them to our district? I couldn't work it out. No sooner had he clocked me than he spun back and continued business with some traders who had gathered around his cart and were squeezing the two young men who were trying to shrug off anyone who touched them.

The time came for us to set off in a crocodile trail of inter-linked coffles into the forest. Torch-lights fired up the night. The coffle scraped the skin on my neck. Young Dafyyd was struggling with the weight of it.

People who couldn't go on were beaten with a truncheon until they did.

After many hours Dafyyd began to stumble about like a dazed newborn foal, his legs buckling under. I wanted to reach out but the coffle separated us by three feet.

Finally he collapsed, bringing down those of us attached to him like dominoes.

Our solemn procession ground to a halt. Dafyyd wasn't moving. The guards tried to rouse him with a few swift kicks.

Garanwyn tried to tell the guards he would carry his little brother on his shoulders, but they ignored him.

Whether Dafyyd's heart had already stopped beating at that stage I have no idea.

He was released from the coffle and swung by his arms and legs into some bushes.

Heavy as a three-stone sack of barley.

I heard the thud as he landed.

It took two nights and three days to reach the sea, which, I discovered, was just like the winter sky: lacklustre, bleached, vacant.

The surf drizzled spit onto the shingle beach.

Makeshift wooden cages were waiting for us.

Way out on the water were enormous ships.

Pulled up onto the beach were small boats called yawls.

The first time I saw the blak men I couldn't believe how their skin could be so dark, their features so broad, their hair so crisply curled. All the stories I'd heard were true because even though it was cold, they wore only cotton strips to cover their privates so they shivered and sneezed and were covered with goose pimples.

I didn't know then that they would rather suffer chilblains, frostbite, the dreaded influenza and even death, than dress like the natives.

The blak men inspected our bodies, our mouths, our limbs, and we were soon loaded face down into the yawls.

As I awaited my turn I imagined telling my sisters back home that I had seen the blak men, with my very own eyes, yes, really and truly; that the stories about slave raiders were not exaggerated gossip to bring drama into our lives, but a terrifying reality which had, fleet of foot and with a sinister stealth, made its way into our homelands.

Just before I was thrust down into a yawl, I looked at those enormous vessels out at sea, ready to carry me somewhere I knew not, and it hit me.

I wouldn't be reporting back to anyone.

Doklanda

When the slow-rocking wheels of the train eased to a sliding stop, I woke up.

It was dark. There was no door. Was I lying upside down or spinning from the ceiling?

I saw the moon dance above my head and a hawk sweeping down about to pluck out my eyes with its beak.

Raising an arm to defend myself, I realised it was the driver holding a lantern, shaking me awake. I could see clearly that he was indeed one of the Tuareg nomads who sometimes made their way to Londolo after a drought or war in their own lands. Submerged beneath flowing robes, they floated about the city keeping themselves apart. He was an immigrant, then, like myself.

'Come,' he said in that soft desert voice of theirs that requires little reverberation to blow across miles of uninterrupted sands. I scrambled to my feet, forgot the basket, and followed the Tuareg and the lantern off the train.

The platform was coated in a sleepy blur as I struggled to keep up with his loping strides.

We mounted a few steps to a landing where I could see a shimmer of light through a slit in the wall. I soon discovered it was a door because when he unbolted it a vicious blast of midday sun and noise exploded upon us like the roar of a furnace flame. I recoiled as if burned, ready to scamper back into the safety of the tunnel, but he turned around to face me, his willowy outline silhouetted against the bright daylight.

'Wait,' he said, and left.

I never saw him again. He had said all of two words to me.

Before I had time to bolt the door and panic my next helper arrived bearing a package of food in banana leaves.

'Hi,' she said cheerily, popping her head around the door as if I were an old friend she was just dropping by to visit. 'You can call me Ezinwene!'

I recognised the smell of Ylang Ylang perfume, from the fragrant isle of Madagascar. It came in a bottle shaped like a voluptuous woman and it was Madama Comfort's favourite. Whiffs of her sickly sweet scent usually turned a corner long before she did, giving us time to walk double-quick in the opposite direction.

I must have looked wild and famished because the young woman immediately handed the package over and watched with bemused fascination as my eyes watered and my hands tore into a dish of chicken in coconut sauce on a pile of tepid semolina.

When I finished I licked my fingers dry, one by one.

Ezinwene was young and came from a family of means, that much was obvious from the two gold crowns on her front teeth. (A rich Ambossan made damned sure everyone knew it.) Her lips were huge and soft and stained ruby from tobacco flowers. Her cinnamon skin glowed with the combination of a healthy diet and expensive moisturisers like cocoa butter and shea oil. Her teeth were fashionably sharpened to a point. Her intricately plaited hairdo rose up in swirling interlocking arcs, revealing she was unmarried. Wooden pendants were sewn into them to ward off evil spirits. Her perfect, naked, cone-shaped breasts were draped with dangling ostrich shell necklaces and her brown nipples were raised flirtatiously to the sky. Gold armlets ran up her arms like coiling snakes. The round platform of her well-fed hips, wrapped in shimmering green silk stencilled with orange flamingos, would secure her a good marriage.

Ezinwene exuded the kind of exuberant confidence peculiar to those whom the gods favoured.

To be honest I hated to come face to face with such wholesome Aphrikan youth, beauty and wealth.

She made me feel like the back end of a geriatric wart hog.

Worse, she reminded me of Little Miracle.

She chattered non-stop but I didn't mind. After so many hours alone I was hungry for conversation. The Ambossans didn't believe in solitude and neither did I any more. Did I really spend time back home happily playing alone with my rag doll? They said that the Europane need for solitude was further proof of our inferior culture, our inability to *share*. Privacy was a foreign concept to all Aphrikans. Life was communal and for we slaves, by necessity, intimate.

'I am so happy to have found my calling,' she prattled on. 'I am here to help those less fortunate than myself. I am of the belief that although we are all created equal, some have lives that are made easy and some will have to endure the greatest tribulations. Oh, look at me and my long words! That means *bad luck*, you understand. Life can seem so deeply unfair, can't it? Take me, for example, I only need click my fingers and the hired help comes running to obey my every command. But even for myself, life is a struggle. No one understands how horribly tedious, how boring, how excruciatingly dull, how mind-numbingly terrible it is to not be expected to lift a finger, quite literally. What on earth is one to do with one's time?'

She leaned in towards me.

'This slavery business really is quite appalling. Oh yes. I

absolutely do not approve of it. It has even given me night-mares. I've heard what happens on those awful ships and in the colonies. You poor, dear, sweet, tormented, unfortunate thing. How you must have suffered.'

She smoothed back stray curly hairs on her glistening fore-head and tugged at the sides of her expensive wrappa, straightening it out with long fingertips embellished with pumpkin-orange nail varnish onto which were stuck diamanté stars. She then cocked her head to one side and half-smiled at me with – well, there's a fine line between sympathy and pity and someone had just stepped over it.

When I was her age I carried a wooden tray full of sweet-potato chips on my shoulder and the knowledge that I was a fully paid up member of the most loathed race in the history of the world, the whytes, or, to use the correct jargon here, a term which the Ambossans invented – the *Caucasoi*.

'Listen very carefully,' she continued, over-enunciating. 'We are at the docks at Kanada Wadi. We need to get to West Japan Quays a little further down where a ship awaits you. Now, pay attention, don't mess this up or we're both stuffed. You will pretend to be my slave from this moment on and we have to leave right away. We cannot wait until night-time because by then news will have spread. Do you understand?'

I nodded my head, resisting the urge to deck her.

She hugged herself with self-congratulatory pleasure as if her mission were already accomplished and she could go home and boast about her dangerous escapade as a freedom fighter.

Was it really that simple?

I wanted to ask her if she'd done this before but I already knew the answer.

She would be careless.

I would be cautious.

The docks at Kanada Wadi were heaving with Ambossan dockers in leather loincloths. Their faces were caked with dirt, their bodies streaked with a gunge of sawdust and sweat. Their hooves were hard and cracked and they possessed the raw masculinity of men who endure strenuous physical labour for a living.

They stank too, of the repellent odour of seamen whose open pores seeped not sweat but the beer and rum they drank all day long because fresh water was in short supply at sea.

Like a gang of big cats on a hunt they began to prowl too close for comfort, sniffing out the pheromones of the nubile Ezinwene, disrobing her bottom half in whatever soft- or hard-porn scene each was capable of conjuring up for his own private viewing; inhaling her saccharine perfume as if it were an aphrodisiac as she pranced in front of them, throwing alluring smiles over her shoulder with the confidence of a woman who has no doubt she will receive admiring looks back when she does.

What on earth was she up to?

The sun struck us with typically nasty tropical ferocity, with no regard for those of us born without enough protective melanin.

The hammering, shouting and clanging of the docks was overbearing. I felt like a limp rag, my hair wringing wet, a pool of sweat dripping from my top lip.

The air was muggy. The waterways steamy. The muddy walkways glutinous and slippery beneath my feet. Everywhere there were pulleys, wheels, wooden crates the size of huts; ropes slumped like great sleeping snakes on the ground.

Cranes soared into the sky like exotic prehistoric birds. There were baskets of every shape and size, barrels which could fit ten of me inside, giant clay pots, iron scales so large they could weigh two Aphrikan buffalo apiece.

Slavers crowded the docks like hulking primordial mammoths with three masts apiece rising towards the sky like towering horns.

Yemonja, the Ambossan goddess of the sea, with her voluptuous breasts and furrowed brow, was most ships' figurehead of choice.

Jib booms protruded like giant swordfish snouts out of bows ready to slice through the seas of the world.

Each ship was studded with round gun-holes. Cannons would be rolled into them and protrude like erect phalluses when approaching the Europane coast.

The slavers rocked and creaked in the water, impatient to set sail again and feed their carnivorous bellies with the succulent delights of human livestock.

Seamen clambered up and down the rigging and swarmed over the decks as they loaded up for the three-month journey of the Middle Passage.

I clutched my stomach.

Slavers sailed to the coast of Europa where they bartered for my people with beads, knives, hats, gourds, bowls, spears, muskets, bolts of cotton, brandy, rum, kettles, even.

It's nice to know what you're worth.

Slavers had just arrived or were getting ready to set sail for the various coasts of Europa: the Coal Coast, the Cabbage Coast, the Tin Coast, the Corn Coast, the Olive Coast, the Tulip Coast, the Wheat Coast, the Grape Coast, the Influenza Coast and the Cape of Bad Luck.

When these ships sailed on to the New World, they exchanged slaves for rum, tobacco, cotton, and then sailed back home to the UK – rich, obese, slothful, satisfied.

Oh, it made great business sense for the Europanes. They received luxury items such as battered old hats and knives and in return sold off healthy specimens of the human race.

We passed warehouses on the Doklanda quayside where three million barrels of rum were stored at any one time. The thick, soupy, intoxicating smell of the wood-soaked rum was enough to make me feel heady.

Then we came upon several little shops selling seafarers' staples such as live chickens and sheep, dried goods, cooking pots and utensils, and then to a shop I knew by name only. I stared at the window of 'Fashion Victim' which sold *Designer Jewellery for the Master with Taste*. A blue plaque bearing the UK Royal Seal of Approval was nailed to the door.

It was high-end, it was classy, it was only for those who could afford to adorn their slaves with expensive 'jewellery' to parade at weddings, rituals, festivals and the like.

Set on a bed of purple crushed velvet was a gold choker inlaid with sapphire, with a hook at the back on which to attach a chain (name engraving an optional extra); there were chunky gold bangles inlaid with amethysts with an interlocking chain (also available in platinum), silver-plated anklets (with matching keys).

A naked seven-foot security guard stood inside the door. His chest was criss-crossed with lots of multicoloured beads, a red-dyed lion's mane headdress raised him another two feet to nearly nine, and he had a sword and shield at the ready. He was whyte, of course. Security guards always were. This one looked very Nordic, with his long flaxen plaits and stature.

Ezinwene had stopped some way ahead and turned around, finally noticing me lagging behind. She shot me a stern reproachful look from eyes that glittered even at a distance. It was the typical slave-madam look. Designed to instil fear and subservience.

I dragged myself away from the Crown Purveyors of Fetters and Manacles and hurried to catch up. By the time I did she was on her way again, walking closer to the ships which loomed ominously above. I read their names: *The Ambossan Hero, Europane Queen, Black Beauty, The 3-Point Turn, The Whyteamoor, O Dear Mama.*

Then I began to notice that the people on the docks were surreptitiously smirking at me: the fine ladies with their topless fashions and supercilious eyes, the fine gentlemen with their invincible struts and luxurious material flung over one shoulder, the robust children led by whyte nannies who were more mother to them than their own.

Ezinwene stopped in front of a small ship moored at the end of the quay and waited for me to catch up, whereupon she tried to usher me up the gangway with what I believed was an impatient, lip-curling grimace. Sunlight bounced off her gold teeth but cast the rest of her in shadow. In the energy-sapping heat and noise and frazzle of the docks it dawned on me that her mission was in fact to lead me onto a slave ship where I would be sold on illegally, or where a sheriff was waiting to take me back to Bwana in chains.

Had the Resistance been infiltrated? Of course.

Everything was clicking into place.

The heat was frying my brains.

I couldn't think straight.

My feet could not, would not climb aboard the ship.

Not another floating torture chamber.

Not another floating coffin.

Not after all this time.

I dug my heels into the sludge of the docks, and felt myself sinking.

Back through the years to when I was a captured child.

The Middle Passage

Trussed up in the bottom of the slaver's yawl, I felt like a trapped fish flapping about in its final death throes as I struggled onto my back, spitting out rotten fish scales.

My head banged against splintered wood as I inhaled the strange new smell of the seaweed which slurped against the side of the yawl, now lurching away from the coast.

I was being pulled in two: my body forced away from the shore, while my heart dragged me back to the landmass to which my whole life was attached.

Two men rowed out to sea, muscles pumping hard, four oars chopping up the waves, ignoring the squirms of we poor captives wedged in between their legs. They were the strange blak men who had taken control of our shipment on the beach, I noticed. Not of my own kind. My own kind? If I had to pinpoint a moment when the human race divided into the severe distinctions of blak and whyte, that was it: people belonged to one of two colours and in the society I was about to join my colour, not my personality or ability, would determine my fate.

The rowing stopped and I was carried up a rope ladder which swayed precariously down the side of the ship.

As I looked backwards one last time towards the coast, the dark forest seemed to charge towards the sea – a legion of black stallions racing to my rescue.

Then I caught sight of birds swooping down into the sea, making little splashes as they dived underneath the water in a carefree display of aquatic ballet.

It was dazzling.

Water glistened on my eyelashes.

I blinked to release it.

The ocean streamed soundlessly down.

The ship was a slaver manned by the blak men. It weighed some 200 tons with six cannons mounted on her gun-deck. I craned my neck at the proliferation of nets and ropes that stretched high into the sky to secure the billowing sails being hoisted towards the trade winds. They were like the wings of the white albatross of legend, ready to carry us to a strange new place.

I was carried on board over the shoulder of one of the men, my hands bound, my body bruised and sopping wet. As the ship rolled from side to side in a gathering wind, I shuffled from foot to foot trying to remain upright. Goats, sheep and chickens in coops were winched bleating and squawking on board. Water caskets were hauled up over the sides alongside sacks of wheat and clumps of cowhides and more captives arrived dripping water over the poop rail, while others were being shoved down the hatch into the hold.

Garanwyn managed to sidle next to me. He was at least a foot taller than me and his bulbous knees bolted his much thinner legs into place, while his knobbly shoulders tried to shrug off a childhood that had not yet arrived at the manhood which would bulk out his frame and settle his proportions.

Yet, like the man he wanted to become, he took my limp, damp hand in his confident clammy one and gripped it. I squeezed back. Warmth charged into me.

Captain Wabwire, the man in charge, leaned against a rail, watching the activity on board his ship, one leg casually crossed over the other.

In the shadow of a sail, his eyes appeared as bottomless hollows.

He swivelled a polished wooden cane between the slender fingers of his hands.

Unlike the sailors who wore their hair shaven, cropped or stuck up in uncombed bushes, his was plaited into neat corn rows. A pristine white wrappa wound around his slim hips, the ends flung over his shoulders with the usual voluminous flourish.

I was mesmerised.

He was a long-necked, snooty-nosed peacock, standing aloof from the chaos of loading his cargo.

He caught sight of me peeping at him through a gap between the waists of two male captives. We were both transfixed. I wanted to drag my eyes away but a fresh deluge of tears poured down my cheeks.

He ruffled his wings, turned and strutted towards the cabins on the quarterdeck, the cane now spinning furiously.

Sightings of this exquisite bird were rare after that.

The seamen's bodies and words had a strange physical presence. Their muscles were crisply defined and densely packed and they spoke a language unlike any I'd ever heard. Clicks and clacks were interspersed between words – sounds made by sucking the tongue against the roof of the mouth. They chucked wide, open vowels into the air while hard consonants rode on the spine of their own reverberation and shuddered down my vertebrae, making me shiver.

I gaped at the nicks of their facial engravings and at biceps imprinted with black-inked tattoos of naked women whose exaggerated buttocks enlarged when they flexed their muscles. One of them pissed over the side of the ship. The others snortled when the wind slapped it back so that it showered a group of us captives.

I winced, not realising such uncouth behaviour was nothing compared to what these lions of the sea would get up to once out at sea.

The men who worked the slavers were the lowlifes of the seafaring community because even *their* chance of surviving the Middle Passage was low. Those who had been press-ganged into it had no choice but to sink to the slaver's moral code, which was – Anything Goes.

As I stood there amid the chaos, a sailor cuffed his barnacled hand around my neck with such force it propelled my legs towards the hatch.

I tumbled down the narrow wooden steps into the lamp-lit darkness while my mind scuttled straight back up again, leaped over the poop rail into a yawl, rowed to the shore at great speed, and ran through the forest for home.

Below deck the storage system was both unisex and utilitarian: planks of wood formed shelves which ran in six parallel rows the entire length of the hold.

The shelves were space-effective and cost-effective, I later found out. There were two available options: the Tight Fit, which allowed for an extra 30 per cent of cargo, but with a downside of increased fatalities. Or the Loose Fit, which offered more space per person, but also resulting in reduced profit.

I was assigned my space on a shelf and secured with leg irons bolted to the wood. I wasn't handcuffed, the women weren't. No fancy bracelets for us, only the men wore chains which connected the irons on their ankles with those on their wrists.

A minor discomfort were the maggots who dined on the

festering gashes caused by the constant chafing of iron on skin. Unfortunately, it was impossible for the men to reach down to pick the moist little squidges out of their ankles.

My ankles were almost thin enough to slip through the irons.

Our shelf was reserved for the female of the species only and we were to spend nearly all of the trip lying prone upon it. We lay on our sides as Captain Wabwire had opted for the Tight Fit – more cargo, less space.

If one of us turned we all had to.

Headroom of less than eighteen inches made sitting up impossible for all but the tiniest.

When I lay on my right, my face was squashed into Hildegaard's back. Her spongy, creamy skin lifted easily off the bone. She became my mattress and my pillow.

When I lay on my left, my nose prodded Samantha's spinal column.

Hildegaard came from a nation that was not my own. I never worked out which one because we never got past the hold's lingua franca of sign language.

She had two long blonde plaits which wrapped around her head twice. Lice crawled all over her scalp, as they did all of ours. We scratched our heads until they bled and became infected. The men were shaved but a woman's locks raised her market price. We picked out the lice of the head in front. Behind the ears were favourite breeding grounds. It was quite effective as displacement activity.

It was a shock, though, to discover your neighbour had died during the night and the lice were still burrowing.

Like the time I woke up.

And Samantha didn't.

Samantha had been a milkmaid on the Throgmorton Estate some distance south from my family home.

She was bony where Hildegaard was fleshy, freckled where Hildegaard was unblemished, had a head of shoulder-length auburn coils compared to Hildegaard's endlessly circumnavigating plaits.

Samantha told me that she was seventeen and had been married a year with a one-month-old daughter, Rosie-May. Her husband, Wilf, had been hired out by their master to a neighbouring farm, but walked over to see his wife and daughter every Sunday after church. He'd gather them both in his arms and hold them for the longest while.

With the advent of summer, the master, Lord Thurston Throgmorton, began his seasonal visit to the hovel she shared with seven other women on the estate.

Those who resisted were no match for his strength.

But Samantha was now married; a wife and mother.

She left him rocking on the ground cradling his crotch, sending the foulest curses out into the night.

A few days later she was on her way to the dairy, Rosie-May strapped to her back, whistling the nursery rhyme *Mary Had a Little Lamb*, noticing that the moss on the heath had turned the loveliest shade of green, marvelling at how the days were warming up very nicely indeed, when two six-footers appeared around the bend, wearing brown capes and high leather boots. They blocked both her path and the sunlight.

Their eyes were flint in the act of ignition.

They ripped Rosie-May from her back and dropped her. Just like that.

Samantha was dragged away towards the valley at the foot of the hills.

When she managed to look back, there, standing in the middle of the track, was Lord Throgmorton.

Triumphant.

The lump at his feet was her little girl.

In the forest they took it in turns – although she never felt a thing.

Spent, her kidnappers rearranged themselves, bound her with twine, set her on a horse in front of the rider, his arms around her waist as he made haste for the coast.

She could feel him up against her, hard, and every few hours he set her down to relieve himself in her.

They took it in turns.

And so it went on until they reached the coast.

As the slaver progressed towards the tropics, it became unbearably hot. Fresh air entered through the wooden gratings and air ports but there was never enough of it. When it rained we heard the dreaded shout, 'Batten down the gratings, fore and aft!'

If a storm raged for days, my bruised lungs wheezed like an asthmatic.

Mealtimes we were fed pulped horse-beans with yam mixed with slabber sauce.

Women and children were allowed to sit on the floor and eat from a communal tub, each with our own wooden spoon.

Samantha didn't have much of an appetite.

She gave me what she didn't eat herself.

I counted more of her bones becoming visible.

Her eyes never travelled far from that warm English morning.

I was the girl her child might have become.

When she stroked my cheek, it was her daughter's.

When she looked into my eyes, she didn't see me.

When she spoke, it was to Rosie-May.

In the absence of family, we all became surrogates.

Hildegaard piled so much food onto her spoon it teetered towards her trembling, puckered mouth. Her moist pink tongue slid out and guided it in without spillage. When she dipped in for a fifth or sixth helping, her adversary, a woman called Bethany who matched Hildegaard for size and voracity, flicked the offending spoon away from the pot.

Slaps, punches, pulls and kicks turned into a free-for-all among the women. The crew crowded into the hold, cheering, goading and roaring as Hildegaard head-butted Bethany so hard her forehead split open, and Bethany wrapped her fists around Hildegaard's plaits, trying to pull them out.

I wished the food Hildegaard put in her throat would catch and choke her.

We were *all* starving.

I began to regurgitate what I ate.

I was becoming a sliver.

One day I slipped my feet out of my irons.

I put them back in and looked around to see if anyone had noticed.

The crew took aside those observed to be not eating.

The punishment was to place hot coals so near the offender's lips, they blistered.

It didn't always do the trick.

The males of my species were kept shackled for their gourmet experience. Food was fed to them from a ladle. If they were too weak to lift their heads they had to eat prone and sometimes choked, a couple of times to death.

When we were good, and the weather was stable, we ate up on deck.

We fouled ourselves. Of course we did. It ran between the slats onto the people lying underneath.

Large, conical buckets at the end of the platforms filled up quickly.

If there was a terrible storm, we weren't able to muck out the hold. (You can imagine.) One gale lasted eighteen days.

Just as well we'd been stripped naked after the first week.

Fresh water became my new god.

And where was He when I needed Him?

We prayed and sang hymns and hoped for the miracle that never came.

Bedsores, cuts, maggots, hunger, dehydration, asphyxiation, my own filth – I disgusted myself.

In the early days I tried holding my breath in a childlike attempt at suicide.

My dreams were filled with wintry breezes.

My dreams were filled with tumblers of homemade lemonade.

My dreams were filled with the laughter of my sisters who had lost all irritating personality traits.

My dreams were filled with my mother and father's love.

My dreams were filled with the aroma of honeysuckle and baking bread and the lavender bush behind the cottage from which we made mothballs and the sharp, refreshing aroma of grass after a night's rain.

When I took a trip into my dreams, I didn't want to come back.

*

Dr Nwonkorey, the ship's surgeon, was the oldest person on board. He had white froth over his patchy brown palette, white foam for a moustache, white weeds for a beard and remarkably white teeth. A layer had formed on mine that only a shovel could scrape off.

Dr Nwonkorey worked his way through the nauseous fug of the hold with a strip of lime-soaked muslin tied over his mouth. He complained that the hold looked like a slaughter house with slicks of blood, watery shit dripping everywhere, slimy mucus running down the noses of men who could not reach up to wipe them – and the sweat, the fever, the dysentery, the vomit, the despair, and a floor so treacherous with human detritus he had to be careful not to slide from one end of the hold to the other.

He had a soft spot for we children and at first would practise a hearty laugh on us. When we merely stared back with dead-fish eyes, he dropped the act and met us with the same.

When he spooned vinegar into my mouth to prevent scurvy, he would pat my forehead with a damp cloth, and sigh, his boozy breath lingering as he moved on.

Up and down the aisle he'd go, naked belly wobbling over his white cotton wrappa as he brandished scissors and blades and cotton thread and poultices and potions and delivered magic spells and incantations, all the while muttering, 'It's hopeless! Useless! What can I do? What the hell can I do?'

One time he came to work so inebriated he bounced down the steps on his bottom. His hair was a matted frizz, his eyes bloodshot, his wrappa soiled. When he landed on the floor he slurred, 'I used to be the personal witch doctor of King Wamukoto Landuleni Eze!'

Then he retched.

We saw less of him: three days, five, ten . . .

Surgeons on other slavers were paid Head Money – pro rata

pay for per capita delivery. A cash incentive to keep the cargo alive. But I don't think performance-related pay was part of the deal with our pissed old ex-witch doctor.

It was never silent below decks. A cacophony of moans and groans, day and night, punctured by screams, which were contagious. If a screamer didn't shut up, they were whipped until they did.

And, if a passenger went insane, there really was only one solution – and it was final.

Bodies were tossed overboard and became dinner for the sharks.

They say the seabed of the Atlantic is paved with the skeletons of those who didn't make it.

If they all got up and swam ashore they could form their own country.

'Get them above hatches!' was always music to my ears.

The fresh air made me so heady I'd almost faint. Some did.

The ocean view was . . . dramatic and panoramic.

Buckets of salt water were thrown over us – a few moments of bliss.

We were forced to sing and dance in a circle, waving our arms vigorously, a cat-o'-nine-tails lashing at any feet that stopped.

The males of my species remained handcuffed and linked by a chain which was in turn bolted to the deck. Given the restrictions, their choreography was by necessity a flat-footed stomp. The deck shook.

It was almost as if they were angry.

Up there in clear, clean, sunny daylight the sailors could see what was to their fancy.

It was expected.

A perk of the trade.

Were not their women in some distant land?

Was life not tough for them at sea too?

Were not the female captives compliant?

Easy, so to speak.

Most nights the wooden hatch creaked open. Women were eased off shelves. At first a scuffle might ensue but as the journey progressed few had the strength to resist. When the hatch closed I'd hear the rumblings of men helpless to protect their own. Most women returned after a few hours, or a few days: crying, bleeding, furious, mute. Some were never seen again.

Hildegaard twitched like mad whenever the hatch opened at night.

Still comely, she'd soon be cherry-picked. We all knew that.

Then one night they came for her.

I watched as they tried to remove her from the shelf while she turned herself into a dead weight, forcing them to yank her off it.

The bones of Samantha's skeletal arms tightened around me as we watched.

As they led her away, Hildegaard rolled her hands into fists and jerked them about. She twisted her naked body, kicked out, spat, tried to bite them.

She was formidable but I was so scared for her.

I wanted to say goodbye but when I opened my mouth, only a croak came out.

If I close my eyes I can still feel Hildegaard's warm, maternal body; how when she smothered me in her arms, I slept as if I was free.

The person allocated her space had been sitting for weeks in a passageway so crowded she couldn't even lie down. Surplus slaves were stored there, or in the nose of the ship or where there was space towards the rudder.

Let's call it steerage class.

Jane was thirteen. She wept with relief the first time she got to lie down on the shelf and stretch her whole body out. (Little did she know.) A prisoner of war, she had been incarcerated in a fort on the coast for months before being shipped out. Hundreds of slaves had been stuffed into an airless, windowless dungeon. She said she expected special treatment on account of her condition – pregnancy. How she prattled on for hours. Maybe her own cabin? A bed? Dress? Basin? Soap? Washrag? Comb? Blanket? Chamber pot? Plate?

Yes, any day now.

Jane had travelled so deeply into fantasy she had lost her way back.

Garanwyn lay on a shelf opposite mine. We found each other's voices only if we shouted above the discordant choir below decks.

When his voice started to break he told me he was becoming a man.

We discussed our destination, but no one was really sure where we were going. Was it that place called the New World? But why? What lay in store for us?

We had no idea.

When I threw up, Garanwyn reassured me it wouldn't last. (It didn't.)

If someone died in the night, he'd tell me to thank God I was still alive. (I did.)

When I fell into depression, he told me freedom was just around the corner. (It wasn't.)

I told him about my leg irons. He told Slade, who slept next to him.

Word came back that I should go up on deck that very night to locate the keys to the padlocks. It was not a request.

My ankles were now as thin as a duck's. How I willed them to swell up.

For the first time in my life people depended on me – not to collect eggs or stop milk from boiling over, or to sweep out the yard – but to save their lives.

I slid out of my irons and crept up the hatch, watched by everyone who could swivel their heads to see me.

The sailors had become careless. It was unlocked.

I emerged onto the deck, my heart punching its way out of my chest cage.

Waves splashed against the ship.

The sky was the star-spangled blue of my homeland.

It was so peaceful and beautiful up there.

A full moon was passing behind clouds, providing enough light for the task at hand but not so much that I was in spotlight.

A single guard on watch was curled over a coil of thick rope. Snoring. Reeking of rum. They all did.

I crept over to a teenage boy so brown he really was almost blak. His lips seemed to spread from ear to ear. Several weeks earlier we'd watched him accidentally drop a sail whilst up the mizzenmast. The Chief Mate immediately ordered a flogging and he was tied to a post and got thirty strokes.

He must have been assigned the night duty no one wanted.

Keys to our chains dangled from a cord hanging from his neck. My fingers quaked as I went to work on the knot. Suddenly he shifted position and fell from the rope, landing with a jolt on his back. He lay there, dazed, looking up at the sky, blinking drunkenly. I had darted behind the rope and lay on my front, peering around it. He turned over onto his side and went back to sleep. The keys were now trapped underneath him. Damn! I thought of the community below stairs. I could not let them down.

I began to search the ship for something that could break chains or a padlock. I darted about in a panic. My hands became my eyes as they delved into baskets and boxes and came up with buckles, rigging tools and, finally, a mallet and a marlin spike.

It might just work.

I dashed hell-for-leather back to the hold with my implements of liberation and gave them to Slade, who worked with the spike, carefully, quickly.

Garanwyn ordered me back to my shelf, just in case.

I lay back down, put my feet back into the irons.

Each man in turn was unshackled. Four, five, six, seven. They worked smoothly, silently, no longer half-dead but invigorated.

I prayed so hard that they would succeed.

I watched Slade, light-foot, swift, make his way up the steps with the poise of a snake about to strike. My Garanwyn was right behind him.

Just as they reached the top the hatch opened and they came face to face with two sailors coming down to pick someone for a midnight fuck.

They hadn't even bothered with muskets – smug gits.

The moon shone down on Slade's and Garanwyn's faces. Frozen.

All hell broke loose. The sailors shouted for assistance. Our men scrambled up and overcame them.

We heard a call to arms and the crew sprang into action. Feet trampled up above, muskets were fired, the hatch was slammed shut, a few of the men tried using the mallet to hammer it open. It was useless. They tried to reshackle themselves. That was useless too.

Curses were flung down at us through the gratings. The skin would be filleted off our backs. We were to be buried alive. No food. No water.

Twenty armed sailors entered and took out all the men who were unshackled.

We fell silent.

And stayed that way.

Four days passed before the hatch was opened again.

We were weak, we were dehydrated, we were starving, we were going to die.

Samantha finally did.

She lay right up against me – rapidly decomposing in the heat – for three nights before they removed her.

There was no space for me to pull myself away from her body.

Her bowels had emptied. So did mine.

The maggots which crawled out of her mouth and nose and ears tried to crawl into mine too.

The smell was – unforgettable.

I went a little insane.

On the fifth day we were ordered to muck out the hold, we were allowed up for exercise, we were fed. Women and children were now also chained to the deck.

They led the 'rebels' out. A show was about to begin.

Slade was not among them.

Then I saw Garanwyn, dragging himself on the ground with one arm. His kneecaps had been smashed in. His eyes were buried beneath bruised swellings. The right side of his face was twice its normal size. His left ear had been severed. His right one a bloodied pulp. His chest had collapsed as if all the ribs had been extracted. One arm dangled from its socket. He had no fingernails. He had no toenails. His genitalia were a mess.

He was the youngest of the men. They had tried to make him talk.

Garanwyn's eyes sought mine and when he found them he mouthed 'Shhhh!'

I thought he might be angry with me, but no, he was still thinking of my welfare.

They strung him up.

The cat-o'-nine-tails whizzed through the air, ripping open the skin on his back, buttocks and legs and slashing it to pieces.

The sailors charged with whipping him took it in turns. Four shifts.

They just wouldn't stop.

On and on it went.

There was no need to see if he was alive before he was thrown overboard.

It was all my fault.

I would live with the guilt for the rest of my life.

The other men were let off with thirty lashes apiece. They had to heal by the time the ship docked, to be healthy bucks capable of fetching a good price.

There were 400 slaves at embarkation, and 227 survived.

Which was about the international average.

*

Captain Wabwire put in an appearance that morning. He hadn't been sighted for ages. He watched the proceedings whilst rocking backwards and forwards on his feet. The canary-yellow caftan he wore that day was encrusted with food droppings. The plaits in his hair were dried-up and coming undone. His eyes had lost their sheen. His skin was dulled. His expression, numb.

He staggered towards we captives as if to make an announcement, as if to lecture us on the futility of insurrection.

But when he opened his mouth to speak, he fell to the ground.

Two sailors rushed to pick him up and escort him back to the master cabin.

It dawned on me that he was pissed out of his head.

After that, our ship sailed uneventfully towards its destination – the paradise island of New Ambossa on West Japan.

Oh Little Miracle

Upon arrival at the port of New Ambossa, I was subjected to the traditional slave-market scramble. We were shoved into a holding pen until at the appointed hour the gates were flung open and a howling mob of men burst in like a pack of starving hyenas about to rip us to shreds.

They grabbed at the slaves they wanted, tied us up with rope or simply dragged us out of the pen by whatever limbs or body parts they could lay their hands on.

I collapsed in the middle of the scrum and was stampeded on. The man who pulled me up wanted me, but so did another, which resulted in a tug-of-war as they each tried to dislodge a shoulder from its socket.

The victor bound my wrists with rope so tightly they bled, then dragged me out of the pen like I was a goat (not for the first time).

I wet myself but I was used to that by now.

He tied me to a post, inspected my scalp and ears, pulled apart my lips and invaded my mouth with fingers that stank of tobacco and left their bitterness on my gums. I filled my mouth with spittle but the foul taste lingered for ages afterwards. He cupped my chest, slapped my bottom like it was a cow's shank and squeezed each thigh to test its musculature. Then he made me sit down and spread my legs so that he could 'inspect' my vagina, pushing those meaty fingers of his inside my virginal self. I didn't cry. I was determined not to cry. At the end, I had to stand up and bend over so that he could 'inspect' my anus too.

I cried.

No one paid any attention.

Satisfied, he went off to purchase me from Captain Wabwire, who was dressed in a spotless cream linen gown with black tasselled borders. He sat straight-backed at a trestle table under a canopy of banana leaves, looking most respectable and dignified after his seafaring ordeal, although I did notice an imperceptible wrinkling of his nose, whereupon he would open a tiny snuff box and take a sniff.

I watched him count up the cowrie-pounds from my sale in little pyramids and enter the transaction in a ledger – no doubt with a flourishing, well-educated, calligraphic script.

Before we left the port I was forced to my knees and branded on my shoulder with the initials for Panyin Ige Ghika – my new mistress.

It took weeks for the different layers of encrustations to shrivel up into scabs and drop off.

Bundled onto the back of a cart, a sack was put over my head and we travelled for hours over potholed roads. My branded shoulder hurt so much I almost bit through my bottom lip. My wrists and ankles were still bound and bleeding. And I was itchy with urine and faeces (yup, that too) which attracted the attention of flies as my naked posterior was exposed to the indifferent air.

Late that night we pulled up at the Roaring River Estate, where I was to spend the rest of my childhood.

I never saw any of my fellow passengers from the slaver again.

Never got to say goodbye to no one, neither.

Pushed into a hut with no windows and bolted in, the next day I was washed down and my wounds were dressed. I was then led up to the Great House where I was presented to my new owners, the Ghika family: Massa Tschepi, Madama Panyin

Ige and, after many miscarriages, the *wonderful*, the *incredible*, the *bestest* in the whole wide worldest, yes she is, you know she is, the *amazing* – drum rolls, bugles, praise singers – LITTLE MIRACLE! – rapturous applause, stamping feet, mass hysteria.

Trussed up in rustling ivory silks, the little brown dumpling sat between her regal parents like a princess.

Madama, whose slick plaits were pulled tight off her face into a topknot, wore eight brass neck rings which stretched her neck to twice its original length. She barely moved her body when she talked and she glided rather than walked.

Massa Tschepi had a mouth full of gold teeth. I couldn't take my eyes off them. Were they real? Surely not.

All were seated on throne-like seats in a room stuffed full of furniture and objects which were even stranger than Percy's aristocratic assembly of stuffed animals.

Who were these people? Like the sailors, they were so dark I couldn't (yet) easily read their faces, nor could I understand a word they said. All those clicks and clacks again. Were they kind or angry? Everything was weird: the furniture, their clothes (which had no arms or legs), the stuffed giraffe by the window – what kind of creature was *that*? Had it once been alive? Really? Even the flowers were odd, and why uproot them and put them in bowls? How come one bunch looked like birds with spiked orange heads and another like purple cabbages on a stem? Cabbages as decoration? And the heat made me feel like I was boiling in a vat of oil. It took me years to get used to it.

And why hadn't my daddy come to rescue me?

If I'm honest, I don't think I ever really forgave him.

Ever.

I started to snivel, which my new owners ignored. Then again, I was beginning to realise these people couldn't see *me*.

Little Miracle sat prized and protected by the plantation titans.

Her juicy Ambossan lips had such a pronounced natural pout it looked like she was deliberately puckering up her mouth. Her nostrils were in a permanent flare. She had ballooned cheeks, and a neck so non-existent her shoulders looked hunched.

She wore one neck ring. Others would be added as she aged.

She aimed a greedy little smile at her new plaything, like she couldn't wait to get her mitts on me.

Her parents called her Missy, and her new 'companion' was renamed Omorenomwara, which took weeks to pronounce properly.

'Omorenomwara,' Madama repeated, over-enunciating. 'It's easy. Break it down into six syllables, O – MO – RE – NOM – WA – RA. Try harder, dear.'

(*The name's Doris Scagglethorpe, actually. Now you try and pronounce that!*)

The Ghikas bought me for their child because there were no Ambossan playmates within a thirty-mile radius, and rather than have her rough-housing with any of the louse-ridden, booger-nosed, scuff-kneed 'field rats' on the plantation, they wanted one who could be turned into a little lady.

Heck, I wasn't about to complain. After the slave ship, I was grateful for all mercies.

My predecessor, a girl called Madisa, had contracted yaws. When her skin broke out into blackberry-type bumps she was quarantined in an out-of-the-way hut.

Food was left under the door, until she passed away.

Little Miracle, jumping up and down (with some effort), told me that now *I* was her best friend.

Her very own friend, she mimed. All hers and no one else's.

She tugged at my long, straight hair until I went 'Ouch!', then giggled. Tweaked my straight nose until I spluttered – giggled some more. Pinched my pale skin until it turned bluish and giggled so much she almost choked. When I began to speak in my language, she almost had a seizure.

I laughed too.

My job was to please Little Miracle.

Her job was to please herself.

We were both about eleven years of age, or rather eleven *rainy seasons* as I soon learned to say, but Little Miracle appeared younger because she was short and rotund, like a young girl still covered in the lumps and creases of an infant's body.

I was tall, thin and angular.

'You ugly,' she said, putting on baby-speak, as if that excused her rudeness, pointing at my face in the reflection of a pool of water after the rains.

'Me pretty,' she said, preening herself.

She was right, of course.

And there was no one in that society to tell me otherwise.

As soon as I could speak basic Ambossan she secretly began to teach me to read and write, as it was illegal for slaves to be literate on the island. I soon worked out that it was because she wanted me to read her the Anancy spider fables at bedtime, and do her homework. Not that I think her tutor was ever hoodwinked, she just knew better than to criticise the one and only daughter of the Ghikas.

Once, while I was reciting the Ambossan alphabet to Little

Miracle, I saw Madama peering sideways around the doorway, a crystal chandelier-style earring trembling in her right ear the only sign that she was furious. When she saw me looking, she slid out of view, but never said a word.

'Follow me,' Little Miracle said, walking off with her flat-footed duck-waddle down the corridor into a bedroom bursting with Aphrikan Queens in various get-ups, a collection which must have run into the hundreds.

A special Doll Maid kept them damage- and dust-free.

She told me their names, each and every one.

Nothing was ever handed down to me. At first I wondered why she didn't give me the things she no longer used. My sisters and I had shared everything. But Little Miracle hoarded everything: clothes, dolls, jewellery, toys. She got hysterical if anything went missing, ensuring one of the other slaves was whipped by an overseer until they confessed to the 'theft'.

Not me, though. *You-Me-Best-Friends*, she kept telling me.

I soon realised I wasn't.

I wasn't allowed to touch any of her possessions without her permission.

If I did, she pinched my arm, hard.

In fact, I couldn't do anything without her say-so. I wouldn't talk to any of the other house slaves, especially those our age, or go for a walk outside alone.

When I broke the unspoken rules in those first few weeks she'd throw a wobbly and threaten to have me sent to the fields.

Her low wooden bed was carved from a single block of cherry wood with a raised headrest and carved side panels illustrated with flowers and spiders.

There was no mattress or pillow; the Ambossans didn't use them.

She had an indigo sheet stencilled with animal shapes.

I slept at the foot of her bed on a sleeping mat covered by whatever wrappa I'd worn that day.

At the beginning of my new life I dreamed of my family at night. Just before sleep I replayed every memory I had of them, imagining I was still there, trying to keep them alive in me.

Even when I didn't go to sleep crying, I woke up with the salt of tears encrusted on my cheeks.

I began to force myself to think of other things at night. My most popular fantasy was to imagine myself as my mistress, the girl with everything. I had a perfect complexion, perfect parents, perfect status, perfect home, perfect possessions.

I'd wake up with a smile on my face.

During my waking hours I was everything my mistress wanted me to be.

During my sleeping hours – I became her.

I had nightmares in those early years too – of drowning.

But when I screamed Little Miracle shouted at me to keep quiet or else she'd tell her parents I was disrupting her sleep.

When she had nightmares, I had to climb into her bed and cuddle her.

'Huggles,' she'd snivel. 'Huggles for Missy-me.'

Madama brought in skilled craftsmen to satisfy her daughter's whims.

We were taught how to print Adinkra cloth together, cut stars and squares onto halved potatoes, dip them in dye, stamp them onto white cotton. We used an Aphro-pick to create wavy lines.

We extracted clay from the base of termite mounds and rolled it to make pots.

We made masks from leather, metal, leaves, vegetable fibres, grass and red abrus seeds, which were poisonous.

We made hair for our masks from raffia.

We made drums from wood and hide, playing them loudly when the grown-ups weren't around.

We learned to weave kente strips too, on a loom her mother bought specially and installed in a purpose-built hut. We were taught a pattern called 'My skill is exhausted' and another called 'My ideas have come to an end'.

She showed all our handiwork to her mother who said she was such a *clever, clever, clever little girl. Yes you are, you know you are, my sweetie-pie.*

Whatever we made became the property of Little Miracle.

I plaited Little Miracle's hair, sewing in brass discs, shells, amber beads, coral and pearls.

Mine was worn in a pigtail.

Every morning we went on her constitutional down by the Roaring River which ran through the estate.

We both loved sitting by the waterfall, the dangerous excitement of all that water leaping over the side and crashing down as creamy froth into the rocky river so far below you couldn't hear it land.

And every afternoon we had her nap.

Once a year Madama took us all the way to the capital to visit a boutique for little girls called 'Angels' where she bought material for Little Miracle's outfits. They were embroidered, painted or stamped with flowers, fruits, birds, fishes.

As we got older, her Missy was having none of that. She

made her mother take her to the capital's edgy fashion boutique, 'Funked Up'. She became the epitome of cool in fluorescent prints splashed with images of the imperial capital of Londolo's high-rise towers, skateboarding kids, and the silhouettes of youngsters shaking their money-makers at raves.

Her mother winced when she saw what her daughter was buying.

She needn't have worried, it was all lip service.

I mean – what did her daughter have to rebel against?

The years coalesced like sap leaking from a rubber tree.

Living in luxurious isolation in the claustrophobic Great House I became languid, my emotions dampened, the boundaries between who I was and what I had been blurred.

Little Miracle and I were together 24/7.

When there were visitors, I wasn't allowed to join in the conversation.

She was the only person who heard my words.

Something changed on the day I turned fourteen.

I woke up and thought, you know what? That girl called Doris? Where the hell did *she* go?

Soon after, Little Miracle came down with such a severe bout of malaria she slept for large portions of the day.

I was bored and one afternoon found myself slumped against a wall in the corner of her bedroom, doodling on a writing slate. Before I knew it, I started writing a diatribe against my mistress.

Little Miracle sucks. Shoot da bitch. Boom, boom, bye bye.

I couldn't stop myself:

She thinks she's it but she's shit. She's like totally spoilt, y'know?

The vitriol poured forth.

It's all me, myself and I with that dumb-ass air-head mistress of mine.

If my sentiments were shocking, I shocked even myself.

Up to that point if you'd asked me what I thought of my boss I would have declared total devotion. There was never any doubt about what I was supposed to feel and I couldn't distinguish otherwise.

Ah, but the river had flooded its banks.

Damn! There was no going back.

When I ran out of words in that exhausting, rainy-season mid-afternoon heat, I flopped my head onto my chest and closed my eyes, just for a second.

Before I could stop myself, I'd conked out – without wiping the slate clean.

Just my luck, that Little Miracle woke up with her fever broken.

Calling out for me, she found me sleeping.

Coming over to me, she found my writing.

Before I could start to explain (somehow!), she suggested we take a walk down by the river.

Not angry, not calm, her emotions seemed suspended.

I followed her across the lawns as the skies broke open.

Within minutes it was hailing down. We traipsed in the downpour through the papaya and avocado orchards and over to where the river began its journey to the falls.

It was like she was in a trance, I thought, watching a soft brown back made progressively more erect over the years through the addition of neck rings which were beginning to do the inconceivable – give her a certain elegance.

A frosty organza wrappa bound her knees tightly, as was the fashion.

She was gauging how to respond, I decided, which was ominous coming from someone who always expressed her emotions spontaneously, without fear of causing offence or reprisals.

We had reached the thunderous roar where the falls began.

She walked right up to the river's edge, then turned around to face me and said, tearfully, raising her voice above the din, 'You have betrayed me, Omo, and I am, like, *totally* devastated. How could you back-stab me when I have always been so nice to you? I thought you were my best friend *ever.*'

A malicious tinge seeped into her voice when she added, 'You will be punished.'

She paused, tilted her chin upwards, and stared past me, the spurned heroine in a tragedy. I saw that this girl had the power of life and death over me and in that moment she was deciding whether to use her authority to forgive me, her 'betrayer', or to exact revenge.

Her verdict was quiet, resolute: 'And sent to the brothel at the port.'

Punishment meant the lash of the rawhide times 100, more?

The brothel was the fate of young women at Roaring River Estate who 'misbehaved'.

A brothel meant the horrific diseases which I'd long heard precipitated an early death.

Why was she doing this?

Because she could.

We stood facing one another.

Mistress and slave.

I did not lower my eyes as usual.

The wet, spiky grass vibrated beneath my bare feet with the drumming of the falls.

How dare she consign me to the worst kind of hell? For what?

I rushed at her with the amassed rage of all those people whose bones lay at the bottom of the ocean; all those people torn from their families and sentenced to labour for life without payment; all those people suffering unbelievable horrors at the hands of their masters.

My surprised, sluggish mistress, disabled by her neck rings and wrappa, tipped backwards, slowly, into the river.

Her mouth opened and closed but if a sound came out, the rush of water drowned it.

Her organza wrappa billowed and unravelled, revealing her naked flesh, and then trailed behind her shimmying like the translucent membrane of a jellyfish.

Swept forwards by the tremendous current, her arms thrashing about, but she was as weightless as one of her Aphrikan Queens.

Rain slammed down on her like spears flung down from the heavens.

She raised her arms, as if to attempt the butterfly stroke, but was flipped over instead so that face down she was forced forwards by the unstoppable power of millions of tons of water and – bulleted head-first over the precipice – she plummeted down, down, down into the abyss.

Where Am I?

A terrible tragedy, they said. A feverish Little Miracle wandering the grounds alone when she should have stayed in bed . . .

Her companion, a reminder of what the Ghikas had lost, was soon despatched to work for the Katamba family in Londolo.

And then I woke up to discover I was no longer freaking out in front of Ezinwene on the gangplank at the docks, but was now lying down in darkness on a boat, and it was moving.

That I had come to this, again.

I listened for sounds – there were none.

I looked around – at darkness.

There was no light – I was sealed in.

I checked my breathing – ragged, but there.

I smelled wood polish, and my own foul breath.

I needed to slake my thirst – swallowed saliva instead.

The energy in the room was dead – I was alone.

I wriggled my feet and wrists to see if I was chained – I wasn't. (Thank God.)

I rose and felt a blanket slip away from me.

The floor beneath my bare feet was smooth, varnished.

I held my hands out in front – walked slowly until a wall announced itself by coming up softly against them.

I felt its panelled dimensions, made my way around, my hands reaching up, spreading out.

A door presented itself when my forehead tapped against a frame.

I searched for a handle – there was none.

I felt a keyhole and peered into blackness.

Using my shoulder as leverage I pushed my weight against the door in the vain hope I could budge it.

Without sight my other senses became acute.

I began to hear waves.

I heard the roll of the ship.

I heard my own stunted breath.

I had walked full circle back to the blanket.

It was made up of patches: wool, linen, cotton, muslin, brocade, velvet, hessian.

I recalled that my people loved quilts.

Our women sewed them back home, when their joints favoured the sitting position and their spines curved and shrank.

I buried my face in the blanket.

The crisp night air must have dried it – for the wind had spun itself deep inside the fabric.

When I heard footsteps, I froze.

When they stopped outside the door, I wrapped the blanket around me.

When the door opened, I sensed it was Bwana.

He was standing there, hidden behind a flaming torch.

I could hear his laborious panting in the dark, smell his cologne, sense his unbridled rage.

He'd charge down from Mayfah in a carriage driven by flame-snorting dragons.

I'd been spotted – of course I had.

Bwana, Bwana, Bwana.

How could I evict my master's name from my mind when he had squatted it for so long?

Chief Kaga Konata Katamba I.

Book Two

THE FLAME

REFLECTIONS, THOUGHTS, EXPERIENCES & SENTIMENTS

CANDID & FREE

ON THE

TRUE NATURE OF THE SLAVE TRADE
& REMARKS ON THE CHARACTER & CUSTOMS
OF
THE EUROPANES

&

AN ACCOUNT

(MODEST & TRUTHFUL)

OF MY PROGRESSION FROM INAUSPICIOUS ORIGINS TO THE HIGHEST ECHELONS OF CIVILISED SOCIETY

Dedicated with the Greatest Veneration

To the Sons of Virtue
&
The Rights of Mankind by Their Most
Respectful & Humble Servant
The Author

Chief Kaga Konata Katamba I

Dear Reader,

I am a reasonable man and a man with reasons:

No. 1 As one of my country's Captains of Industry it is my duty to maintain business standards because the 'Great' in Great Ambossa &c was not put there by pussyfooting, pie-in-the-sky dreamers but through hard-headed, hard-working, self-made entrepreneurs such as myself.

No. 2 The right to property is the right of mankind, whether it be land, oxen, house, ship, articles, child, wife or slave. When that right is violated man's liberty is attacked.

No. 3 It is therefore in defence of my rights that I had to undertake the arduous re-capture of the wretched slave girl Omorenomwara. Do I not have more important tasks to undertake than wasting valuable time in pursuit of a runaway?

No. 4 How many slaves have been accorded the rank of personal secretary to Grand Masters such as myself? How many slaves are required to undertake simple office tasks such as writing letters with an ostrich-feather quill dipped in Indian Ocean squid-ink on specially imported Egyptian parchment? Oh, what backbreaking work indeed! How many slaves are thus privileged and what is a man to do when that privilege is abused?

No. 5 When is a beating more than just a punishment? When it is a lesson in self-improvement, inasmuch as it will greatly benefit the recipient if he has the ability to learn from his mistakes. It is true that there are limits to the brain capacity of the Caucasoi but it has been proven that some kind of moral foundation can be learned. When that fails, the switch and the rawhide serve useful functions. As do the thumbscrew and the rack.

No. 6　A good businessman never allows those in his service to run roughshod over him. He is the boss, he must be obeyed. It is a delicate balance. One is firm but one is kind. One gives an inch but one guards the mile. One is respected but one is never, ever a friend.

No. 7　To those of you who say, 'Poor Omorenomwara, let her go!', I say read on.
To those of you who say the Trade is cruel, I say read on.
To those of you who say the Trade is just and necessary, I say read on.
To those who are betwixt and between, I say read on.

Humble Origins – Personal Tragedy

Dear Reader,

It woe betides me to be the bearer of bad news, but for those ridiculous personages who pontificate with arm-waving dramatics from the Soap Box of Self-Righteousness that the Trade is cruel and inhumane, who bemoan the sufferings of these wretched creatures as if we and they are one and the same, be warned that your fallacious assertions are a complete waste of time because the groundswell of public opinion is against you, and will ever remain so.

Other personages, however, deliver Sombre Pronouncements gained through the Wisdom of Experience, much Serious Contemplation, Erudite Debate, as well as Rigorous Scholarly Research and the Analysis of Vital Statistics, all of which thereto leads them to discover certain Objective Truths.

Henceforth it is my duty and pleasure to acquaint the Reader with the latter.

To commence, for those new readers who are unfamiliar with my path towards Property, Prosperity and Enlightenment, let me retrace my footsteps back through the savannahs of time, the meandering rivers of memory, the overcast forests of the past, to the blue skies of my youth.

My people, the Katamba Clan, were hunter-gatherers who for generations had roamed the southern reaches of GA.

How humble! I hear you gasp. Yes, indeed, the honour of Chiefdom, Dear Reader, was conferred upon me by the House of Masters for Long and Outstanding Services to Industry. Let it be understood that, quite unlike others who reap rewards without earning them, I was not born to inherit the Golden Stool of the Kingdom but the gold bars in my vaults were stockpiled through decades of self-sacrifice and an upwardly mobile mind.

And so it was that during my early youth I was spurred on by the dreams of the achievements of manhood which possess all young boys eager to make their mark upon the world.

As the eldest son I should have been my father's favourite, but it was not to be. I was neither strong nor fast enough to please he who was the bravest and strongest of all hunters.

It was Kwesan, my younger brother, upon whom he bestowed his favour.

On that fateful day long ago, my father sent Kwesan and me to catch prey over the land our clan had recently chosen as hunting ground. It was our first time hunting without adults and after hot and tiresome pursuance of a young impala, my brother, who always boasted that he was far stronger and swifter than I, suddenly took off ahead and disappeared from sight in woodland just as the mantle of darkness began to fall.

I called after him to wait for his older brother, as I panted behind him like a three-legged cheetah.

His laughter echoed back light and happy and tinkling from beneath the trees.

I ran to catch up with him but lost my way in the scrub and spent hours trying to find my way home.

When I finally did so the impala was being roasted around a camp fire and a glowing, victorious Kwesan sat in pride of place next to my father, who was lavishing him with praises.

I was at a loss to account as to why I had failed at the task,

whereupon my father stood up and delivered the pronounce-
ment that I was the greatest disappointment to him; indeed,
he asked aloud, 'Is my son Kaga more woman than man?'

This produced much mirth amongst my gathered clan.

Following the most wretched, sleepless night, early the next
morning I decided I had had enough and left. I took to
wandering, until I found myself at the coast and was immediately in thrall to it.

What would it be like, I wondered, to feel those frothing
undulations carry me to the far-flung corners of our planet?

I decided to find out and soon after gained employment
aboard a schooner, the *Adana*, which was moored some
distance along the coast.

But I was not to know then, Dear Reader, what fate had in
store for me, when Young Kaga, as I was then called, earned
his sea-legs aboard the *Adana*.

It was my misfortune that my eager yet mawga young self
became the natural target of my older cross-grained, foul-
mouthed companions who considered me scant more than a
punch bag on which to vent their spleen.

Oftentimes when those scumbags had turned in and were
sleeping off their rum, ribaldry and rage, I stood alone on the
quarterdeck as the ship sallied forth, its sails flattened against
the wind, skimming the sea like a seagull unburdened by the
woes of the world.

A fine eight-knot wind could clear my head and settle my
inner turbulence. Hope swelled within my breast and I resolved
to climb the rope ladder of life until I got to the top. Then I
would hoist each rung up behind me, burn it and have a
three-day feast to celebrate my victory.

As is the way with our perambulations, procrastinations

and peregrinations on earth – Time Passed. Young Kaga became seasoned by life at sea and the Kaga you see before you today began to emerge, he who is described by *others* (I make no immodest claims myself) as: strong yet sensitive, powerful yet peaceful, a money-maker for the benefit of the nation and an extoller of high morals for the spirit of the Empire of GA.

Thus armed, I grasped the opportunity to realise my dreams when it presented itself.

We had just touched the wharf one damp morning in the heart of the rainy season, and were disembarking at Do Va from aboard a tea clipper which had sailed in from the South China Seas, a safe but long voyage during which, thankfully, the pernicious pirates of that region had kept their distance as our formidable vessel could outrun and outgun any of theirs. As my trembling sea-legs adjusted to solid ground, I was approached from amid the hurly-burly of whores and porters and messengers and thieves on the docks by a brisk, elderly gentleman with a monocle who wore green silks with gold threads which swished most ostentatiously about him, as did the attentive page boy at his side who cooled him with a fan of spoonbill feathers.

Chief Ambikaka had heard of my reputation as an honest, reliable, respected First Mate, and invited me to dine to discuss a matter of mutual interest.

My eyes fastened on the humungous gold ram's head hanging on a chain about his neck. It was obvious he was no mere mortal but a god in the pantheon of Big Business. That afternoon I was guest of honour at a lavish feast in the white-washed courtyard, where purple and lilac bougainvillea dripped from every balcony.

Chief Ambikaka set me down with high-ranking fellows

such as himself, all of whom sat cross-legged on mats. Their naked torsos bore a sprinkling of grey hairs and their stomachs spilled over skirts of freshly cut grass. Gold nuggets set into rings flashed in the sunlight. I suspected good tidings were in the offing.

Alas, first I had to endure songs in my honour rendered by a decrepit kora-playing griot who sang but two notes and strummed but another two as he droned on glorifying my heroic and mythic qualities. As the afternoon sun began to blend into evening's fading light I was most relieved when the noise finally ceased and the waiters spun into action – a fluster of flamboyant yellow turbans and kente lap-cloths.

We were served ducks spitting in their own juices on platters, yams roasted to a golden brown, fried spinach spiced with chilli pepper and garlic, and plantains roasted whole so that the yellow flesh oozed out of burst, blackened skins.

As we consumed this mouth-watering feast, Chief Ambikaka turned to me, gold dust sparkling in his eyes. I was to be offered command of the latest addition to his fleet of merchant ships, a 200-ton slaver called *Hope & Glory* which was to sail to the Grey Continent twice yearly to increase his already considerable fortune through the almost limitless bounty available through the trade in slaves.

I would make a trustworthy captain as my references, which he had already sought, were impeccable.

The *Hope & Glory* would carry forty cases of muskets, 32,000 gunflints, coral necklaces, Aphrikan prints, bead jewellery, quills, papyrus, household objects such as kettles and musical instruments such as the talking drum, with which to barter for livestock. My host joked that the guns would encourage the Europanes to start more wars which would result in more prisoners offered up as slaves.

Once at our destination – the island of New Ambossa in

West Japan – we would exchange the slaves for sugar, rum and tobacco.

And once back in GA, these luxury goods would be sold for a small fortune.

Furthermore, as a special incentive to remain loyal to my paymaster, I was to receive 10 per cent of the overall profit made for every slave shipment safely arrived in New Ambossa.

It took me one second contemplating the invitation, and another before offering my assent.

Captain Kaga Konata Katamba I.

Such jubilation was bursting in my heart that I could not contain it.

That evening I sank my knees and swirled my hips with Chief Ambikaka's sleekly oiled wenches who had bounteous breasts and bullet-catching buttocks – while the hi-life music vibrated into the skies above the compound.

You may imagine how I felt that night as I lay on a rug in a suite in the chief's compound, my appetite satiated by two appetising whores who reclined under my arms, the drums and rum still pumping through my blood vessels, kept awake into the dawn hours by extravagant fantasies of the business I would soon start building.

I praised the gods for my excellent good fortune as I nestled between squashed breasts and smooth arms and thighs which warmly imprisoned my own.

Captain indeed!

Some Are More Human than Others

Like all men who are driven to roam the oceans, I had heard tales of the Grey Continent throughout my seafaring life.

Europa – the name tripped off the lips of every seaman, adventurer and merchant who dreamed of accumulating riches through the trade in slaves. Yet only the bravest and hardiest dared venture to its stormy coasts, because if the wheezes, coughs, and sneezes of the deadly influenza did not catch you, the wild savages surely would.

Yes, Dear Reader, the natives of those lands are just now emerging from the abominable depths of savagery which we civilised nations left behind in prehistoric times.

With my trip to Europa in sight, I embarked upon a period of study.

The more enlightened among you will already be aware that there are three stages or, if you like, classifications of humanity according to the exact science of Craniofaecia Anthropometry, a tried and tested science which measures skull sizes within the rigorous and most esteemed field of Physical Anthropology.

These classifications are:

No. 1 – The Negroid, who is indigenous to the Aphrikan continent.

No. 2 – The Mongoloid, who is indigenous to the Asian territories.

No. 3 – The Caucasoinid, who is indigenous to the hell-hole known as Europa.

We all recognise that the Negroid head has a wide prominent forehead, the back of which is spacious and rounded, and that it has what is termed a prognathous (or protruding) jaw. Over millennia the capacious skull of the Negroid has been able to accommodate the growth of a very large brain within its structure. This has enabled a highly sophisticated intelligence to evolve.

Additionally, the prognathous jaw itself denotes determination of character and a strong sense of direction. The Negroid skull has, therefore, produced the following traits: ambition, self-motivation, resourcefulness, self-discipline, courage, moral integrity, spiritual enlightenment and community responsibility.

It is also worth noting that due to its position on the evolutionary scale, the Negro is also very Sensitive and capable of Great Depth of Feeling.

Needless to say, Craniofaecia Anthropometry proves that the Negro is biologically superior to the other two types. Indeed, while the Negro belongs to the *genus* known as 'Mankind', the Mongolo and the Caucasoi belong to a broader definition of 'Humankind', which ranges from the fully evolved species 'Mankind' to the lesser evolved species classified as 'Neo-Primate'.

The Caucasoinid skull, on the other hand, is, unfortunately, consigned to the bottom end of the scale of Humankind. It is long, narrow and somewhat square at the back, with an orthognathous (less prominent) jaw. This skull type contains a far smaller brain because it has been unable to expand beyond the limits of its small cranial structure. Furthermore, the narrowness of the skull denotes a brain that is a bit, as we laymen would say, squashed up.

The orthognathous jaw itself denotes weakness of character, limited imagination and restricted intellect. The general consensus is that these cranio-structural defects also produce the traits of infantilism, aimlessness, laziness, cowardice, poor coordination, moral degradation, and a nonsensical language or languages; so unintelligible, in fact, that it has not yet been verified by linguistic experts whether Europa possesses one language, classified as Mumble-Jumble, several languages, or merely one language with several dialects.

Furthermore, the Caucasoi is unable to calculate mental arithmetic beyond what they call their 'ten times table'.

Because the Caucasoinid brain is so stunted, it has also naturally led to somewhat blunted emotions. Along with the beasts of burden who work the fields, the Caucasoi is incapable of acute emotionality because, due to its Neo-Primate state, it is but a few steps up from the animal kingdom with its primary preoccupations of Perambulate, Agitate, Capitulate, Somnambulate, Ejaculate, Procreate, Masticate, Procrastinate and Hibernate.

Nor, when the Caucasoi receives physical 'pain', does he suffer in the same way as me and thee. Beating the hide of a Caucasoi is more akin to beating the hide of a camel to make it go faster. Be not hoodwinked into thinking that the blood shed and the skin torn of the Caucasoi is a crime against humanity, no matter how much they shed crocodile tears to convince the gullible among you otherwise.

Surely even you diehard liberals are by now doubting your old verities?

Should any vestige of doubt remain, however, please rest assured that these categories and conclusions are derived from *precise and systematic measurements* of the bones of the human skull by leading doctors who carried out empirical research over many months on one hundred skulls before arriving at their conclusions.

To put it in simple terms, the Caucasoinid breed is *not of our kind*.

On the other hand the piggy-in-the-middle, Mongolo, is exceedingly desirous to align himself with the Negroidian type. Yet the truth is that he possesses a mere 35 per cent of our admirable qualities.

Or, to present the facts another way:

Imagine a brain operating at full capacity with 100 billion neurons (Negroid).

Then a brain with 35 billion neurons (Mongoloid).

And finally a brain with 20 billion neurons (Caucasoinid).

To go one step further – it also appears, then, that the removal of certain specimens of the Caucasoinid *genus* from Europa to Aphrika and its dominions is, in fact, an Act of Mercy.

Consider for a moment, oh you men of cynicism and misinformation, that the Trade is a chance for those poor souls to escape the barbarism prevalent on the Grey Continent where unspeakable horrors take place as a normal way of life.

Some of these I have witnessed myself first hand and as my narrative unfolds you will hear tell of them.

As you will soon discover, the Europane slaves have been saved from the most horrendous deaths, punishments, morally reprehensible indulgences and serfdom, whilst being given the opportunity to adopt the manners and customs of civilised men.

Furthermore, the Europane tribes enslave each other. It is a most natural state of affairs for them.

As soon as I myself had grasped the facts, I must confess that it was with great excitement that I embarked on my journey to Europa, and with great relief too. Not only would my moral fibre remain intact, but it would be strengthened.

Indeed, I now realised my trip was, additionally, a Mission of Liberation – the Saving of Souls.

*

Nevertheless, with the terrible accounts of the Grey Continent ringing in my ears, there was also much trepidation in my heart, at the barbarism I would encounter on those shores.

Captain Katamba I will spare the reader the run-of-the-mill details of my first voyage to Europa, suffice to say that the seas were, as usual, vicissitudinous.

The worst came upon us on our seventy-fifth day out when a night-time nor'wester rapidly ripened into a tempest so powerful that if we continued skudding we ran the risk of running the *Hope & Glory* under.

Alas! I awoke to discover it was too late to bring her to the wind. We could not reach the foresail to cut it away nor the reef points to do the same. The forward deck was quickly attacked by the infamous Atlantic rollers which swept over us and the crew could do no more than huddle together whilst the helmsman struggled to keep us upright. It would be only a matter of time before the keel rolled over showing its wooden underside to the tumultuous skies with my crew and myself, good men and true, flailing about beneath it.

I prayed to Yemonja with more fervour than ever before. I was a young man. I had a fortune to make and a family to create that would one day carry on the name of the Katamba Clan.

As if in a miracle, Yemonja heard my cries and the storm broke. The rains abated as swiftly as they had arrived. The swell of the waves subsided so that the sea soon resembled a tranquil pond again, and the skies cleared and poured forth sunlight and warmth.

I then understood that Yemonja was smiling on my mission.

From then on in we ploughed the waters peacefully until we approached the coast of Europa.

The Grey Continent – it seemed harmless enough, at first sight: a deserted, somewhat featureless beach viewed from a distance, snaking as far as the naked eye could see beneath an insipid sky through which the sun could not penetrate. The trees which encroached upon it looked quite normal from the distance of our ship – perhaps sun-dappled woods or even a majestic, ancient forest? But as we rode the breakers in our yawls, I became aware that it was the dreaded jungle.

Suddenly such a wind began to gather behind us that we had no need to row as waves pushed us helplessly towards the coast with the force of it, and before we could catch breath we were thrust up onto a beach made up of pebbles and sharp shards of rock which glinted like the blades of knives.

The underside of the yawls skidded and scratched on the shingle and it was with great foreboding that I hauled my yawl further up the beach and secured it there.

The wind had seemingly arisen out of nowhere as if to whip us with evil spirits. Brooding clouds had amassed in the skies with a deathly quiet, making the shore overcast and ominous, and as I surveyed the forlorn beach it sunk home that we had arrived on terra firma most sinister.

The country called Europa.

The region called the Cabbage Coast.

Indeed, it will be readily understood that I felt most imperilled.

I decided to tarry no longer than was necessary. Our business contact, the renowned yet notorious Ambossan factor

Byakatonda, who had lived on that continent longer than most sane men could withstand and apparently gone native, (spawning such a proliferation of mulatto children bearing his features he could form his own tribe), should have been waiting for us with hundreds of slaves in barracoons for our selection – but he was nowhere in sight.

I turned seaward, towards the merry wooden belly of the *Hope & Glory* bobbing innocently far away in the waters, and weighed up the possibility that it was not too late to abandon this mission altogether.

However, as you may by now be aware, Captain Katamba was not a quitter.

No sooner had I ordered my men to branch out along the perilously slippery beach to explore this bleak landscape than I noticed savages beginning to emerge from inside the jungle.

First one head appeared nervously around a tree, then another and another until dozens of the wretches began creeping out with all the stealth of burglars who will rob your property with one hand and slit your neck with the other.

These creatures brandished a farcical yet nonetheless disturbing assortment of weapons: saucepans, wooden spoons, hammers, pitchforks, spades, penknives, rocks, hoes, truncheons, spears, screwdrivers, swords, fishing rods, spanners, saws and whatever other implements they could lay their measly hands on.

As they crept in a cowardly way towards us, I heard them whispering rapidly in their nonsensical 'language'. This too was farcical. A language without the c!icks, c!ucks, c!acks and !tsks of normal speech sounded dreary beyond belief, more akin to the low monotonous moan of cattle than the exuberant sounds of human communication.

Did they come bearing gifts as a gesture of hospitality?

Were they greeting us with smiles to welcome the newcomers onto their soil? Not a bit of it.

I asked the question: what crime had we seamen committed to elicit such unprovoked hostility? What had we done except to pull up on a beach and wander about while we awaited our business partner?

As they drew closer I registered contempt on the faces of each and every one of them; although, in fairness, to suggest that I could distinguish one from the other is somewhat an exaggeration as it was quite evident that their ghost-like pallor rendered them all looking, quite frankly, the same.

I suspected they might be males of the *genus*, but I could not be sure.

We barely exhaled, my men and I, shivering as we were faced with two evils: the cold weather which pricked my naked skin (but for my loincloth) like needles, and the threatening approach of the savages.

I purposefully hesitated as I surveyed their shifty progress.

What, precisely, was a young man with no military experience to do?

In those moments of indecision I wondered if I should try and reason with the enemy, persuade them to lay down their arms. Would they understand or rather, like their four-legged compatriots in the animal kingdom, would they charge in ruthlessly – teeth gnashing, claws ripping, spears shaking – for the kill?

Paralysed, I watched.

Naturally the savages were overdressed, as I had been told they would be. They wore grimy layers of cloths and matted wools which were coloured in browns and greens so dingy they could blend into the filth of the earth without need of camouflage.

Their cloths were cut, quite comically, into the shapes of the human body. It was as if without arm sections and neck sections and leg sections these simpletons would not know how to dress themselves.

Upon their heads they wore strange objects which I was later to learn were called hats.

Their feet were clad too, in objects called boots which were made of animal hide. They rode tightly up the leg to the knee, for some unfathomable reason.

Some, though, wore the foot objects called shoes, made of either animal hide or even stranger – wood. What crazed mind conjured up that idea?

Would you believe that these beings were also hirsute beyond decency?

Wherever flesh showed it was covered in hideous hair like that of a monkey or gorilla, especially upon their heads and sprouting from their chins, like dirty woollen thread.

The enemy began to gather speed, emboldened by our apparent inaction which they stupidly mistook for defence-lessness.

I came to my senses, resolute that there was no way I was going to die there – not then, not like that.

'Stop! Come no further, my friends!' I called out, raising a flat palm to them with as much authority as I could muster.

'Stop! At once!' I repeated.

They were now so near we could almost smell them and I could see their alien eyes which were of the colours which should never be seen on a human face. It was quite creepy to look into them and see a grey sky staring back. Or to catch the stare of another and be plunged into a bottomless aqua-marine ocean.

I issued another warning, ordering them to drop their weapons.

But then a saucepan seemed to shake in the air.

A wooden spoon was raised like a dagger about to plunge.

A fishing rod became a javelin in the wrong hands.

A rock was thrown very aggressively out to sea.

I finally allowed my temper to rise to the surface and called my men to arms.

And make sure you don't miss!

Muskets were hoisted atop shoulders, and fired.

I admit that I may have been a tad rash in this respect, but I had to act decisively, did I not?

Approximately ten were felled in the first volley, twice that number in the second. The others fled back into the jungle, caterwauling, and those who remained squirming on the beach were finished off.

When they were all gone, an eerie quiet once more descended upon that pitiful shoreline.

The soundless air was chilly as the heart of a poisoner.

The sea sucked up the shore with a viper's hiss.

The trees were malevolent assassins spying on us.

Before us lay the bloody carnage of warfare.

As I surveyed the gut-wrenching vision, a terrible swelling rose in my stomach. I struggled to subdue it, but, alas, I could not.

Captain Katamba, Leader of Men, rushed into the sea, and well, yes, he threw up.

Oh, I could have flung myself onto the water and drowned in it. Yes I could!

However, just as swiftly I was rescued from the abyss of self-destruction by Shangira, God of War, who had a word in my ear.

Firstly, I was victorious, which was to be celebrated; and secondly, it was not I who was a murderer, after all. I, who was possessed of the most benevolent of intentions, had never personally killed a man (we can include 'living soul' here) in my life and my record remained intact.

I had not fired a single shot – my men, or rather the crew, had.

As I waded through the sea back to the beach, having thrown up all that was inside my stomach, I saw an Aphrikan chap marching across the pebbles, followed by a veritable legion of savages, all armed, this time, with muskets.

It was Byakatonda, of course, accompanied by what appeared to be his own personal guard.

Tall, thin, and in concordance with rumour, he had gone quite native: a hat upon his head, wooden shoes, woollens with arm sections draped over his upper half, and sackcloth material with leg sections on his lower half.

All shit-coloured.

It was unwise to remonstrate with him for his tardiness, however, considering we had business to undertake and his men outnumbered ours. Yet I wanted to inform him that *he* was to blame for this fiasco. It was *he* who had left us unprotected and at the mercy of savages in the wild.

He beat me to it.

'Captain Katamba!' he called out angrily. 'What the blazes has been going on here?'

Heart of Greyness

Dear Reader,

Byakatonda had sojourned some nineteen seasons on the Cabbage Coast, and it showed. He had lost the loose-limbed lope of the men of the Aphrikas and walked as if a rod had been rammed up his fundament.

As I waded back through the shallows towards him, his nose streamed, yet he did not send it hygienically to the wind with his thumb but pulled out a dirty, viscous rag and blew into it, thus multiplying the germs and prolonging the disease!

He then proceeded to blast me in a grating, nasal voice about 'A massacre on the shores of Europa!'

Apparently the enemy, who had surprised us, were actually close allies of Byakatonda himself. Good fellows, if you will. They were merely being curious and, by necessity, cautious.

What an impetuous fool I was, he ranted, spittle landing on my cheek. My rash behaviour could ruin his hard-won rapport with the locals. Had I considered that?

I then exercised something I suspected he knew little of – self-discipline – and explained that we had been threatened by what we saw as bellicose savages intent on malfeasance, and that he should remember that I was on those shores to put a casketful of cowrie shells in his coffers.

At that he began to calm down until, without warning, he clasped one of my hands in his, and shook it!

I immediately withdrew said hand and raised the other to defend myself.

'My dear Captain, hand-shaking is the custom here,' he guawed, revealing teeth as dark and uncoordinated as his attire. 'It is a salutation of goodwill. One gets used to it then one adopts it.'

That, I suspected, was his problem.

'Please, let us put this regrettable affair behind us because, as you have justly remarked, you and I must do business.

'May I now extend a warm welcome to you and your men,' he declared, extending his arms in a gesture of ceremonious invitation, before adding in a conspiratorial whisper, 'amidst such barbarism you would not imagine. Life is cheap in these parts, but easy on the trigger, eh, Captain?'

I had not pulled a trigger on anyone, but let him think me a hot-headed brawler. Let him be wary.

I was to spend the next twenty-four hours with Byakatonda who was, unfortunately, most prolix.

'Pardon me for mentioning it, Captain,' he shouted over his shoulder as he suddenly strode off up the beach leaving me, his guest, to trot behind him like a donkey. 'But you'll freeze your bollocks off running around in that loincloth of yours. Now come, come, into the forest we go!'

I followed him into the jungle which was as evil as I had anticipated – sunless, soulless, colourless. It was seething with foreign insects, thick with rotting foliage and grave with an air of despair and devastation. Alien creepers threatened to block our path, the contorted arms of grotesque trees threatened to reach out and strangle me, the ground was matted with diseased leaves, the damp climate chilled my bones. Shrill sounds shot out into the silence. Something hawked up in the trees. From inside the undergrowth came sounds which were neither human nor animal.

Demons brushed their icy lips past mine.

I felt *watched*.

It was like returning, Dear Reader, to the earliest days of the world when the trees and vegetation of the wilderness spread their tendrils and talons without the restraining hand of civilised man.

As we penetrated deeper into the dark heart of Europa my host began to prove cordial enough, prattling on about an impoverished upbringing on a maize farm in the outback of Great Ambossa. (As if *I* should admire *him*.)

He showed no interest in the country he had left behind.

The jungle had claimed him.

The jungle was his home now.

We finally approached a high wall in front of which ran a river. Our party hastened around it as Byakatonda told me it offered a circle of protection for the settlement inside.

'Against what?' I asked in my youthful innocence.

'The natives are a bloodthirsty lot, squire. Without these fortified walls they'd be slaughtered in their sleep by marauding enemy tribes from up north. Those shipped overseas are the lucky ones. Surely even you knew that?'

What a know-it-all he was.

'My *dear* fellow, as an esteemed captain of the sea I know many, many things, for example that we civilised nations are not without the urge to conquer and defeat ourselves, a minor fracas here and there, the occasional full-blown war. This is common knowledge to all *learned* men.'

Byakatonda stopped short and grabbed my arm, pulling me towards him.

'Listen to me, *sir*,' he hissed. 'I'm talking about murder on a scale you would not imagine – one hundred million, and counting. Let us not forget the thousands of mini-wars since time immemorial. Sometimes they even go into battle and declare it is on behalf of their pagan idol – Xtia – the very one who commands *Thou shalt not kill.*

'Now – look at this!'

We had come to a spot where a bridge crossed the river and he pointed up at two rows of poles lined either side, upon which were stuck what appeared to be heads.

Surely not, I thought, before coming to the incontrovertible conclusion that it was indeed a parade of dismembered heads.

I promptly keeled over and regurgitated what little was left in my stomach.

'Be warned,' Byakatonda spat down my ear-hole as I was retching my life away.

(Ye gads! Give me a fucking break!)

'They are hung, disembowelled, beheaded and quartered, that is – the body chopped into four parts. It's been common practice for over three centuries for those who commit crimes against their big Chief, the King. A powerful deterrent, don't you think?'

I knew not what to reply. Massive iron gates in the wall opened to release a procession of trance-like natives clad in black clothes.

I struggled to my feet as we moved aside to let them pass.

The lead native wore a vivid purple robe and carried two wooden sticks in front of him, the shorter horizontal one crossing the longer vertical one.

Six of the taller males balanced a long wooden box on their shoulders.

I nearly jumped out of my skin when they started up a communal chant rendered in a babble of uncouth sounds which went something like this: *ourfatherwhoartinheav* . . . and so on and so forth &c.

*

A dead person was in the box, Byakatonda informed me, as we watched them disappear into the thicket, who would shortly be buried in the ground, as was their custom. It was peculiar because they did not thrash and wail with woe at such times, nor use official mourners, but maintained what was called a 'stiff upper lip'.

As we passed through the gates of the settlement, the bitter aftertaste of vomit made me so queasy I felt my legs almost give way.

'What can I expect inside?' I asked my host, trying to control the tremor in my voice, leaning one arm on his shoulder for support.

'I dare not tell you,' he smirked. 'Except to say, welcome to my world.'

As we passed native warriors on guard I saw they were covered head to toe in cumbersome iron. How could they possibly fight freely in battle dressed so?

Once inside the wall, Byakatonda informed me that he had won the natives' favour through keeping up a steady supply of buyers for the slaves they captured for him, although he liked to go out on the hunt himself from time to time.

Several winding paths branched out from the gates with square-shaped wooden dwellings lining either side. Yes, square!

Natives loitered in the guttering like slugs in their own slime.

All were emaciated and wore rags darkened with vile filth.

Some lay stiff on the ground, flies buzzing around the death-gasp of open mouths.

Occasionally one of the cadavers stirred, which was rather a shock.

Supplicant hands begged as we passed.

Swaddled infants were held out by withered mothers who sat back on their haunches like chimpanzees.

The first little bundle I looked into contained something so grey and still, it was more stone than child.

I asked my host if mental illness was also rife in these parts.

He replied that they were called the poor.

I was most relieved when we came to a crowded square. But yet again I was at a loss for words when I witnessed a mad spectacle of many colours.

Females paraded around wearing garments whose torso-frames crushed their ribs so tightly breathing must have been impeded. The material on these garments tightened around the neck appearing to choke the wearer. Circuitous structures hung from their lower halves which expanded their hips to ridiculous proportions, and shoe objects were so narrow and pointed as to deform their feet.

Quite how they managed to stay alive is beyond my comprehension.

The males strutted about in torso garments which were nothing like our stylish lion or tiger pelts, but which were designed to make their shoulders appear twice their normal width. Upon their bottom halves were leg garments which came down to the knee, in some cases tied with ribbons! Objects upon their heads were so wide their faces fell into shadow.

That they should dress like this *and* go abroad in daylight?

'It is called "the fashion",' my host chortled, slapping me on the back as if we had become great companions as well as mere compatriots. 'For which they are prepared to suffer pain and even permanent disfigurement. Come! Let us go to the gallows where that crowd is amassing over there.'

At the far end of the square hundreds of jeering natives were jostling for position. Byakatonda deftly wove his way to the front.

'Perfect timing. This lot are burglars. You may not approve the punishment but we'll all sleep a lot better without that bunch of ne'er-do-wells roaming the streets at night.'

Directly before us was a horse-drawn cart on which stood five blindfolded natives whose necks were attached to a rope hanging from a single beam.

A gong was sounded and the cart sped off, leaving the victims dangling by the neck, writhing and gurgling for an eternity, until they eventually went limp.

At which point the crowd settled down into a satisfied silence and began to disperse.

I had barely digested what had happened when, at the opposite end of the square, another crowd raised a loud cheer.

'I spared you that one. They put a fellow's head on a block and chop it off.'

In the next breath Byakatonda told me that soon enough he would take me to his house for a hearty meal and thereafter we could begin the business at hand.

To be quite frank, Dear Reader, I had quite lost my appetite.

Yet no one could have prepared me for what I saw next.

I smelled a terrible burning. Perhaps they are roasting one of their strange animals, I wondered?

Byakatonda conducted me to the third corner of the square and as we neared I saw that one of their females, of middle years with a skein of black hair, had been tied to a stake in the middle of a fire.

She was being burned alive.

Yes, alive.

Whoosh! Her hair went up in flames and although she screamed, no sound came out.

My body went into convulsions for a third time but my stomach was empty.

What can I say, Dear Reader, but the horror, the *horror* . . .

She was apparently a woman who is called a witch, that is, one accused of consorting with their chief demonic figure, called the Devil.

The fate of a witch is to be bound, weighted and thrown into the river. If she sinks she is innocent, although she is by now of course dead. If she floats she is considered guilty of witchcraft and they will set her alight.

Did anything in this hell-hole make sense?

Murder in the Square was the settlement's Saturday-afternoon entertainment. The next day they went to the temple to worship the god who told them not to carry out any of these unspeakable acts.

'You have to remember that they are not like us, Captain, not like us at all,' Byakatonda said, studying me intensely to gauge my reaction.

'I do not need reminding of that,' I countered, looking up at a sky drained of colour, drained of life, drained of humanity, drained of sanity.

Would that I were gone from this abominable place.

I had seen and heard enough.

Byakatonda lived some distance from the market and although the landscape was bleak I was relieved to be invigorated by a light breeze. As we made our way there he continued to fill me in on more of the other customs and traditions of this foul society.

The previous Saturday Byakatonda had seen a native strapped into a basket filled with wasps until he was stung to death; a couple of months earlier one was put into a barrel spiked with nails and rolled downhill. The rack was popular for forcing confessions too – stretching a person until their bones popped out of the sockets.

Unable to hear any more, I decided to put an end to this litany of evils and asked what the hell this thing called a Saturday was. He explained that it was the natives' system of ordering time into what they called days. Seven of these days constituted something called a week, and four of these weeks constituted a month, although the amount of days in a month varied from between twenty-eight and thirty-one. And three hundred and sixty-five of these days constituted a year. Except in the years when they didn't.

I tried to see the reason in it.

I'm *still* trying.

I asked why he had chosen to spend his life among the heathen tribes, to which he replied, 'Here I am someone – the big blak chief among the little whyte natives. In Great Ambossa I was a nobody. So why do you think?'

I admired his honesty, if not his sarcasm.

We passed barren fields draped in a sinister diaphanous mist. Evil-looking pagan idols had been stuck in the centre of the fields. Wooden sticks attired like natives with hair made of straw.

As my head began to clear Byakatonda's conversation took a more humorous turn. I was told that the natives were awfully superstitious. This is what they do for good luck.

They must touch a piece of wood, cross two fingers over each other, hang a horse's shoe on the front door, pass a black cat in the street, and repeat 'White rabbit' three times as soon as they wake up on the first day of each month.

'Why not a pink pig?' I joked, beginning to feel myself again.

Conversely, it was considered unlucky to walk under a

ladder, to break a mirror, wear the colour green, spill salt or pass another person while walking upstairs, and the thirteenth day of their creation called a Friday is so unlucky some never get out of bed on that day for fear of what might happen to them.

By the time we arrived at his dwelling, my spirits had been lifted.

It was all quite hilarious.

My host revealed that when he eventually returned to GA to live a life of luxury, he planned to form the International Society for the Suppression of Savage Beliefs and Customs.

One began to warm to him, finally.

The Saving of Souls

Dear Reader,

We have now arrived at that part of my story concerning the purchase of slaves.

Byakatonda's domicile was, thank goodness, constructed in the Ambossan mode of architecture. It did not imprison like a square box but its walls curved into a circle. It was not built of flammable wood, but of solid, high-quality, low-maintenance mud.

Annoyingly, rather than sit cross-legged on the ground and eat with our fingers like normal people, I was directed to sit at a table and forced to struggle with steel implements more suited to farming or warfare than eating.

A 'winter stew' was served, which contained the following: meat so tough and stringy its threads got trapped in my teeth, a cabbage-vegetable-thing which consisted of thin, green, watery membranes as tasteless as wet leaves, and floating on top of the stew were dumplings made of flour and water which rather resembled the corpses of bloated mice.

When I asked for chilli pepper to spice it all up, my gracious host retorted that his palette could no longer take it and if I wanted it I should have brought some off the ship with me.

Charming!

He was a loathsome, cantankerous fool after all.

I was offered a drink called tea which looked like dirty water and tasted like boiled straw.

I do assure the reader that somehow, however, I managed.

It transpired that my host lived with one official wife and knocked up as many unofficial ones as he could muster. The official wife, who went by the appellation of Janet (JAAA-NET), was, unsurprisingly, a native. Wisely, she was kept out of sight.

He boasted that he had spawned many half-breeds whom he occasionally caught sight of as they scampered around the lanes and fields of the settlement like little orang-utans.

'Dinner' over, we ventured behind the house to a massive yard where the slaves (chained, slothful, thankfully docile) were corralled in a cattle pen. Apparently it was no longer safe to store them in cages on the beach due to the warmongering northern tribes who created such a nuisance.

Byakatonda complained that the all-powerful Association of Ambossan Slave Traders planned to build a fort on that very coast in the near future, which would probably scupper the nice little business of independent traders such as himself.

He introduced me to his trusted 'boy', Tom, a stumpy, wrinkled, white-haired Europane of some sixty seasons.

I immediately clasped my own hands firmly behind my back so that he could not grab one and shake it.

'God-days Capitin-sir. Wi gotte fyne bunsh wiggas fo yoo. Strang, helthie buks ind wenshez. Wi bin waytin longe tyme yoo aryve. Wi alle redy fo yoo. Me beete thim if git oute of hande sew yoo goh and chooz, sir. Jesh goh rite on in ind pik em oote.'

Yes, indeed I would.

I entered the pen and embarked upon the task at hand. I prodded for fast reflexes, squeezed muscles for strength, joints for pliancy, inspected private parts for venereal taints, teeth for good health, and carefully assessed the young females for the curvacious potential which could triple their price.

The chosen ones were led by Tomashara-whatsit to the empty pigs' pen on the other side of the yard.

The procedure was going tolerably smoothly when all of a sudden one of the natives, just as I was bending him over to examine his anus, erupted in a fit of pique. He spun around and shook his fist in my face.

I had already noted that he was sinewy but solid, not in the first bloom of youth but not too old to do a good day's work in the fields of West Japan either. Lurid red hair loitered past his shoulders.

Two of the guards immediately pinned his arms behind him while he frothed and fumed in Mumble-Jumble, which Byakatonda translated for me, so that I would know what I was dealing with.

I rather wished he hadn't.

'You must help me, sir! You are my only hope. I am Jack Scagglethorpe, a hard-working, God-fearing, law-abiding citizen from the north. This lady here is my dear wife Eliza and these are my girls Alice and Sharon. Those kidnapping devils came into our cottage while we were at dinner and before I could get up and protect my family I was sent flying to the floor with a blow to my head which knocked me out. They'd already taken my Doris last Spring and on the way here they dragged my eldest Madge into the woods. We heard her screams. Oh Lord, we heard her screams.

'We are good folk, simple folk, poor folk. I beg you, get us out of here. We only want to go home and live in peace. Oh dear Lord, let us go free! Let us go free!'

At which point Byakatonda sent the fist of his hand into the fellow's cheek – which shut him up.

I told my host that it was obviously beyond this creature's

comprehension to understand that he was being removed from Abject Misery. Perhaps my host needed to educate the stock before sale?

He told me that it wasn't his job to inculcate the stock with the benefits of Ambossan civilisation, thank you kindly.

He then ordered the native to be gagged, dragged out of the pen and put in a very clever wooden contraption through which his head and arms were inserted.

There he would remain until he had learned his lesson.

A shame to let that one go, I thought, because notwithstanding his violent temper a man of such vigour would fetch a good price in New Ambossa.

No sooner had he been shut up than the yellow-haired females surrounding him started up a fuss too – like a gaggle of clacking, flapping ducks.

Tomashara-whatsit raised his stick and brought it down on the back of the youngest, a child with a profusion of matted, dirty-yellow curls who was having the most horrendous temper tantrum.

That did the trick. Silence.

I agreed to take all three yellow-heads. The two young ones had potential.

After selecting 200 slaves I was beginning, I admit, to flag when I came to one who assumed a somewhat pompous demeanour – looking me directly in the eye as if we were equals!

I had just lifted a big wedge of loose fat from underneath his upper arm and was ready to move on when he too began to talk and before I could stop him, Byakatonda again began to translate:

'Look here, dear chap, there's been a terrible misunderstanding. The name is Lord Perceval – of the Montagues. Perhaps you've heard of us? One of England's oldest aristocratic families. Hark, sir, there's been the most godawful mix-up. I was negotiating the sale of a batch of prisoners to one of those new, rather brash, upstart traders, when he accuses me of trying to defraud him with low-quality goods and thereupon demands a 50 per cent discount. A row ensues, I smite him, calling him a guttersnipe, whereupon he directs his hired brutes to put me in irons too! Moreover, I discover that these rogue middlemen have also been carting off my very own property, kidnapping the serfs who work my land, if you please.

'Now look here, I'm not a worsted-stocking'd knave or a scapegrace or a scoundrel like this lot. I'm not a slave, I own them.

'DO – YOU – UN – DER – STA-ND?

'I demand my immediate release, old fellow, and I shall see that the King of England looks favourably upon you. Trust me, I am one of the best connected men in the realm. You are heretofore invited to spend a weekend as guest on my estate, if you so please, where we can discuss mutually beneficial business interests.

'Are you a hunting or fishing man yourself?'

'What a pompous idiot,' I remarked to Byakatonda, who replied, 'Oh, I've heard it all before: But I'm a prince! But I'm an aristocrat. But I'm a landowner! Like we give a damn. He's just another wigger to us. What do you think, can you use him?'

'I cannot use someone who has clearly never lifted a shovel in his life.'

'Then let's move on.'

And we did.

By nightfall I had chosen my shipment, haggled for an agreed price and retired early for a well-deserved night's sleep.

Except that the bliss of the subconscious eluded me because my conscience was in moral turpitude.

You will readily understand, Dear Reader, the dilemma I faced as one who was new to the Trade. Chief Ambikaka and

I had agreed on the purchase of 400 slaves. This would ensure they fitted snugly onto the platforms in the hold.

Bunk beds, I called them.

By my calculations, all going well, the financial profit from this cargo, when we finally returned to GA after depositing the cargo in New Ambossa, would be somewhere in the region of C£52,000, 10 per cent of which would be mine – C£5,200.

I calculated that should I add another 150 slaves, making a total of 550, the gross profit would rise to somewhere in the region of C£71,500 – 10 per cent of which, C£7,150, would be mine.

If I withheld this additional cargo from my employer, however, and undertook a secret sale on my own account, I would accrue an extra C£19,500, plus the C£5,200, bringing my total profit to the tidy sum of C£24,700.

One would be quite rich indeed!

Yet, after much tossing and turning into the early hours, I came to the conclusion that I simply must do the decent thing because, if truth be told, I am not a treacherous man.

I would carry an extra 150 slaves and I would tell Chief Ambikaka, who would be as delighted with the resulting profit as his trustworthy captain.

I reasoned that some of them might not last the trip, but I calculated that even if fifty were to die at sea it would still be worth it.

With a personal profit in the region of C£7,150 I would be able to purchase a second-hand seagoing vessel and immediately begin to trade as my own boss.

When dawn broke I awoke my host who was naturally delighted to be making more money out of me, and we embarked anew on the selection of slaves.

I even took that red-haired scallywag who had spent the night in the wooden contraption. Fret not thyself, Dear Reader, he was still alive and quietly repentant.

I took the pompous one too although, truth be told, he was thrown in for free. They just wanted to get rid of him.

It was time to bid farewell to Byakatonda. An odd, unlikeable fellow with whom one could, nonetheless, do business.

Sailing the Seas of Success

Dear Reader,

There is little reason to trouble you with the minutiae of the long and tiresome journey to New Ambossa, suffice to say that running a slaver meant having to be responsible for the welfare of the cargo – rather as a parent for its children.

Nonetheless, they made such a noise in the dormitory below decks that I had little peace of mind the entire trip!

Many of them indulged in the Sulks, some even died from it. It was nature's way of sorting out the wheat from the chaff, I suppose. A few managed to fling themselves overboard in some kind of ritualistic suicide pact, although my crew did everything in their power to stop them.

As forewarned – the smell of a slaver could carry five miles with the wind behind it.

I must now confess, however, that alone at sea for months on end – what hot-blooded male would not long for female company?

Yes, the very idea was repugnant at first, but I was forced to give in to pressure from my Chief Mate who said it was 'mighty unnatural, sir' (implying *what*, exactly?) for a captain to decline first pickings.

Salvaging my manly reputation, I was therefore obliged to survey the females as they danced on deck and decided, strangely, that one of the yellow-heads was the least offensive. She was perhaps a little thin and immature, but I was drawn to a certain grace and dreaminess about her – as if her body was there but her mind was somewhere else.

She went by the appellation of Sharon (SHAAA-RON) so I let her know pretty sharpish that she was to answer only to the name of Iffianachukwana.

I quickly broke her in and was only forced to put her under the thumbscrews just the once, after her first night in fact, when she had run around my cabin scratching her chest and arms like a lunatic and throwing my beautiful, hand-painted, porcelain washing bowl to the floor where it smashed into smithereens.

(Hysteria, it seemed, ran in the family.)

After that little outburst she quietened down, wise, no doubt, that there would be plenty queuing to take her place in the spacious captain's cabin with spectacular sea views.

Soon enough Iffianachukwana had picked up a smattering of the Ambossan language and spent her days carrying out her duties: she looked after my bedding, cleaned the cabin, polished up my jewellery collection and rubbed my feet, as and when required. She also served me dinner, as befits a man of my rank, on all fours, so that I could eat from the tray laid upon her back.

When the *Hope & Glory* finally sailed into the harbour at New Ambossa to a salute of cannons from the shore, I stood proudly on deck in my finest regalia. I wore a bronze headdress with two antelope horns, a bronze collar decorated with cowrie shells, ivory armlets, copper and brass bracelets, a beaded skirt and heavy brass anklets. (How one longed for the day when it would all be custom-made of gold.)

We unloaded from the hold:

400 pounds of beeswax
2,500 goatskin hides
20 tons of wheat

10 tons of lambswool
and last but not least
323 slaves

It will be readily understood, my Dear, Dear Reader, that those who had succumbed to Fate would not have been strong enough for plantation life. While those who lasted the course were testament to my ability to select stock with strong constitutions.

Luckily for me, the cargo exceeded expectations as it was the heyday of this international migration of labour and a seller's market. Notwithstanding the decrease in numbers for sale, I still walked away with a commission of C£7,700 and soon after purchased my first sea-going vessel.

After my second trip to Europa, I began to buy my own stock of slaves, and soon owned a modest plot of land in the central mountainous region of New Ambossa.

Upon completion of my tenth successful voyage for my employer, Chief Ambikaka, Captain Katamba was ready to go it alone and did so triumphantly.

Nevertheless, the hardships of life at sea eventually wore me down and I desired to stretch my legs, raise them upon a stool, pour a tumbler of pina colada (or two) and sip the sweetness of my success.

Thus it was that in due course I joined the legion of absentee plantation owners who return to Great Ambossa to enjoy the delights of polite society in Mayfah.

My eldest son, Nonso, whilst still very young, was eventually despatched to manage the estate, a task he undertakes admirably, being by nature an enthusiastic disciplinarian.

(Alas, the high hopes I had for my second boy, Bamwoze, were bamboozled when he tried to elope with his mulatto whore. It pains me to discuss this further.)

Every once in a while I return to audit the plantation.

Soon after disembarkation, Iffianachukwana grew heavy in the hips, her breasts swelled with milk, and she began to breed.

Pray, do not be shocked. Yes, they are half-breeds, but they are *my* half-breeds. The first child she bore me, Kolladao, is now a successful overseer.

It may surprise you to learn that long after my first voyage Iffianachukwana still remains my only plantation whore.

One has grown somewhat used to her.

And that modest plot of land has grown into one of the largest plantations in West Japan – 'Home Sweet Home'.

And it is.

The climate is perfect, my sugar yield expands yearly and my slaves, so long as they behave themselves, are always to be found happy and smiling.

The Betrayal of Kindness

Dear Reader,

Finally I must turn our attention to the delicate matter of that wretch Omorenomwara.

Let us examine the facts, Dear Reader, because, as I have proven time and again, the facts are all that matter.

Omorenomwara was residing on the West Japanese island of Little Londolo where she had been for some years the property of the well-connected Ghika family whom I knew of through great mutual friends, the Kensahs. She had been companion to their only daughter, Little Miracle, and had been taught, quite uniquely for a slave, to read and write.

Unfortunately the charming and by all accounts delightful Little Miracle died tragically when, not yet recovered from a bout of malaria, she slipped and fell into the river on their estate and drowned in the waterfall. Her parents never recovered and the young slave served as a constant reminder to her owners of what they had lost. They sought to be rid of her forthwith. The Kensahs heard that I was seeking a maid of quality for my recently acquired second wife, Pleasure, and thenceforth sale and safe passage to Great Ambossa was speedily arranged.

When the young Omorenomwara was ushered into my office that first morning, I detected an air of rare intelligence. While it is true that the Caucasoinid *genus* is generally as thick as pig shit, there are to be found, I admit, exceptions.

Moreover, there was something familiar about this yellow-headed stalk of a girl, as if I recognised her somehow.

It was a tad disconcerting.

As she had spent years working for a good family her Ambossan was quite proficient.

'I have been told that my handwriting is exemplary, Massa.'

I chuckled to myself. Exemplary. Really.

Yet I had no cause to complain because she quickly became indispensable, although not, as she must have fancied, invincible. She proved herself loyal, discreet and competent, and I saw little reason not to trust her and treat her well.

Yes, I was blind, as I discovered to my cost.

When I returned home late that balmy Voodoomass evening, merry with alcohol, hoarse from singing along to festive songs, tired from dancing and my stomach bursting at the seams after a feast of broadbill soup, mashed cassava and peppered roast giraffe, I was told that she had disappeared without trace. I was so dumbstruck that I slumped onto a divan and had to be resuscitated with smelling salts.

When it became clear that she had indeed absconded, gossip spread around Mayfah like sewer rats.

When I went out for my early morning constitutional the next day on Hy Da Plains, riding my favourite camel around the Serpentin Wadi, I was greeted with such smug smiles from my neighbours that I felt the urge to slice off their lips and grind them into the sand.

I decided that when I found the little bitch, as no doubt I would, I would be forced to exact a harsh penalty to recover my self-esteem and standing in the community.

Let us not forget that punishment for a runaway is usually the loss of a limb or a tongue, or even death.

It is quite the done thing.

I immediately sent out news of her escape and soon

enough was notified that she had been spotted down at Doklanda, in the company of a well-known debutante from one of those misguided liberal-lefty Qua Ka families.

I decided to head the hunt myself.

ADVERTISEMENTS

BANK OF UK
Our Credit is Your Profit

LLOYDS OF LONDOLO
Be Assured
Your Ships are Insured

ASSEMBLY OF THE HOUSE OF GOVERNORS
Ambossa Rules the Waves

WORSHIPFUL COMPANY OF SLAVE TRADERS
BUILDING THE NATION

The General Council of Holy Men
The Missionary Position: *There are only 600 True Gods*

Worshipful Company of Rum-makers
Savouring the **Sweetness**

The Royal Aphrikan Company
The Royal Family Favours Us

Wool Wi Che Arsenal
Gunning for You & Silencing Our Critics

Advertising Rates Negotiable

Book Three

Oh Sweet Chariot

A cluster of moths crashed into each other in a tiny, heart-shaped space.

I tried to see who was standing in the doorway of the ship's cabin, obscured by lamplight.

I was so sure it was Bwana.

If he'd found me, he would torture me, and I would probably die.

Once upon a time I'd had the hope of a decent future. Then it was stolen from me and Bwana had benefited from my free services for the whole of my adult life.

He *owed* me.

I felt the fighter spirit stir within me and sprang up ready to defend myself.

I knew what I was capable of.

I had done it before.

I could do it again.

But when a shrivelled Ambossan woman stepped out from behind the lamp I froze.

Thank God it wasn't him.

She lowered the lamp, illuminating a face whose deep crevices fanned out from its centre.

A black bombazine wrappa rustled as she walked.

'Don't be startled,' she said, shaking her head, setting her pronounced chicken wattle quivering. 'We going to get you home safely. The name's Harrida and I'm on *your* side.'

I recognised the accent of the Amarikan south, which had

vowels so drawn out they went to sleep before the end of a word.

'You been dead to the world, girl. You got a nasty shock passing out there on the docks. Poor Ezinwene had to drag you up the gangway with everybody most likely wondering what was going on.'

She beckoned me to sit down.

'Now get some of this soup down you. It's got bushmeat and sweet potato in it. Bet that sounds good.'

'I was worried that she would betray me,' I blurted out.

'Ah no, she's a good girl – young but trustworthy. She helped us once before and we'll use her again because who'd suspect the flirtatious debutante Ezinwene of such clever subterfuge? Praise be the gods!'

She handed me the soup.

I sat down and ate, savouring, thinking that surely we were on the open seas by now and far away from the danger of the docks.

The rhythm of the rolling boat beneath us reassured me, as did this kindly lady.

It turned out that Harrida had been born the only daughter of a wealthy cotton planter in the Lone Star Administrative District of Te Xasa in Amarika.

'Slavery never sat right with me,' she said. 'Just me and my daddy lived in a great big old house with more rooms than I could count and forty domestic slaves working round the clock so's we didn't have to lift a darned finger. Hundreds more were literally worked to death in the fields just so's my daddy could make more money than he'd ever have reason to spend. There were so many half-breed girls who looked like me too, I lost count. Yet none of them was allowed to come talk or play with me and most of them ended up getting their backsides whupped for one thing or another. My daddy said he'd kill anyone who ever laid a finger on me. Nope. It just didn't sit right.'

As soon as she was old enough, she left, financing her independence by selling the jewels inherited from her dead mother. She began working for the Free Ferry Service which sent missionaries to convert Europane natives to Voodoo.

Runaways were hidden in secret cabins. None had so far been captured.

'You will soon be free, my dear,' she said. 'Free,' she repeated, letting the word take flight, like a solitary seagull speeding across a sparkling ocean on a glorious day.

Hallelujah!

In the morning we'd be at the mouth of the River Temz, then we'd enter the Ambossan Channel and eventually dip down towards the Atlantic and be on our way to Europa.

I had finished eating and drank from the gourd of water she offered.

She told me I could go on deck as it was almost dark but I had to stay out of sight.

'Your life is in our hands and our lives are in your hands. Remember that.'

As I made my way out she hunkered down, spread her shawl on the cabin floor and emptied the contents of a goat-skin pouch onto it.

Out tumbled cat's teeth, claws, bunches of coarse animal hair, the jaws of a rodent, a little bundle of herbs, a snuff box, a candle.

I hoped it was on my behalf.

Alone on the empty deck I sat out of sight on a coil of rope and peeped over the railing. I was surprised to see we were still only passing through the outer reaches of Londolo – zones 8, 9 and 10. I recognised the prosperous town of Green Wi Che, known for its shipbuilding yards, several of which we passed. We soon skirted the wide riverside factories of the arsenal town of Wool Wi Che, famous for manufacturing the finest spears, shields, crossbows, poison darts, muskets and cannons in the world.

Grotesque hippos lay entwined on top of each other in the mudflats, their rubbery, slimy skins like those of giant slugs, their eyes and ears a putrid pink. Two open-mouthed alpha males were squaring up to each other, jaws stretched wide, teeth interlocked inside.

A herd of ugly water buffalo traipsed like disgruntled hunch-backed farmhands through the mangroves.

A Temz crocodile pretended to sleep on the riverbank, mouth casually open, waiting to snap down hard on its next gullible prey.

Glimpsed between trees a powerful young hunter with shiny black thighs and thin calfs was hot on the heels of a wild boar.

A flock of egrets passed overhead, an exquisite flurry of white wings set against the red-streaked sky.

Soon we came to grassy plains where a herd of giraffe was grazing, wobbly-legged calfs taking refuge between their mothers' legs.

Further downriver an ungainly herd of elephants approached the water, making every other animal run for cover.

Far away I could just make out the mountain ranges of the Essex Massif.

Now that I was leaving, it all seemed quite scenic.

At a bend in the river a signpost announced:
WELCOME TO THE CITY OF DARTFOR, TWINNED WITH CASABLANCA.

Coned rondavels, whitewashed villas and mud huts with corrugated roofs rubbed shoulders with each other on the hills. Municipal mud tower blocks rose high above them, laundry hanging colourfully from windows.

As the ship sailed silently past, Ambossan voices ebbed and flowed as people walked along the promenade or sat in cafes, while their children played beach football with green coconuts beneath the advertisements for the Acoca Aloca fizzy drink, the red-and-white squiggle of its logo emblazoned on riverside billboards.

Under the arches of a bridge skateboarding teenage boys with wild Aphros, beaded corsets and leather jockstraps hurtled up its sweeping walls, turned, hovered mid-air, then skidded down again with a whoop and a flourish.

Crouched in the shallows was the after-dinner crowd, chatting and shitting.

A row of young adults sat flirting on a low harbour wall. The girls wore their hair shaved with a bushy topknot just above the forehead, their faces painted a bright yellow with white chalk dots circling each cheek and kohl-black lipstick. The boys sported thin hennaed dreadlocks and had a green line streaked down the centre of the nose.

Tips of cigarettes rose and fell like fireflies.

Two ancient fishermen with wrinkled stomachs dined at the end of a pier, scooping up rice from a large green ravenala leaf.

As we left Dartfor City a harvest rave was in full swing in an outlying field. Groins banged hard against crotches. Buttocks slid up and down thrusting pelvises. Legs shimmied in between each other while heads rolled from side to side. Drummers sat on a stage banging out super-fast rhythms while dancers wearing grass skirts shook their cheeks to the beat, exposing themselves to the crowd.

The drums pounded on in my bones for miles afterwards as the ship rolled deeper into the Ambossan wilderness.

★

If I reached out I could almost touch the forest ferns.

The skeleton of a disused train carriage became visible where the trees thinned out, a plume of smoke coming out of its chimney.

The shriek of a jackal made me start.

Lemur eyes stared out as luminous orange lamps from the branches of trees.

I could hear howler monkeys creating havoc inside the rainforest.

Waterborne creatures rippled in the river.

Airborne creatures flapped around me.

The darkness wrapped me up.

The darkness held me.

The darkness carried me.

I am walking down the lane towards our cottage and see Pa returning from work with his two grandsons who are strapping lads – Robert and John. They're Sharon's two boys.

Mam is sitting on a love seat cradling her latest granddaughter who is called Doris. She's the first child of Alice.

Mam has filled out now and is ruddy-cheeked and she never talks of dying any more.

Madge is sewing the hem of the wedding dress for her niece Rebecca's marriage to a turnip farmer who owns 300 acres. Rebecca is Sharon's too.

Madge has never married and never will.

Sharon married a stable hand whose bushy-bearded good looks were supposed to make up for the absence of a princely pedigree. But she's still looking over at the hills yonder, just in case.

Alice, sadly, is in a mental asylum.

Ah no, just kidding. She sees me first, comes running down the lane to give me the sister of all hugs.

There are three other teenagers there too. Two girls and a boy.

The girls look the spitting of me and the boy is a dead cert for Frank.

They're helping Frank secure the last door on a beautifully inlaid cabinet he's making. They're teasing each other and laughing and the door nearly falls off and Frank tells them to behave but you can see he's not at all angry because he doesn't stop grinning at their antics.

He's not changed a bit. (Not had another woman since, either.)

The look on his face when he sees me is – priceless.

I didn't want to return to my cabin.

My first night of freedom would be nothing like my first night of incarceration.

I found a sheltered spot on the deck, piled with empty sacks, and lay down.

I spread my wrappa over me.

The clouds and ship sailed with ease in the same direction.

The stars were close enough to pluck and wear as jewellery.

A pair of star-diamond earrings.

Stars threaded onto a silver necklace.

I felt my muscles unclamp from my bones.

Released, my limbs sank into the improvised mattress of sacks.

My scalp let go of its tight grip on my brain.

My thoughts floated light as an air bubble towards the sky.

I was going home, oh Lord.

I was going home.

Eeny Meeny Miny Mo

A warm, light-fingered mist seduced me into morning.

The ship was swaying from side to side so we must have moored for the night.

The rainforest loomed in front of me, a high wall of vegetation.

My mattress had moulded to the foetal curve of my shape.

I stretched out, wriggling my toes, raising my arms above my head, feeling the rocks of my vertebrae pull away from each other.

I rotated my head from side to side to ease away the cricks.

I yawned loudly, just for the pleasure of it.

I felt so light-hearted, so youthful, so full of hope.

Morning dew brought out the smell of fish, embedded in the sacks.

What was for breakfast, I wondered. Boiled yam? Boiled cassava?

Soon it would be porridge: large flakes, creamy milk, sweetened with honey.

Rolling over, I climbed to my feet and strolled to the river side of the ship, to breathe in the quietude, to bathe my face in the moisturising mist, to overhear the unintelligible conversation of birds, to gaze upon the watercolour Temz which now seemed so beautiful draped in its gauzy bridal veil.

Yellow-billed storks waded through the rushes.

A wadi fed into the river, a gaggle of white swans paddling down it.

That day the Temz would carry me downstream until it pulled me far away from Great Ambossa.

I was looking up towards the heavens, as the rising sun began to bleed a pastel pink through the nebulous grey, when a ship pulled up alongside ours, with all the stealth of a silent assassin.

And there he was, standing high on the gun deck.

Two hundred feet tall, three hundred feet wide.

An expensive black-and-gold striped wrappa was tied around his waist, one end flung over a shoulder.

I heard Harrida behind me, 'Come inside! We will deal with this. Come inside, dear. Come inside!'

But she did not know the nature of this beast.

No way, Bwana. No way was I going down.

I dashed to the forest side of the ship.

I climbed over the railings and dropped into the river, not caring that its aquatic citizens might relish a slender white drumstick for breakfast. I dog-paddled my way through the river, gripped the roots of a fortress of trees and tried to lever myself onto their unyielding limbs.

My mind was more agile than my body. I kept slipping, but finally managed to clamber up onto the bank.

Just before I disappeared into the trees, I turned around.

Bwana was spewing orders. Men were running up and down the decks of both ships. Harrida was scurrying back down below deck, hands cupped over her mouth.

When I scanned the length of Bwana's ship I saw Ezinwene hovering on the quarterdeck. She had wrapped her arms around herself, her hair was undone, she looked bedraggled. Did she have a black eye?

As soon as she spotted me she ducked down behind the railing.

Hoisting my wrappa up, I let my legs propel me over mulch

and twigs, over stones and moss, through ferns and bracken, over mud pools and rocky streams.

My feet quickly sored. They did not complain.

My legs scratched against thorns. They did not complain.

My hands bashed against the bark of trees. They did not complain.

I listened out for the barking of the dogs that would surely come.

The canopy was an impenetrable ceiling which blocked out the light, the sun broke through only where a tree had fallen and now lay upon the forest floor being devoured by insects.

Birds of paradise flew high up in the leaves. Blue macaw parrots argued in the raucous voices of angry humans.

Chimpanzees swung from the aerial roots of plants which dangled from the canopy like snakes.

Mossy twigs could have been vipers.

Black leaves could have been scorpions.

Small rocks could have been porcupines.

I scuttled into the undergrowth where vines conspired to choke me.

Whenever I saw the sun, I followed it, hoping it would stop me running around in circles, hoping it would take me away from the river.

I came to an open space where trees had been burned down and which now sprouted a new carpet of soft grass so inviting it took all my willpower not to fling myself upon it.

To rest, just for a moment.

A black vulture with a glossy wingspan of ten feet was swooping down towards the carcass of a jackal.

Turning to my immediate right, I fled the wide open space, re-entering the shade and shadows of the forest.

I returned to its breathing – the crushed twigs and leaves

underfoot, the insects, the birds, the falling fruit, the howler monkeys who were making such a din.

Passing the reddish-brown bark of a guava tree, I grabbed a bunch of its fruit, stuffing them down without even peeling their hairy skins.

I had sustenance. I could go on.

Oranges, mangoes, star fruit, berries – I could survive in the rainforest.

I listened for barks but none came.

I listened all night while I scrambled through the undergrowth.

I listened in the morning when I was sure they would have found me.

I listened in the afternoon when I climbed into the cradle of a thick tree and slept, for a few minutes.

When I awoke it was dawn.

Huge black ants were biting my body raw.

I climbed down painfully from the tree and ran until I found a stream, splashed in and watched the ants drown.

Overnight my legs had swollen to twice their normal size. I wrapped my feet in leaves and hobbled along as best I could.

My soles were butchered.

My sores oozed pus.

My cuts were bleeding.

I heard children shouting.

Behind some mangrove trees two thin Ambossan boys were beating two gaunt cows with sticks as they chased them around a paddy field churning up mud in preparation for rice planting.

I crouched and watched. If I approached they might run off and tell their parents.

I decided to wait until they were finished and follow them home.

I struggled to keep up and out of sight as they larked about, their little voices echoing under the canopy, picking berries as they walked, climbing up a coconut tree, slicing open a coconut with a knife, sharing its milk, singing songs, prodding the cattle, cursing them.

I could smell pottery cooking.

Four older women were firing pots in a dell, adding layers of grasses, branches, leaves to the flames. The boys greeted them.

I must be nearing a settlement.

Impulsively, desperately, I walked into their midst.

Looking up, they stopped what they were doing.

One of the women approached. Her hair was a coxcomb of animal fat, the holes in her earlobes were so stretched I could've slipped my hand through them. A brass ring hung from the middle of her nose and she wore a brass torque. Her breasts were stringy and juiceless and a dirty beaded skirt showed off withered thighs.

Her face was inscrutable but she took my hand, gave me water and fed me a piece of fried fish.

One of the boys poked me with a stick as if I was some strange, possibly dangerous, new animal he'd just discovered.

Slapping him on the leg, the woman then helped me up, and I was assisted into their nearby home – a kraal of stone and loam huts thatched with millet.

Everyone gathered to watch my arrival but no one said a word.

I was offered a straw mat underneath the spacious branches of a guango tree.

My helper dabbed some ointment onto my wounds, ordered a bowl of rice to be brought to me.

I whispered my thanks, saying I hoped my strength would return soon, then I'd be on my way.

I prayed I would be safe there.

I heard the uncertain pounding of corn near the huts behind me and hens clacking. I heard mats being shaken out by confident, impatient adult hands. A crying baby was shushed. There was the squelch of a cow being milked and the brush of twigs sweeping the floor of the kraal.

No one spoke.

No one said a word.

I should have left but – I was exhausted.

The hot afternoon stretched out its long limbs and yawned itself into evening. I closed my eyes, just for a short while.

I awoke to see Bwana heave his bulk into the kraal.

His expensive wrappa trailed from his waist in a long, mud-drenched twist of cloth like a tail.

A forked rawhide whip dangled from his left hand.

I eased myself onto my feet in the vain hope of running but the helper woman pinned my arms from behind.

Flanking Bwana were two hunters whose naked bodies were painted with white geometric patterns.

One held a spear, the other a machete.

Up close he was a blur of exaggerated features swimming in a film of sweat. His breath was so revolting my eyes watered.

I could touch his fury.

'I will beat you until you can no longer beg for mercy. I will cut off one ear so that you will hear better with the other. I will chop off one foot so you can no longer run. I have been a kind master to you. Now I will be a stern one. *Thus* will you know the difference.'

He beckoned to the hunters, who ripped off my wrappa, spun me around and tied my hands to the tree with twine.

Warm liquid spurted down my left leg.

Justice is Served

(from *The Flame*)

Dear Reader,

I am not a violent man but one who has, on occasion, to make sure that acts of deterrence and punishment are carried out.

Imagine how I felt when I strode into the compound in the forest two days later and found the wretch cowering with self-pity underneath a tree.

Something inside of me flipped.

Judge me not, Dear Reader, when I confess that I cared little, in that moment, whether the wretch lived or died.

The skin on her spindly back was pale, and when the first lash sliced it open, thick blood trickled down it in thin red rivulets.

What could I do but turn and walk back out of the gates of that compound as the sound of her blood-curdling cries tore through the evening skies?

Night had fallen by the time I returned to the compound to find her on the ground, not moving.

My men stood guard while the local women tended to her.

Something inside of me flipped again.

Tears of rage flooded down my cheeks. After such a good working relationship, it had come to this!

I was forced to admit the old adage – you can take the child out of the jungle, but you cannot take the jungle out of the child.

The humane thing to do would have been to finish her off, but I was not and will never be a murderer.

She was to be nursed back to good health and transported henceforth to Home Sweet Home.

There she would discover the nature of a hard day's work.

Hereto a word of caution, Dear Reader:

The Stages of Evolution must be respected and the Laws of Nature adhered to.

Chief Kaga Konata Katamba I learned the hard way that one must never ever treat the Caucasoinid breed as we do our own.

Alas, until the next time.

Paradise Island

The trackers took it in turn to deliver the two hundred and one lashes ordered by my master.

My back was gorged with the kind of deep gashes a finger could slide through.

The knuckles of my vertebrae were exposed underneath, like the parting of white flesh on fish to reveal its skeleton.

The rawhide splintered my delicate little ribs and lacerated the skin on my thighs and behind.

Bwana trusted the women of the forest to look after me until I was ready to be moved. They pressed herbal poultices onto my back which kept getting reinfected and the pain felt like my raw wounds were being doused with vinegar.

For the longest while I lay face-down on a mat in a darkened hut wishing I was dead.

That brought back memories.

Bwana had decided to banish me to his plantation on New Ambossa, a journey conducted in some style, relatively speaking, aboard a schooner which ferried supplies and Ambossan personnel from the UK to the West Japanese Islands. I shared a cabin with three slave girls, each a personal waiting maid. Their mistresses were three sisters betrothed by their families to marry planters they'd not even met.

The three maids, who catered to the whims of their capricious mistresses, kindly took it in turns to check up on me while I indulged in a lot of sleep.

They were just kids, and so excited about what lay ahead. They had no idea.

I could go anywhere on board, of course, because there was nowhere to run to.

When we sailed up the coast to Mo Bassa Bay, the girls insisted I go up on deck to view the miles of shimmering beaches, the stunning colours of tropical plants and palm trees swaying in a warm breeze inviting me to lazy days of sunning, napping and convalescing.

Once we arrived at the bay I was put in chains and escorted to a man waiting to collect me and a consignment of rice. He was an old trusty called King Shaka who lugged the sacks onto his cart and told me to climb in between. Then he hurtled off inland towards the Mount Diablo Mountains, me bouncing about like a floppy rag doll, hair in two damp plaits, each jolt of the bumpy tracks threatening to tear open the fragile new tissues forming across my back.

Bwana's plantation was approached via a narrow mountain path with heart-stopping twists and turns; one wrong move would've sent us head-over-heels into the plantation valley which lay a dizzy five hundred feet below.

It was cool in the mountains but as we descended Lucky Valley, the humid air draped itself languorously over the surface of my lungs so that I could barely breathe.

Sugar-cane fields stretched for miles, surrounded by cloud-piercing mountains and trees bearing mouth-watering fruits: sour sop, star apple, sweet sop.

Mid-morning the wooden wheels of the cart staggered through the plantation gates under a filigree sign cast into an iron arch: 'Home Sweet Home'.

To think that I had been on the fast track to freedom.

A dormant rage began to race through me.

My heart leaped from my chest.

What had I done to deserve this?

I decided that as soon as I found a way, I would be gone.

Somewhere. Somehow. Someday. Soon.

This time I'd slit my throat before capture.

At that thought, I picked up my heart, cupped it between my hands and placed it back behind my ribs, where it belonged.

King Shaka took a right turn up a pathway lined with logwood trees.

High up to the right was the Great House, Massa Nonso's *crib*.

I had watched the boy grow up, seen him claw his way up from the lowly position of privilege, wealth, education and inheritance to become, de facto, master of all he surveyed.

Whereas Bwana and Madama Blessing had been devout disciples of his younger brother Bamwoze, Nonso, the overlooked heir, had issues.

I'd not seen Nonso for many years. Just what kind of young man had the child I'd once known become?

The air was so muggy it was like a layer of grease had been slathered over everything.

The cart lurched from side to side as its wheels mounted deep ridges of solidified mud before coming down on one side or another with a thud.

We lumbered past sugar-cane fields where walls of hard, militaristic stalks grew to over twelve feet high. A gang of slaves was advancing on the cane like a phalanx of soldiers, hacking at it with urgent repetitive movements. Male and female – they were all stripped to the waist. The familiar KKK brand was burned onto tanned skin, clothes and hair were bleached blonde and crisped hard by a sun from which there was no respite, and their muscles had ripped and fused into fists of knotted rope straining underneath translucent Europane skin.

I remembered from my time on Roaring River Estate how a strapping First Gang like this chopped up the cane, followed by a weaker Second Gang who cleaned up after them, and bringing up the rear were the youngsters and elders grouped into a Third Gang.

Little Miracle and I used to pass them in the fields when leaving the plantation by carriage.

They were strangers to me.

I remember wondering how they could work so hard, for such long hours, in such heat.

I remember feeling so removed from them – and thankful.

As we rolled past, everyone looked up and, for an instant, froze.

These silent otherworldly people, sizzling in the fuzz of heat, premature lines etched into each jaded face, transported me back to my own time on the islands so many years ago – so many light years away from the coffee houses and dance raves and high-rises and high society and all the glamour, garrulousness and gaudiness of the metropolis.

Here time passed so slowly – it didn't, really.

In that moment the isolated bushmen encountered the urbanite I had become.

I could not reach them, nor they me.

They turned their attention back to the cane and I remembered this much – that at harvest time their days would practically never stop and their nights would hardly begin.

As we trundled down the lane one of the women released a contralto which grew wings and soared above the cane:

Gahd save we grashus chief
Long live we nobel chief
Gahd save we chief
Send him victorias
Happee and glorias
Long to rane ova us
Gahd save . . .

It was so stirring the song stayed with me long after it faded into the distance. Where had I heard it before?

Finally we came to a halt in the shadow of some low-lying thatched stone warehouses which were slumped alongside a river like grumpy old men: straw hats pulled down low, mulling over old hurts, planning new vendettas. A sulky mulatto, covered in dust, loped out of a side door wearing a leather flap over his privates. His slim, tapered muscles had the perfect cut and carve of a twenty-year-old but his face had the enraged *Why me?* of slavery scrawled all over it like graffiti. Scratching his balls, he mumbled a greeting to King Shaka, registered me with a sharp tilt of his chin, sullenly offloaded one sack at a time, initially doubling over with the weight of each one before attempting to straighten up.

He too seemed vaguely familiar, yet I could not explain why.

King Shaka explained that just behind us was the factory quarter: sugar mill, water mill, distillery and boiling house.

Way behind that was the Dong River Falls, which ran through the estate as the Dong River before passing out into open country.

Down in the south were the slaves' quarters.

To the east lay a forest of pines – provider of timber and tinder.

*

King Shaka walked down to the riverbank, picked up two gourds and dipped them in. Like most whytes on the islands he was so brown he could pass for mixed himself. The skin on his thick, square back sagged into folds underneath rounded shoulderblades. He wore a white loincloth which showed off creased cheeks and his stiff, thin, bandy legs rocked sideways when he walked.

He returned with a gourd swinging low from each hand.

Throwing back my head, I poured the cool mountain water into my mouth in huge, lip-smacking, greedy gulps, then watched as he unwrapped the green-and-white spotted bandana which had been tied around his forehead to gather sweat. Grey hair hung limply around the fringes of his peeling baldness. Squeezing liquid out of the cloth, he put it out to dry on the cart, smoothing it down, his movements meticulous.

He could control the little things in life.

Climbing down from the cart, I stretched and shook out my limbs, feeling the blood trying to circulate through the ruptured vessels in my back. Close up I could see that King Shaka was older than I had at first thought, perhaps in his seventies, quite an achievement in a society where few slaves survived beyond middle age.

His face was marinated in bitterness.

He perched himself on the cart and spoke to me in the language of the islands, which had evolved from the various tongues of the people who inhabited it. He told me that he had been born Arthur Ethelbert Reginald Williams, the fourth son of a humble fisherman who lived in a village called Margate in England. As a boy he'd been kidnapped when out picking cockles early one morning by men who had sailed in on a slave-raiding expedition.

He never got to say goodbye to his mum and dad.

Six decades later, he still thought of them every day.

Once he had arrived in New Ambossa, he was renamed King Shaka. It had long been popular on the islands for masters to give slaves the names of leading Aphrikans. Heading the lists of 'Most Popular Names for Slave Girls and Boys' were: Muganzirwazza, Amina, Cetewayo, Sonni Ali, Cleopatra, Nehanda, Tipoo Tib, Nzingha, Tutankhamun and Yaa Asantewa. King Shaka had been in residence at Home Sweet Home since the days when Bwana was running the joint and had been promoted from cane-cutter to odd-job boy.

'Lissan,' he whispered with a cursory glance over his shoulder. 'Don't tri buk sistem becorze sistem bruk yu down furz. Massa Nonso? Him wurz dan him poopa. Yu betta *beleev*. Ah beg yu, don't tri eskape becorze nowhere a-go, nowhere to hide and patrols goin ketch yu quick-quick an chop off yu fut.'

He waited cock-eared for a response, prompting a reassuring nod from yours truly. King Shaka would not go down for Spearheading the Revolution against our Aphrikan Oppressors, then.

I would have to watch him because, I suspected, he would be watching me.

Once we had both rehydrated King Shaka took me behind the warehouses into the heart of the factory quarter to find Massa Rotimi, the estate manager. A formal introduction had to be made.

I knew then that I was being denied an audience with young Massa Nonso. Skilled slaves were a valued commodity on plantations and as yours truly was a white-collar slave and not a manual labourer, I'd hoped Nonso would ignore his father's orders and find desk work for me. The bosses were businessmen, they weren't stupid. Why throw extensive office experience down the toilet? And hadn't I suffered enough?

One look at me and this Massa Rotimi would surely see I was too weak to work out in the fields.

Our first port of call was the sugar mill, where cane juice had to be extracted within twenty-four hours of cutting or else it would start to rot. I found myself thrust into a large yard clogged up by a stream of carts delivering massive bundles of cane which were offloaded and carried into the mill. It was absolute chaos as slaves collided with each other trying to work faster than was sensible, under the bellowing orders of an overseer who stood on the back of a cart waving his arms about in a frenzy.

Conical smoke-stacks thirty feet high billowed smoke which darkened the sky, sending a smattering of black ash to rain down upon us. Gigantic blades rotated in the wind, powering the crushing rollers inside.

When the wooden door to the mill was flung open with such violence it nearly smashed into pieces, I knew it had to be the man in charge – Massa Rotimi. He strode out, bald, bullish, stabbing the ground with a carved wooden staff, barging into the crowd, shouting at the overseer to clear up the backlog of deliveries, then he fixed his scowl on the newcomer hovering next to King Shaka, who, I noticed, shifted a little as if to create physical distance between us, as if he didn't want my reputation to sully his. When Massa Rotimi looked me up and down with disdain, I had no doubt that he knew *exactly* who I was.

My job interview took place as he swept past, muttering out of the corner of his mouth that I'd been assigned to work in the mill and boiling house – immediately.

'Now get that damned hair cut or those rollers will scalp her!'

Well – nice to meet you, too.

Before I knew what was happening the dutiful King Shaka

pushed me down by my shoulders so that I dropped to my knees. He whipped a penknife out of his pouch and began slashing away at my hair until only stubble remained.

Inside the mill I encountered a beast with a vicious set of teeth being fed ripe cane stalks by a statuesque woman working at a speed I could not hope to match. She was introduced as Ye Memé, and she greeted her new co-worker with a warm smile, my first proper welcome; although I noticed that her teeth were rotting, typical of plantation slaves for whom sucking the sweetness out of cane was an addiction. Yet even then, and even bareheaded, she was still a big-boned, sloe-eyed Viking beauty with proud sculptured cheekbones which held her skin smooth and taut.

Ye Memé showed me how to force-feed the herbivorous monster, but the syrupy stench of the cane set fire to my olfactory glands and whatever strength I possessed was quickly sapped. Before long I was crippled by new pains shooting across my back and ribs, yet when I dropped to the ground for a breather she gasped in horror, yanked me back up onto my feet and yelled over the rackety clunking of the mill's machines that impromptu breaks weren't allowed and if I didn't speed up I'd risk the lash of the bullwhip, and so would she. The factory overseer, she explained, liked to sneak in with the express purpose of catching slackers on whom he could vent his spleen.

I returned to work stuffing the Mouth, which masticated the stalks – grunting, spitting, dribbling, swallowing the sap-saliva down into its digestive system with burps and belches, until it was pissed out as gushing white foam, then sent on its way via a sluice to the boiling house. The crushed cane was pulled out the opposite end of the machine by another shaven-headed woman who threw the trash onto the floor. Children ran in and out to carry it to the boiling house, where it provided fuel.

Ye Memé told me that the jaws of this monster had ripped off more arms than she cared to remember: the rollers were fast, deadly, unstoppable.

'Be cyaful. Sloppiness mangel yu, or wurz – mek yu ded.'

As the mind-numbing, body-wrecking hours drew on, I summoned up all my mental resources not to succumb to my most desperate desire: to flop onto the stone floor and damn the consequences.

I had to survive, not just that afternoon, but the following days, months, years. Non-stop drudgery preceding an early death? I knew the stats – one in three slaves didn't survive the first three years in the New World.

Bwana was right: '*Thus* will you know the difference.'

How I despised him.

When a tremor began in my legs, I tried to resist it.

When my whole body became wracked by spasms, I collapsed on the ground.

Thank God for Ye Memé, who stopped work at great risk to herself, helped me back up, cradled me in the damp warmth of her soft-breasted, six-footer self while calming me down with a motherly, 'Hush-now, furz few week bad-bad, den get betta.'

Had the overseer caught me 'skiving' that day, and sliced my back open again, I know in my heart of hearts I would not have survived.

Ye Memé had saved my life.

At some point our shift was relieved. I crawled out into the yard which, under the hissing flames of torchlight, was still congested with carts delivering cane. Ye Memé took me to a spot underneath a date palm where other workers were resting on mats. She sat cross-legged, shared her meal of rice and black-eyed peas and fetched a gourd of brackish water for us to drink.

Appraising me in my state of stupor, she said, not without a hint of remonstration in her tone, 'Feeld-wurk wurz. Yu luky, gyal. Yu luky!'

Assuming my day now over, assuming it was time for bed – wherever *that* was – the lead lids on my eyes slammed shut, only to fling themselves open when Ye Memé's strong, sweaty hand gripped mine and yanked me up for the second time that day.

'Wurk! Iz wurk we hav to do. We nyot here to be happee. We nyot here to rest. We here to make plentee-plentee monee for Massa Nonso. Iz wurk what we do, gyal. Wurk! Wurk! Wurk! Now come!'

This was the point when I realised that the gap between myself and blue-collar slaves had well and truly closed.

Slick, sarcastic, sophisticated, opinionated, literate, numerate – no one gave a flying fuck here. I was now one of the anonymous masses on an island in the middle of nowhere where life was cheap and death came easy.

When we entered the boiling house it was so hot I wanted to pass out.

We joined other women who were hunched over kettles boiling cane juice. Ye Memé taught me how to skim the scum off the top, then ladle the sap into ever-smaller kettles until it started to harden. Dripping with sweat and steam, I looked around and saw my future: haggard, hunchbacked women whose arms were streaked with the darkened, congealed skin of old burns.

After hours spent bending over, I discovered that when I tried to straighten up to carry the kettles into the purgery, I couldn't. My back had fossilised. Instead of walking, I shuffled. Instead of standing straight, I was bent double.

Then I had to pour the juice into coolers and vats and leave it to crystallise.

Ye Memé must have taken me to her hut at some point, and put me to sleep on a mat on the floor next to her children. I have no recollection except that some time later, while the night was still soaked in the pitch black of the moonless countryside, she splashed cold water onto my face to rouse me from the most impenetrable slumber, then massaged my legs to get them moving because they had become two heavy iron rods: no nerves, no muscles, no mobility.

My Viking friend hauled me back to the mill, as I tried to keep up with her strides.

'We must hurree. If we late, we git beet. Cyant be late.'

Ye Memé was a single working mother raising five children in a plantation society where most children grew up in broken homes. Prized for his sexual prowess and physical strength, one minute a male slave would be head of a household, the next he'd be sold off to a master on the other side of the island or abroad.

Motherhood was far from straightforward too, because managing to actually keep your children depended on your master's whim. A canny master would let the family stay together. Happy workers were more productive, after all. However, should it make greater economic sense, or should his finances nose-dive, or should he be simply cold-hearted, malicious or just plain indifferent, they'd all be sold off.

Mother no more.

And in the absence of proper child-care provision? Well, there was Granny Doda, Granny Abir and Granny Makeda, the plantation ancients. Only when they were too weak to lift a machete and too decrepit to work in the factory quarter, were they put out to pasture, subsisting on the goodwill of their neighbours, whose rumbustious toddlers they looked after.

Although they had all been born on plantations in New Ambossa, each knew of distant ancestors from the nations of Portugal, Spain and Belgium.

Some mothers kept newborns strapped to their backs while out in the fields, or laid them down in the shade of bamboo, close enough to hear their mighty little screams for milk and a cuddle, but not always allowed to rush over to tend to their needs.

My new friend Ye Memé had given birth to thirteen children. Three died soon after birth, unsurprising considering she slashed cane until a couple of weeks before they were born and, because she lacked rest after that, her milk dried up. Four had been sold off. Dingiswayo was being raised by an older woman in the quarter, Ma Marjani. Of the five remaining – Yao, Inaani, Akiki, Cabion and Lolli – all were under ten years old and every night my friend prayed that her nine-year-old, a shy boy called Yao who was at an age when he might be sold off, would not be taken from her. As Yao and his younger siblings were all over three years of age they had found employment working from sun-up to sun-down in the Third Gang.

Ye Memé was one of the lucky ones with five of her children still under one roof.

But just how she managed to make sure her children were well fed, her hut spotless, her allotment thriving, *and* work eighteen-hour days during harvest time without ever once complaining never ceased to astonish me. Born into slavery, with no name but her slave one (there was a grandfather from the Danish nation, she'd been told), it was all she knew and she had no memories of a better life elsewhere.

She got by on five hours' sleep a night, spending early

Sunday morning at the shrine and the rest of the day catching up with her chores.

No one forced Ye Memé to take me on as house guest, Lord knows I gave nothing back in return, at first. No one told her to protect me from the advances of men who saw me as fresh meat, to raise her sizeable fists to ward off those for whom *No* spelt *Yes*. Men loved her even though she was taller and broader than most of them:

'Yu tink a likkle bwoy like yu can tell a big wooman like me what a-do?'

Then she'd flounce off, rolling her hips in the exaggerated Ambossan way, chest thrust out, chin stuck up in the air, knowing the man she'd just belittled was leering after her with the most almighty hard-on.

A succession of nights and days tumbled into each other as I stumbled from the fog of work to the fog of sleep and back again.

After a while I started to adjust to my new life of drudgery in the slave wilderness.

I began to get my mojo back.

Instead of sleeping soundly through one Sunday, I awoke at midday to a hut devoid of everything but sleeping mats, some blankets and a clothes chest. I went outside, momentarily blinded by the dazzling sunlight.

The slaves' quarter was like another world on a Sunday: busy, lively, normal. People were caught up with household chores, sweeping out huts, sewing garments, repairing roofs thatched with twisted-millet or walls of huts made out of reed and red clay, weaving coiled baskets, putting cassava flour through a sifter, cooking stews over fires in big Dutch pots.

Everyone wore their Sunday-best – a stylistic composite of

Aphrika with Europa. The women wore floor-length calico petticoats, white billowy blouses and headscarfs as flamboyant as those of the Ambossans. On their ears were large hoop earrings and through their noses were small bones. Men wore calico pantaloons held up by thick leather belts.

Blind Bimbola, the local hairdresser, whose eyes were always closed – because they had never opened – was sitting on the stoop opposite ours singing a spiritual very loudly and very out of tune: *All ting brite an boot-i-fal/ All creetyur grate an small/ All ting wize an wun-da-ful/ De lord Gahd made dem all.* All the while she was plaiting Yao's sister Akiki's thin, white-blonde hair into cane rows so tight it pulled back the skin on her forehead. Held in the vice of Blind Bimbola's mighty thighs, Akiki squirmed and pushed out her lower lip in a melodramatic sulk. Upon seeing me smile at her over the way, however, she poked out her tongue.

I began to walk down the lane – to *stroll* – relishing this alien concept when the only walking I'd done since arrival had been to rush to work in a panic and stagger back to sleep.

Women returned from the allotments carrying baskets on their heads piled high with mud-encrusted yams and sweet potatoes, the serrated green leaves of aloe vera and the crinkled green leaves of callalloo. Or they set off for the river, heavy little stools on their heads on which to sit and scrub clothes in shallow water; on top of the stools were baskets full of washing. Hands swung at the side or grasped those of their little children, as they greeted me with a friendly 'Y'all rite, sister?' or a 'Howzit?'

Fiddle-playing came from somewhere over the roofs of the immediate huts to my right, accompanied by harmonised group singing and a joyful mess of crashing tambourines. *Happee burt-day to yu/ Happee burt-day to yu/ Happee burt-day dear Zikabiva/ Happee burt-day to yu.* It was a song I knew from my homeland. I'd not heard it since.

Further down the lane Yao and his brother Inaani, who was a year younger, were stuffing their youngest brother, five-year-old Cabion, into an empty barrel. They then tried to push it in a straight line, which it refused to do. They were in hysterics. I found myself laughing out loud, too, which felt weird. What a miserable sod I'd become.

Looking straight ahead, I noticed for the first time a magnificent ninety-foot silk cotton tree with whitish flowers blooming. People were lounging in the alcoves of its buttressed roots which spread out to meet the ground, smoking tobacco from long-stemmed clay pipes, knocking back rotgut liquor from tankards and rolling dice.

The slaves' quarter was a hotch-potch of higgledy-piggledy shacks struggling to keep the aggressive wilderness at bay. In this tropical, humid climate of scorching suns and torrential downpours, everything grew rapidly and threatened to reclaim the entire settlement.

The roots of trees burrowed underneath the ground until they pushed hairy elbows and muscular forearms up through the middle of huts without a by-your-leave.

Ferns and bushes had to be continuously chopped down at the base but within days grew back longer, thicker, wilder.

Black Widow spiders lived underneath innocent-looking leaves and while their bites did not kill, they hurt like hell.

Other spiders spun webs six feet wide, trapping birds and frightening small humans who ran into them only to end up with a mouthful of stringy, powdery web.

The lime-green stinkie bug, shaped like a diamond, flew senselessly into all objects, including this one, leaving an unpleasant smell in its wake.

Red ginger proliferated, its flower like pink brushes, its leaves shaped like bananas.

Out of the halved bellies of calabashes grew yellow daffodils. Daffodils – I remembered them. The Ambossan settlers must have brought them from Europa as exotic specimens.

Hanging heliconia sprouted freely everywhere, their purple, red and golden flowers shooting sidewards out of long stems like small fishes with parrots' beaks.

The elegant bird-of-paradise plant grew four feet tall, topped with an imperious orange crest.

Several trees bore orchids, and fences and walls spilled over with bougainvillea: white, orange, magenta.

Aware that for the first time the pain in my back seemed to have completely disappeared, I felt brave enough to reach behind and actually touch it, running cautious fingers across its sensitive grooves and cavities.

Not an inch remained of the silky-smooth skin of which I had once been so proud.

It was a wreck.

It was vile.

It was ugly.

And so was I.

No man would ever love me again.

I slumped trembling against a lemon tree just as a giant swallowtail butterfly flew past and landed on a leaf close by. Nearly six inches wide, with cream and black spotted wings. I stared into the strange red eyes of this creature, and it seemed to look into mine.

Framed against the pure blue sky it was so beautiful, I wanted to cry.

Such beauty on these islands. Such beauty.

As it fluttered away, my gaze wandered over to where the

ground had been cleared around an old ebony tree. Even though space was at a premium in the quarter, no one had commandeered it for a drinking session, no children were using it as a maypole.

When I walked over to the tree, I saw that the trunk was as scarred as my back. Something had attacked the bark, slicing bits off. There was blood on it too. I wiped some onto my fingers. It was gooey, it was lumpy, it was red, it was fresh.

Feeling my stomach somersault, I turned away, glad to spy Ye Memé standing down a side passage underneath an ackee tree whose seed-pods were bursting open like little bubbles of crimson blood. Holding court among a gathering of women, a basket of green bananas at her feet, Ye Memé was dressed up in a brilliantly white blouse and a calico petticoat with burgundy roses embroidered at the hem. Her baldness was covered by a white headscarf tied into such an extravagant bow it added another ten inches to her height, making her appear some seven feet tall. Her tanned skin had been oiled, gaily painted wooden bangles ran up her arms, big, brass discs were inserted into the flesh of her earlobes and a chicken bone was shot through her nose.

Honestly, the woman was *such* a glamazon.

I faltered some steps away, aware that I was wearing a wrappa so old and filthy it had lost all colour and design. The women in the gathering were so dressed up and seemed so confident, so at ease with each other, so at home.

Ye Memé, sensing she was being watched, turned and caught me hovering. She beckoned me over and drew me protectively under her arm.

'Laydies, dis here mi new skinnie-like-bamboo frend, Omorenomwara. Lissan, all she do iz wurk, eet an sleep. She na talk, she na laf, she don't let none a-deze wotless brudders about here poke her in de bushes. Mi gyal here iz sofistikyated, ya hear? So-fist-ik-ya-ted. An she nyot like yu mamas at all becorze she uze her brain box and studee everyting an sayin nuttin. I know dis becorze I watch her like hawk.

'So, everybawdee, yu betta treat her nice-nice or I goin box yu in de head so hard it get mash-up an yu end up dribble like fool. Lookee hear – I *know* wot yu bitches all like!'

The women chortled. All heads, which had hitherto been directed up at Ye Memé with a combination of awe and resentment, now turned towards me. Their respect for her was, I noticed over time, often tinged with envy. They each offered me a traditional hand-shaking gesture.

Ma Marjani was Ye Memé's closest friend. She stood with such a rooted connection to the soil, it was like she was growing out of it. She had the forceful, emphatic gestures of a woman used to lifting a bundle of cane half her body weight or a hogshead of rum. When she shook my hand it was more of an assault than a greeting.

Then there was Lyani, who was petite and pretty, and played on it. Men fell for it, women didn't. I envied Ba Beduwa's hair which dripped like molten oil down her back. It didn't need cutting because she worked in the fields. Short and round, Amadoma looked doe-eyed up at Ye Memé. Then there was cool, cylindrical Kicongo, who had lost a hand, and fifteen-year-old Olunfunlayaro, a mulatto, whose prematurely enlarged breasts would ensure men treated her like a woman. Her father was a rapist, her mother dead.

Most of these women had been born on a plantation, survived the three-year seasoning period long ago and grown resilient. You either died or you survived, and if you survived you found the inner strength to thrive. They weren't weedy like me and it was obvious that the only fools these women would suffer were their masters. As they silently appraised me one and all, I realised I'd better shape up.

When I lived on Little Londolo as a child I hadn't mixed with the field slaves. There was no escape from the Ambossan world then, nor at Bwana's. Everywhere I turned my masters were breathing down my neck. So I diffused my resentment with downcast eyes, controlled my body language so that I never appeared sullen or threatening, monitored my speech so that my words never gave offence.

Now here I was in the all-whyte world of the slaves' quarter, where we ran *tings*, more or less.

Perhaps now I could be myself – whatever that was.

Outside the quarter Massa Nonso reigned supreme with a regiment of overseers to keep his troops under control. The pecking order inside the quarter was somewhat more complicated. Masks of humility were dropped and people emerged – as themselves. At work Ye Memé bowed to the overseer's superiority yet somehow kept her dignity. Inside the quarter she was a boss woman, a good boss woman at that, who got what she wanted through charm rather than bullying. And this boss woman filled me in on the flogging of the runaway Salehen that very morning, by the ebony tree, *Yes! Ova dere.* He had lasted two nights out in the pine forest before the bloodhounds ran him down. He was only twelve.

'Him get two hundrid an fiftee stroke which nearly kill him but nyot kwite. Massa Nonso nobuddee fool, he know dat bwoy can mek plentee-plentee monee fer him dooring his lifetime but if Salehen try again? Him loose his foot, fer sure.

'Ten day bak, Ole Man Garai try eskape. *Mi born free an mi want fe die free, dat's all,* he told Massa Nonso dat evenin when he kaptcha, just as de sun disappear fe de nite ova de moutain an just afore Massa Rotimi put his foot on a tree trunk down by de riva, an tek it off wid an axe.

'Ole Man Garai dispenzabal, yu see. Him ded frum hemredge

last week. I organize his burial ole kuntree style – in de grownd.'

There was something matter-of-fact in the telling of the tale, as if she'd become immune to it.

'Every week he flog innocent folk as precorshan nyot to do rong, him deklare, like it fe we own gud. What him call deterant. Prublem iz, we see his face. Massa Nonso like to draw blud. An wen I say he like it, I mean he *like* it. Y'understan?

'Tek woman when he feel like it too – all a-dem massas de same. Prublem iz, seems like Massa Nonso feel like it all de time.'

Ye Memé told me that he left her alone these days but those nights when he had come to her hut to do what he did in front of her whimpering children, she knew it was to break her. Men always wanted to break her.

Some of the women chose suicide, but not her. 'Afta, I cut mi eye at him an mek shure he see it. Mebbe he like mi spirit becorze he shift mi frum First Gang to factrey kwarta afta dat.

'Biggez prublem fe us iz our gyal-chiles. Soon as dey ole enuf, dey forced a-do nastee-nastee tings wid de massas. Yu can imagin. We try to protec our gyal-chile. Truth is, we cyant.'

She paused, looked up at the sky. All the women stayed silent too, lost in their own thoughts, eyes turned every which way except into someone else's.

'All a-we hart so brukken-up on dese islands, Miss Omo.

'So brukken-up.'

Out here in the island outback, away from the towns, hidden between mountains, it was as if we were at the ends of the earth, and with no law but the master's, and in the absence of a restraining hand, it was indeed hell on earth.

Bwana's children were all spoilt rotten, including Nonso, except that as his father's heir he was expected to be more serious and responsible than the others. He was often reprimanded, even beaten. He became timid.

Bamwoze, however, was allowed to develop a mischievous personality, which endeared him to his parents.

Nonso hid his resentment well.

But I had watched him snap off lizards' tails. Watched him pluck the legs off spiders, slowly. Once he swung a puppy by its tail in the orchard, checked that no one was watching, and bashed its brains out against a tree trunk.

Something stopped me letting on that I knew Nonso. It seemed distasteful to admit a deeper acquaintance with him and reveal my formerly elevated position at Bwana's. It might complicate my burgeoning friendship with other slaves. Instead, I found myself asking about escape routes. What lay beyond the pine forest?

There was a palpable bristling. Kicongo's eyes narrowed in blatant suspicion. Lyani let out an artificial giggle. Ma Marjani tchupsed slowly and loudly.

My cheeks burned.

Ye Memé came to my rescue.

'We don't talk about dat here, Miss Omo. Iz dangyrus. All yu need to know iz dat Massa empliment Nayborhood Watch on dis here plantashun. It protected by guards against Maroon invashun. So, it hard to git out an it hard to git in an dose dat git out git fetched rite back in again. I ask meself, why de heck dey forkin bodder, enh?'

The women concurred with a chorus of *Dat's right* and *Yes'm.*

Hang on a minute – who were the Maroons?

'Come-now.' Ye Memé led me away by the arm. 'We'll go

bak home an brew some nyice tea wid fresh molasses to mek it sweet-sweet.'

We began to walk back to her hut.

She – straight-backed, loose-hipped, soft-kneed, so that she bobbed and floated, even with the basket of bananas on her head.

Me – stiff-hipped, awkward.

While we walked Ye Memé warned me to watch what I said in company, even among the ladies. Did I notice that Lyani wore a silver chain?

'Well, sumbuddy wid-a lotta-lotta monee must-a give it her which probablee onlee mean one purson – Evil Inkarnate Hisself, Massa Rotimi. An I don't trust dat Olunfunlayaro eever. All-a-we look afta dat gyal becorze a-fore her mudder ded we promise. But tings so bad on dis here plantashun sum folk do anyting to get favar wid de massas an she wurk up at de house. So be cyaful what come out yu mowt, yu hear?'

I did hear, but I had to pluck up the courage to ask about the Maroons. Ye Memé would read between the lines.

'So, Miss Omo, yu nyot let dat one rest?'

'I can't.' I was surprised that my reply came out with no negotiation in it.

'Well, all right den. Just dis once. Maroon is runaway dat live free ina de hills long time. Folk say sum settlment goin bak almost one hundrid year. De massas hate dem becorze dem rade plantashun an burn crop, steel animal an farm tools. Hambush folk on de road too. Most a-dose dat run away to join dem is new slaves, com drektly frum Europa, and cyant stand dis plantashun life. Anyhows, as I told yu a-fore, most a-dem runaway git kort an git ponished, so why budder, enh?'

She turned to look at me but I kept my eyes on the lane ahead, swallowing hard.

'Beside, yu skinnie self nyot last out in de forest one nite an even if yu find Maroon camp, which is hiley unlikely, dem nyot accept wooman like yu. Mi hear dey want strong men an yung breedin woman an dem iz suzpishus of strange runaway. Anyways, I need yu here wid me becorze yu mi frend. Dis yur home now. Git uzed to it, like me. Dis mi home, betta or wurz. Onlee one I know.'

Ye Memé, the feistiest woman I'd ever known, had admitted that she needed me, and now I knew for sure that there was indeed a route to freedom on this sorry island in the middle of nowhere surrounded by sharks.

I couldn't ask her *how* to escape, though, not then, and deep down I knew I wasn't yet ready to run the risk of suicide, because it was either freedom or that. I'd never let those bastards flog me ever again.

If I could help it.

Instead I asked if she knew of anyone who had joined the Maroons?

'A few. Magik iz one dat reach dem. He com from ova da wata long time ago, same place as yu. Beaten-up bad-bad like yu too. A melankoli fella, but oh bwoy, dat man so tall an criss an respecful all-a de wooman fall fe him, but he fall fe none-a-dem. Not even Ba Beduwa git her vampish claws into him an dat sayin sumting! Him put to wurk strate off in feelds a-fore dem realize him karpenter an he sent to wurk up at de big house afta dat.

'Sundays him carve tings fe folk in de quarter an don't charge nuttin but just aks to join famlees fer dinner. Yu see how we all love dat man? Magik, we call him. Magik Fingas, becorze everyting he mek so bootifal. Den, soon as he feel betta he just tek off. Four year later he return on rade as leeder of group-a Maroons call demself Maroon Guerrilla Armee.

'See dat bench yu sit on in mi yard? One dat heavy an shinee an simmetrikal an look like it goin last ferever? Magik mek it. Yes, Magik! One in a millyan man. We all miss him, still.'

'What was his real name?' I asked, my voice so measured the sentence came out as flat-lined.

Ye Memé rummaged around in her mind before replying, 'Mi cyant recall if I ever did hear it.'

We were nearing her hut – *our* home.

'Lookee-hear, Omo-dear.' She stopped to set down her basket and turned to me. 'I been meaning to aks yu dis. I want mi bwoy Yao to have more storee in his hed dan what go round in mine about dis damn place, which, kwite franklee, give mi flamin hedake all de time! Yao will neva git outa dis hell hole exept to be sold to some odder plantashun, but de wurld out dere will get into his hed if yu help him reed an rite. I have contakt in de big house who will git book fe me.

'Den yu can help de odder pikney too when dey get older an can keep sekrit. Dat why yu stay in mi yard lawng time. Furz, dem always send newcomer to me to look afta becorze I iz boss-woman, but den mi feel so sorree fer yu when yu come ina de mill, so mawga an mizerabel an unda fizzikal suffrance, dat mi decide a-tek yu on. Now yu git betta, yu must mek world bigga fe mi pikney. Hagree?'

It would be a rebellious act. The masters didn't want literate slaves. Yet I had been taught by Little Miracle, and not only got away with it, but it had been to my advantage.

Of course I would teach Yao and maybe, some day, it might be to his too.

In any case, how could I refuse?

It was payback time.

I was glad to earn my keep.

★

Lolli, Ye Memé's youngest, was outside the hut holding hands with some playmates while skipping in a circle singing *Ringa ringa roza/ Pokat fulla poza/ A-tizzoo, a-tizzoo/ We all fall down* – whereupon they all collapsed on the ground in hysterics. Upon seeing us, Lolli jumped up and charged, leaping into her mother's arms, letting her sweep her up and throw her so high into the air that she squealed, knowing that when her mother caught her it would be with large, safe hands.

Lolli had sun-kissed ginger curls, freckles and lime-green discs for eyes which started spinning when her mother planted wet, noisy smackers on her cheeks, neck, stomach, bare arms, her tiny legs. All the while Lolli was squeaking, 'Do more, Mama, do more!'

Even in hell there was such love.

The hole that my children had left and Frank had once filled never felt more hollow than at that moment.

As I was coming alive, my memories of what I had lost became more acute.

It was so long since I had been loved by another, I couldn't imagine ever being loved again.

A Balm in Gilead

A hand beat slowly against a goatskin drum. A second drum went against the beat. A third added to the mix and then a fourth and a fifth until suddenly tambourines began to crash and rattle all around me, the demented bow of a fiddle leaped and scratched, sticks ran up and down the wooden pegs of a xylophone, the sound of a buffalo horn blasted long, bombastic flattened notes until the whole cave resounded with the truncated rhythms and rib-rattling reverberations of Aphrika.

The congregation got into the spirit too, flinging their arms and legs all over the place, as if wet, heavy rope had replaced muscle and bone. People spun on the spot, heads rotating faster than the bodies to which they were (theoretically) attached, and everyone broke out into a babble of tongues – the product of overactive imaginations (if you ask me) rather than divine intervention: *Ferttia! Amanop! Agapopopop! Tububibi! Lelelele! Lawqum! Papzaraz! Peetimo! Chewe! Ququq! Bbezaal!* – and so on and so forth.

There was so much noise in the cave it must have been heard all the way from the overseers' quarters up to the Great House which, I quickly understood, was the whole point.

It was my first Sunday morning at the shrine, and amid the ruckus of this lively communal therapy session I stood tight-lipped. I had always pretended to talk in tongues at Ambossan services but as this shrine was only used by whytes, with none of the blak masters present, I didn't have to. All that rhythm and vitality was simply too nerve-racking and exhausting at any time of the day, let alone first thing in the morning.

It hit me just how much I longed for the good, old-fashioned church organ of my homeland: the drawn-out mumble and rumble of its pipes which produced the kind of sombre, soothing music the Ambossans despised, but which I, nonetheless, considered to be the sound of the soul of my people.

I missed it.

Carved deep into the hillside next to the Dong River Falls, the cavernous shrine had painted wooden effigies of the gods inserted onto rocky ledges and murals painted onto walls. Embroidered cloths hung as tapestries. On the altar were bundles of dried herbs, heaps of powdered glass, phials of rum, plaits of hair, chalk, stones, bananas, palm wine in gourds, candles.

The high priest was a slave called Father O'Reilly (we sometimes got away with it), who wore a flap of coloured beads and a headdress of three tall plumes. White pointillist dots were speckled all over his tanned, hairless, lithe body. He'd just delivered a sermon in the melodramatic oratory of the Ambossans, his tremulous voice oscillating between at least three octaves: from a belly-rumbling lower register to the more hysterical nasal shrieks of his head voice. He preached how the Great God Obulattanga had moulded humans out of clay and, when he had completed the task, gave them to the equally Great God Olaranjo, who brought them to life through breath.

His speech was perforated by the enthusiastic cries – *Praise be de Arishans!* and *Tell it like it iz, Fadder O!* – of the righteous standing around me.

It never ceased to shock me that people believed these stories to be a true and accurate rendition of how we humans came into being. Granted, my own religion featured disconnected ribs and talking snakes but at least we began life as a *human* part, not as flipping clay statues.

I stood with Ye Memé and her brood at the front, Lolli's warm hand fidgeting about in mine like a trapped little mouse.

Ye Memé appeared to speak in tongues too, trying to project such uncharacteristic piety (head dropped, shoulders sloped forwards) that I had to suppress giggles from rising to the surface. She didn't entirely convince as one of the humble devout.

Sweet Amadoma had sewn a white Sunday outfit for me – a lovely, floaty, feminine blouse which covered up my disgusting, butchered back, and the kind of ankle-length, swishy gathered skirt worn by the ladies to Percy's balls up at Montague Manor back home. I hadn't worn a skirt since I'd begun my new career as a slave and what with my shaved head covered up by a pretty cream headscarf, I looked, for the first time in years, I admit, quite *fetching*. Going into the service I had even received one or two admiring glances.

Amadoma had also sewn a new Sunday outfit for Ye Memé, patterned with the orange crest of the bird-of-paradise plant embroidered around the border. Earlier in the week she had approached the stoop, almost tripping over it, hugging the bundle of material to her chest. Ye Memé and I had been enjoying the last few hours of a Sunday evening, the blood-sucker sun finally going down over the mountain having drained us of every ounce of moisture.

The children were playing *Wha de time, Mista Wolfee?* over by the silk cotton tree.

'Oh! Anudder one?' Ye Memé had exclaimed. 'Why, tank-yu kindly, Likkle Miss Amadoma.'

Amadoma then rolled off down the lane with the slow, satisfied demeanour of a mission accomplished, hands crossed over her stomach. It was as if delivering her gift was enough. Ye Memé was unreadable, but when she saw me sneakily observing her (as was my wont), she slipped into a lopsided grin and rolled her eyes into a *Wha cyan mi do, enh?*

Now back at the shrine, Father O'Reilly suddenly ceased his preachifying, turned his back on the congregation, dipped into a basket, draped himself in a white cassock with a large red and gold cross appliquéd onto the front, and strung a rosary of red coral beads from his neck. I heard the shrine doors shut and looked behind to see them barring it with a plank of wood. A boy stepped out of the congregation, gave the priest an effigy of Christ on a wooden cross, lit a chalice filled with incense and returned to the suddenly stilled crowd, swaying the chalice as he wandered among us.

It was the bitter, heavy scent of myrrh which I hadn't smelled for so long I almost fainted when it was whisked directly underneath my nose. It was heavenly. For a moment I was back singing *Loving Shepherd of Thy Sheep* accompanied by the old organist Mr Braithwaite inside the damp chapel at St Michael's Church, surrounded by a family I'd taken for granted until I lost them.

The high priest started to recite a prayer which the congregation knew off by heart. His voice quieter, manner serene.

In de name of de Fadder an de Son an de Holee Gost.

O mi Gahd, I glad to be here in dis place at mass an I iz veree sorree to sin against yu an by de help o-yur grace I will nyot sin again.

Dear Jesu, have mercee on all de poor peepals who hav neva heard yur name.

I love yu above all tings. Aaah-mi!

The priest produced a chunk of cornbread in a bowl, offered it to the crucifix.

Dear Hevenly Fadder, please accept dis here bred which iz goin becom we Lord body. I offer yu all mi joy an all mi sorrow. Aaah-mi!

He poured some palm wine and water into a goblet and offered this too to the crucifix.

Ye Memé's voice rose above mine, loud and sanctimonious, and I couldn't help but recall how often I'd heard my dear friend whisper through gritted teeth, 'Iz dere a Gahd on dis island, Miss Omo? Iz dere? Well, mi neva see him, mi neva heer him, an him neva help me wid nuttin.'

Dear Hevenly Fadder, I pray dat mi offerin become a part-a we Lord's, jus as de drop-a water now a-part-a de wine, which soon change into preshus blud. Aaah-mi!

I got into the spirit too:

'Lord Jesus, present within me, I adore you. I thank you for coming to me. Help me and all your children to keep close to you.'

After all these years I found myself praying in a public place of worship to my own God.

'Dear Lord, thank you for all your graces at mass. Help me to remember them when I leave church and go home. Help me to be in all things, at work and at play, a true child of our Father in heaven.

'Dear Jesus, bless us all, now and always. In the name of the Father and the Son and the Holy Ghost. Thanks be to God, Amen.'

(PS And please help me to find a way to escape, asap. Thanks!)

Then the drums started up again, the doors were opened and the congregation resumed its noisy convulsions.

Most Sundays after the service I taught Yao to write, using a slate and chalk.

Classes began with the Ambossan numbering system of

addition, subtraction and multiplication – all to express one simple number, which I had learned, with great difficulty, while handling Bwana's accounts. It was more complicated than the counting system I'd known, the 10s, 20s, 30s of back home, and Bwana had scoffed to hear me count thus, like I was a backward child, he said, typical of my *genus* who cannot comprehend basic arithmetic.

The Ambossan number 12, for example, is expressed as 20 minus 5 minus 3. The number 45 is expressed as 20 times 3 minus 10 minus 5. The number 525 is 200 times 3 minus 80 plus 5.

Yao was hungry for any activity which exercised more than the muscles in his body. He didn't need to be cajoled into study, he understood the luxury of an education. No exercise brought complaints, no class was too long, there was no whining such as *Dis too borin, Auntie Omo.* Instead, my model student was excited at the new thoughts coming into his head, making it feel bigger, he said.

Counting up to 40,000 may have been a mouthful (10 times 2,000 in two ways), but he soon mastered it. As he did the Ambossan alphabet, consisting of one hundred and fifty characters. It was really quite easy, once you'd learned it off by heart.

We sat side-by-side on the floor inside the tiny, claustrophobic hut for two hours until noon, the other kids banished, the door closed, sweltering, the hatch ajar to let in streaks of sunlight which radiated on the clusters of his knotted golden hair as he applied himself, head down, to the lesson at hand. I stroked his curls as he worked, untangled them or wrapped them around my fingers, remembering that I had a son of my own, somewhere, out there.

And two daughters.

I discovered that I was a natural, patient teacher, enjoying passing on what I knew so that one day, perhaps, this child could do something useful with it – for our people.

As his brain cells multiplied I watched him grow in confidence, assume a knowingness which made him stand out – perhaps a little too much. Yao was already a striking child, tall for his age, like his mother, with a back not yet bent by cane and a spirit as yet unbroken.

Sunday afternoons Ma Marjani came over to ours to teach me to cook food New Ambossan style, at the behest of Ye Memé, who was always busy tending to the allotment and washing her kids.

Ma Marjani was raising Ye Memé's son Dingiswayo as her own – a strapping eleven-year-old, with a stubby-blond brush which ran the length of his shaved head. He strutted about the quarter in a pair of outsized, hand-me-down cotton pants worn so that the waist hung (somehow) *beneath* his bum. It was in poor imitation of the local teenage troublemakers who walked with an exaggerated, determined, lopsided limp, arms swinging. I always thought they looked like drunken conscripts marching to war, trying to appear sober, or punch drunk ones returning home from the front line. They'd grab the bulge in their crotches sporadically, and give it a good squeeze too, presumably to check it was still there.

How many times did I hear Ye Memé say within earshot of these boys who had commandeered the silk cotton tree and were trying to intimidate all passers-by:

'Jus tink how dose great slave rebels of de past must be turning ina de grave to see dis lot. Dey rise up to lead rebellion against de massas on dese islands an giv demselves good, solid, historical nik-name like Willyam Konkara or King Alfred, nyot stoopidness like Bad Bwoy, Totallee Kross or Machete Monsta like dat lot ova dere. Dose boy pikney intent on selfdestrukshun, like dem have powa, but wurz kinda powa, violent one. Miss Omo. It so sad, enh?'

Then she'd shout out, 'Sumbuddy should send fe dem fadders an tell em to clip de damn earhole of dose *eeedyots!*'

Ye Memé's younger children sprinted towards the cool older brother they saw only on a Sunday when he walked up the lane with the silly swagger that made men smile wistfully and women shake their heads at the sight of another aspiring gigolo. Sitting on the stoop with the little ones gathered at his feet, he showed them the blade he'd bound with twine with which he could kill and gut a crocodile – *Yes, mi do it! Like dis so!* Pretending to be an action hero he felled the beast again and again for the benefit of his rapt audience.

Occasionally I caught Yao walking behind his older brother, trying on the skanky, high-shouldered, lopsided limp – and shuddered.

Dingiswayo took Yao, Inaani and Cabion to pick ripe ackee from the trees, teaching them that they must only pick red pods which had burst open to reveal the pale yellow arils inside, otherwise it was poisonous. Akiki and Lolli were made to stand at the base ready to catch the fruit in a basket.

The party returned up the lane, Dingiswayo in the lead, the basket on top of his head, Akiki and Lolli proudly trailing at the back, sneaking glances to see if their little playmates could see they were part of Dingiswayo's posse.

Like everything else she undertook, Ma Marjani's cooking was an entirely physical experience. With a work-a-day wrappa tucked over her chest, her brittle, burnt-straw hair tied back with string, her browned, brawny, scarred arms were ready to do business.

She kneaded dough as if pummelling an opponent, then split open the head of a coconut with an axe. She shred callalloo by ripping it into thin strips and mashed boiled pumpkin by bashing it with her fist. She broke a marrow in two like it was a loaf of bread, scooped out the seeds with the spoon of her hand, diced it, fried it, and instructed me to lay the seeds out on a cloth in the sun to dry. She rolled yam balls between her palms and tossed them in a sizzling pan until they were crisp and golden. On the rare occasion we had fish she scored them and de-scaled them, de-boned, barbecued, salted, fried, stewed or smoked them.

'We cane peepal wurk so hard we hav to eat good-good on rare okashun we git de chance. Once yu cook good, yu will get a man, dats fe shure.'

'But I don't want one,' I replied, too quickly.

'What? Yu mad? Yu don't want a fella to give yu a likkle someting like dat Qwashee who got his eye on yu?'

Qwashee worked in the First Gang and lived alone in a hovel barely twice his height and width a few doors down. He was often to be found hovering outside his door when I was around. He had no charm or looks to speak of. He was balding, aquiline, skinny, had weedy shoulders, short legs, a long spine, yet whenever he spoke to me – 'Mornin, Miss Omo' or 'I hope de day bring yu joy, Miss Omo' or 'Mi have two hen egg fe yu, if yu don't mind acceptin' or 'Yu sleep tite now, Miss Omo, an wake on de morrow refresh and hinvigorate' – I surprised myself by feeling touched.

I wanted a kind man. A gentle man. A good man.

Ma Marjani was everything I was not and, because she was, wasn't afraid to tell me so: 'Miss Omo, yu too mawga gyal' or 'Mi neva did trust a quiet purson.'

When I did manage to open my mouth to speak, she might say, 'Yu too damned speakey-spokey' – her wintry grey eyes clouding over, even as she offered me her toothy yellow smile.

But she was devoted to Ye Memé who had given her a child, and I was part of the package.

The country she lived in was the country she was born in: 'Mi born ina dis island an mi mammy too an she mammy an pappy an all-a-dem bak-a-yond dat, far as I know.'

Ma Marjani knew about cooking and she knew about cane. She knew that she could bear no children and that the son she was bringing up as her own was becoming the kind of man she loathed. She knew that she was a *nobudee, becorze we all nobudee here*, and she knew that the new slaves from the shores of Europa hated being on her island because they had known a country called Freedom and they were always running off in the name of it.

Those born on the island showed little curiosity about the places we newcomers came from. When I tried to tell Ye Memé or Ma Marjani about the teeming metropolis of Londolo they looked blank, even bored, and turned the conversation back to whether *Ba Beduwa child reellee faddered by Kicongo man? An if Kicongo ever find out? Why! Miss Beduwa end up wid-a stump fe hand too. Nobudee shud mess wid Kicongo becorze she will mess wid dem badda.*

Under Ma's guidance my cooking speciality became gelatinous cowfoot stew with butter beans and scallions. The rest of the cow's meat was eaten by the masters, except for its genitals, which formed the basis for cowcod soup – 'provan to aid virilitee'. The same claim was made for Strong Bak Drink, about which Dingiswayo, stroking his crotch, confidently told Yao, 'It mek big-man like me strong, long and hirresistabel to de hos and bitches dem' – unfortunately within hearing of Ma Marjani who called him over and whacked him upside his head with an iron pan. This reduced him to the tears of the little boy he really was inside, followed by the protracted sulk of the teenager he was desperate to become.

Ma cut her eye at him, laughed like a pan-scraper, and threw a 'Wotless bwoy!' his way.

(Taking me aside, she whispered, 'Wha cyan mi do? It's de hinfluence of dose older boys. Gyal, it mek me worry so much bout mi likkle chile.')

When Ye Memé was seeing a new paramour – 'Laydies dis here mi new gennalman frend so be *nyicee-nyicee* to him, yu heer!' – he had to be one with more resources than most. The men who lasted the longest managed to bring a whole chicken to jerk every once in a while.

Most of the time we had to make do with dumplings, sweetcorn, yam, greens, breadfruit, cornbread and the fruits of the island.

But when times were good, and our stomachs were full – and those are the times I will for ever savour – we would sit in a circle around a large round raffia mat on a Sunday evening, citron-scented candles stuck into the neck of gourds to keep insects and mosquitoes away. Ye Memé sat at the head, Ma Marjani to her left, me to her right and the children gathered around. We dug into portions of whatever meal I'd had a hand in making, everyone talking at once, teasing each other:

Yao jumping up, trying to outdo Dingiswayo's swagger.

Lolli trying to stick out her bottom and push out her lips like her mother when she was being feisty, flirty or tchupsing.

Cabion trying to pinch food from Inaani's plate and Inaani snatching it right back while Yao distracted Cabion's attention.

Akiki mimicking my speakey-spokey voice.

Ma Marjani pretending to throw a strop like Lolli – who was the mistress of them.

Dingiswayo trying to act manly and cool and above such childishness until Lolli and Akiki jumped on him and tickled him until he pleaded with Ma to pluck the little terrors off him.

And Ye Memé. Dear Ye Memé:

'Oh mi Gahd! Yu peepal mek such noise an kayos an mess I don't know what a-do wid yu all! Is dis mi familee? How can dat be when I iz so well-mannard an shy an butta-no-meltish? Oh Gahd up dere, if yu really heer me, an we nyot extablish dat fact *yet*, give me anudder famlee becorze dis lot iz one big unrooly pane in de bottok!'

She'd throw her head back and laugh – her beautiful, full-mouthed, rotten-toothed, throaty, raucous, up-yours cackle. We'd all throw our heads back and let it all out too, seeing who could laugh loudest, longest, silliest, by snorting, trilling, ululating, honking, until our eyes ran and our sides hurt and we begged each other to stop.

We let our laughter stream up into the sky and ricochet between the mountains.

It was almost as if our lives were normal.

As if we were free.

My children: Yao, Inaani, Akiki, Cabion and Lolli slept each night sprawled out around me and their mother, their warm little limbs flopped over mine, messy, sleeping heads cradled under my arms or open-mouthed and dribbling onto my stomach, heads so light I could barely feel their weight. When they awoke screaming or in a cold sweat, I caressed them back to sleep, stroking prematurely defined muscles, massaging calloused hands or picking twigs, leaves, sugar sap from matted, sticky hair which would only feel the cleansing lather of coconut shampoo when their mother bathed them in the Dong River on a Sunday.

In My Master's House

I stepped out of sleep into the ghostly vapour of dawn's dew-soaked clouds as they began to float up and disperse over the mountains.

White oleander blooms had been planted to ornament the pathways, their sweet fragrance competing with the nauseous stench of the quarter's night-time shit buckets.

The flowers never failed to take my breath away, and sipping their milky sap could do just that, slowing down a heartbeat until it came to a final, irreversible stop.

Toxic – the story of the islands.

Hurrying through the half-light, we were all going up the hill to our jobs-of-work – in my case, the cane fields. Yes, Massa Rotimi had demoted me to make way for cute little Lyani, who was now working alongside Ye Memé – until she was ready to give birth to his child.

I now worked in a gang with Ma Marjani, Kicongo, Ba Beduwa and Qwashee.

I was a cane-cutter, which went like this:

The slip of a machete could mean loss of a body part.

Stalks, stumps and sharp leaves left me riddled with cuts.

Bending over all day to cut the cane was crippling.

Setting fire to the fields to destroy the weeds and pests, but not the cane, created fumes which left me wheezing for weeks.

(Sometimes people were trapped in the thicket and burned alive. I'd not seen it, but I'd heard the stories.)

Prolonged exposure to the sun left me with permanent headaches, severe dehydration and burnt skin.

And should I survive all of the above, venomous snakes were lurking in the undergrowth to nip one of my ankles with poisonous fangs.

Yet two years after arriving at Home Sweet Home I'd acclimatised to an alarming degree.

Detesting my work, I took perverse pleasure in moaning about it. I relished Sundays and dreaded Monday mornings. My limp, rag-doll arms were now those of a toned, pumped-up muscle-woman. I could cook up a storm out of the most humble ingredients and cuss out the baddest *brudder* – all of which made me more likeable to the women in the quarter.

But freedom had become an abstract concept: my home over Jordan, my campground, my gospel feast, my promised land – something outside my comfort zone. It didn't help that most of those who tried to run away didn't make it out of the man-trapped forest and if they managed to climb the perpendicular mountain slopes they were caught by the patrols on the mountain roads.

I often had to witness the kind of punishment meted out to runaways for whom death would have been the easy option.

Pepper, salt and lime juice rubbed into whip cuts meant getting off lightly.

Having your nose sliced off meant you didn't.

Massa Rotimi once nailed a repeat offender's ear to a tree, left her there for thirty minutes, then sawed it off, as if cutting through the gristle of beef.

He repeated the procedure with the remaining ear.

As for Massa Nonso, I'd seen him in action too, at a distance, hiding myself deep in the crowd so as not to be recognised.

One time he forced a runaway to lie down and another to shit in her mouth. Two men forced it open, and when the deed was done, clamped it shut.

No kidding.

I had seen men castrated and women lose a breast. I had seen limbs removed, skin scalded, cheeks branded.

Once a man was hogtied and roasted over a spit, alive.

Another was suspended under a spit of pork so that the scalding fat removed his skin.

As for my own getaway?

Only one essential ingredient was missing – courage.

These days I was stepping out with Qwashee. He adored me and wasn't fazed by my repellent back, although when he cooed that it had 'karakta' and 'told storees' he was pushing it a bit far. Yes, horror stories, I countered.

I shared his hovel on some nights but not all, let him love me up, while I offered him all the love I did not hold in reserve for another.

After so long it was time for *closure* with Frank, I knew that, yet the stories I heard about the Maroon Magik man had rekindled a hope which, without proof, became faith – blind faith.

One morning a long line of us traipsed through the battalions of tall cane on our way to a remote field about four miles away. I could see Ma Marjani stomp up ahead as usual, bare-foot, bare-backed, with an energy that could be mistaken for an eagerness to get to work. I had long ago decided that like many of us – child, woman, man – Ma was just plain furious, although she'd never admit it; and while her fury was chan-nelled into cooking and killing cane, others found an outlet in sex, violence, singing, gambling, drinking, sugar, tobacco, even religious fervour.

Qwashee trod the ground lightly in front of me, shoulders loose after a night of love-making; my bald-headed, bony-arsed man who was thin as a whippet but *strawng like croc*. Every so often he'd glance back with a shy, reassuring smile – revealing his motley assortment of stained, misshapen and missing teeth – to check that I was okay, although he knew full well that I was *hunkee-doree dis mawnin, speshally, tank yu, Mista Qwashee*.

When I told Ye Memé we were stepping out together the Sunday evening after he'd taken me for a stroll – *mebbe yu fancee a likkle afta-noon perambulate, Miss Omo?* – around the quarter (where else?), she pretended not to hear, although she must have known. (Secrets in our confined world? Are you kidding?) When I repeated it, loudly, she mumbled something about me getting 'a *real* man', and flounced off down the lane, joshing with passers-by with such cheeriness you'd think she and her children had just been emancipated. But her shoulders were so thrown back the blades almost shook hands with each other, the skin in between squeezed into crushed, reddened folds.

'Real' men were both loved and loathed at Home Sweet Home. They talked dirty and fucked hard and could wind and grind the most *screw-up*-faced woman into submission, and if she didn't want to go down, he turned on the charm – *Gwan, do it fe me, baybee. Be a gud gyal fe yu big poopa*. Real men were so damned sexy women got wet just looking *at dat fine-lookin hunk-a beef ova dere*. Women cried, fought, poisoned, even killed over them, but when their real men let them down, they complained about having to put up with *dat bastard filandara* and *dere iz no good man in-a dis place*. But the good men – not tall enough, broad enough, well-endowed, sexy, handsome, confident, cocky, muscular or sweet-talking enough – weren't *real* men so they didn't count.

My dearest friend Ye Memé had had more than her fair share of them. All the fathers of her children were *real* men. And what was she?

Alone.

As soon as we reached the field we set to work. It wasn't easy, but it wasn't complicated either. You picked up a machete and severed the cane for the Second Gang to collect. Ma Marjani always worked faster than most. To wear out the body was to tire out the mind. It didn't help to think too much.

The slave drivers who kept us in control were themselves controlled by the overseers – usually blak men working for a short while on the islands before returning to Great Ambossa with enough cash to purchase a home in the capital, Londolo. The slave drivers were whyte trusties who kept their positions of privilege through exerting a certain whip-happiness. One was a young mulatto called Ndewele. His mother was part of the slave aristocracy, only glimpsed by we masses from afar, because she lived behind the Great House and never came down to the quarter.

She was Bwana's mistress, under his protection, and the mother of his children. Her name was Iffianachukwana and it was said that she was the kind of whyte person or mulatto who would own a few slaves herself if she was ever freed. (It wasn't unheard of for freed slaves to do this.) Rumour had it that this was on the cards when Bwana popped his clogs, which would be sooner rather than later, I thought to myself, if he kept stuffing his fucking face with fu-fu!

Her son, Ndewele, was slight and russet-coloured, which contrasted with his very blond frizzy curls. The long, pinched symmetry of his rather melancholy face reminded me of my father's. Mostly he tried to affect a haughty disdain, as if destined for better things, sitting astride his horse or sprawling out on a mat in the sun, hat pulled down low over his extraordinary violet eyes. He'd suck on straw or chew a lump of tobacco while we sweated around him. I could see he was masking a terrible boredom and frustration with the only thing he had going for him – superiority.

As Iffianachukwana's son, Ndewele had nothing to prove and little to fear, but, rather than turn him into a budding despot, this brought out the best in him. He was a lenient slave driver.

I worked next to Qwashee, knowing that each time he swung back his arm and brought it down, it was to will me to do the same. We worked twenty slaves in a row and sang.

Out there in the fields the vibrations of sound reverberated from deep within our bellies with a power to match our physical exertions. We had to be loud enough to be heard in an outdoor space filled with a chorus of a cappella voices, and we were always so full of soul because we poured our hearts into the music. Even the overseers and drivers could sometimes be spied gazing off into the middle distance, as if transported.

The newly arrived Border Landers among us broke down when we sang:

> Shud ole akwaintance be forget
> An neva bring to mind
> Should ole akwaintance be forget
> An ole lang zine . . .

Preoccupied with trying to tune up my amateurish warble so that I didn't balls-up the harmony, it wasn't until Massa Nonso blocked out the sunlight astride his dappled grey mare that I noticed him loom above me like an equestrian statue with its forelegs raised.

I looked up into the face of the man who owned me. Horrified.

Those clear, cocoa-brown eyes, which had registered every attention lavished on his younger brother, now slid behind puffy lids and had the colour, substance and emotional calibre of newly delivered horse dung.

Topless, he revealed a distended stomach as crusty, dried up and coarsely haired as coconut husk.

His horse kicked up the ground with a hind leg, shook its mane, sneezed phlegm right into my face and, if that wasn't bad enough, proceeded to graze my lips with its huge, wet, flared, rubbery, smelly nostrils. I had to stand there and take it (even a horse had more status than me), while its passenger struggled to make a sentence come out of his mouth.

He produced vomit instead.

Gunge dripped down his bare chest like porridge.

Christ! He was drunk as a skunk when it was still, by the sun's reckoning, only ten o'clock.

He slumped over, head level with his mare's.

With conspiratorial familiarity, he slurred thickly, as if his mouth was still full of bile, 'Look *you*, the interfering old sod is on his way here for a surprise visit accompanied by that smarmy, smart-arse brother of mine, Bam*weasel*. Since my holier-than-thou book-keeper has absconded back to Londolo and been telling tales out of school, *you*, our naughty little runaway, will immediately relocate to the Great House to sort out my ledgers so that they are shipshape and Bristol fashion when the old sod arrives. Otherwise, he'll have my guts for garters and I'll have yours. Understood?'

He thumped the mare which about-turned and cantered off, its long, shapely legs kicking up the soil with bespoke, U-shaped shoes.

*

Hidden behind a parade of conifers and reached via a long driveway lined with logwoods, the wall of the Great Compound was painted with the most audacious geometric symbols layered onto each other: triangles, squares, circles, hexagons, pentagons, stars. Embedded in the images were tiny versions of the evil-eye motif of the ancient sun god Horus.

Interspersed with these were picturesque 'naive' paintings of daily life on the plantation:

Head-wrapped slave women strolled down flowery lanes in Sunday-best whites twirling lacy parasols.

There we were singing our hearts out with an eye-rolling passion at the temple.

Or lazing on the banks of the Dong River smoking clay pipes.

And our children danced around a maypole with giddy smiles plastered all over their rosy-cheeked little faces.

All this in such an attention-grabbing array of colours I almost got a headache just looking at it. There was garish yellow boiled from marigold; reddish-orange boiled from bloodroot; bright purple boiled from mulberries; various shades of green from spinach, grass and red-onion skin; pastel pink from roses; screaming-red from cherries; black from charcoal; white from slaked lime.

Statues of the gods were mounted on top of the wall in between giant, white-painted, clay balls.

The wall was intended to both display wealth and inspire awe in the workforce. I recognised the distinctive artwork rendered by Ndebele artists who would have been brought in from Aphrika to do the job.

As I walked around the wall of the compound to the back entrance, I tried to digest what was happening to me now. It was mid-morning and yours truly wasn't bent over with a machete in her hand – so no complaints there. Whether I would return to the quarter that night or sleep in the compound, I didn't know. I couldn't think about when I'd see Ye Memé and the kids or Qwashee again, and I certainly couldn't entertain the thought of seeing Bwana again – so I blocked them all out.

I looked back down the drive, across the lush, green, rain-nurtured meadows and over to the cane fields so far in the distance you couldn't see or hear the workers and beyond that to the mountains. Up here among the gods, where the only sounds were of the parakeets and macaws, was a view so breathtaking, so removed from the beleaguered population in the valley below, that one could feel so spiritually elevated one could convince oneself one was in the Garden of Eden.

King Shaka was waiting for me at the back gate, his eyebrows arched in the style of *Well! Yu iz a dark horse, ain't it*. He told me to follow him to a pump in one of the courtyards where I had to scrub up behind a screen and put on a clean wrappa.

Then he led me into the whitewashed main residence with its palm-thatched roof and white-painted wooden veranda which surrounded the whole house, parlour palms placed either side of the totem-carved doorways.

'Massa Nonso sleepin,' he said.

This time he raised a single eyebrow.

'Everybawdee must be kwiet. Come, mi show yu what a-do.'

My naked feet squeaked down the corridors across the parquet strips of highly buffed floor. The smell of beeswax commingled with the saccharine fruitiness of vanilla-scented candles which floated in silver bowls of water placed on round, marble-topped, single-stemmed console tables, their gold-leaf cabriole legs on mounts made of leaping golden fish, no less.

As we walked towards the front of the house, the shadows

of the domestic slaves flickered in open doorways but no one showed themselves. The soothing bouquet of bougainvillea swept through from the open windows of the rooms inside and muslin curtains blew in the breezy whirr of fans suspended from the ceiling by shiny brass hubs.

As I passed the kitchen, situated in an annexe to the right, I was struck by the intense, nutty aroma of Green Mountain coffee beans being roasted and rattled on a metal tray. It transported me back 3,000 miles to Bwana's house in Londolo, where sacks of the stuff were imported every year to satisfy the family's caffeine habit. I used to help myself to the cold, oily dredges in his morning cup.

King Shaka mooched ahead. I followed him. At the end of a corridor he dropped down a step to unlock Nonso's narrow office door. Inside was a small chapel of a room, stuffy and unventilated. Disturbed by the fresh air, dust particles swirled all over the place, making me sneeze and cough as they swept into my nostrils.

The room was crammed with shelves and cabinets. On the wooden floor were papers which had been ripped up, scrawled over, coffee-stained, crushed into balls, even made into models of birds which had failed their flight test and crashed to the ground.

In the middle of the room was a mahogany desk whose four legs ended in elephant's paws.

On top of it were the plantation ledgers and a huge pile of papers.

King Shaka waved his hand around the room and said, 'Sort it out. Bwana send letta sayin him comin. Soon reach.'

He swayed back down the corridor with a stiff back that knew it was being watched.

At the end he turned around.

'Mi cyant wate till him daddee git here an bust his arse!'

I heard him chuckle as his feet padded back through the hushed house.

I was alone.

That hadn't happened for years.

I began to clear up the detritus, starting with the desk.

Soon enough I came upon a stash of letters from Bwana to Nonso.

Dear Son of Your Father,

Trust you and the family are in fine fettle. Joyous salutations to dear Salmé and the children. Your mother sends her best regards also, as does our prodigal son, Bamwoze. Yes, indeed, you will be pleasantly surprised to learn that we, as a family, are now reconciled with your miscreant brother after his wayward dalliance with that half-breed.

Bamwoze and I jest about his youthful rebellion these days, chuckling over a tumbler or two of that finest white over-proof from the estate. This we partake of in my study most evenings as the sun goes down over the city, man to man. I confess that my heart is gladdened to have our erstwhile dissenter now soaking up the wisdom of his elderly father with due respect.

I have decided that the disgrace Bamwoze brought upon our great family has been consigned to the annals of history. You, therefore, will make space in your heart to forgive him too, although as well I remember, you were the most vociferous in declaring that we should banish him and any of his future offspring from the clan in perpetuity.

His aberration is to be dwelled upon no more.

To make amends, he has agreed to marry a delightfully placid and, I must say, very winsome young girl called Adiba. One of the daughters, you may recall, of my business associate, Chief Ezanaka, the CEO of Baringso's Bank.

Now that Bamwoze is of sound mind again, I have persuaded him, with no additional inducements whatsoever, to relocate to Home Sweet Home after marriage to join you in the management of the estate, anticipating no inconvenience to yourself, naturally. In these trying times two at the helm is better than one, you will agree, and, with complementing qualities, the pair of you will make a fine team. (Now, now, no squabbles. You are both grown men!)

You, Nonso, are possessed of a quite remarkable enthusiasm and what we can pleasantly describe as incredible potential. Bamwoze, on the other hand, shall bring to the business partnership a sharpness of intellect, impressive eloquence, an authoritative bearing and, of utmost importance, a (renewed) mastery of social etiquette which will maintain, nay improve, relations with our neighbours for we must depend on each other in times of uprisings.

Not a day passes that we do not hear of slave revolts on the various West Japanese Islands, in particular the vicious rebellious forces on the island of Haiti, where our people have been the victims of what can only be described as a genocide, and those evil Maroon terrorists on New Ambossa are always ready to jump down from the trees to slit a poor man's throat as he goes about his everyday business. Have you had any trouble from them lately?

One is particularly cautioned by the stories one hears about the original terrorists, the Mongolo indigenes, Carawak or Arib or whatever they called themselves. They were similarly bellicose, treacherous and bloodthirsty when Man first arrived, although our hardy predecessors succeeded with much effort in eliminating the problem. Bone idle as the wiggers they were too, when brought from barbarity to neo-humanity and required to put in a good day's work for their supper for a change.

Such a cautionary tale is in the forefront of everyone's minds, and you will be glad to know that plans are afoot to send troops to *the island to mount a full-scale war against the current crop of subversives. Eradicate the pesky critturs once and for all.*

Enough! Enough! 'Tis too depressing!

On a more agreeable note, Blessing, naturally, is delighted that her 'Bamzy-woo' is back embosomed where he belongs. In truth, it pleases me to see her mood improved again. Your mother deteriorated terribly these past few years pining for her little 'Bamzy-woo'. Nothing worse than a sour-faced old woman traipsing around the house muttering to herself, eh?

But with lightness in my heart, I declare that those dark days are over!

I look forward to the estate audits in three months' time, as usual.

Drop me a line or two. A few words will suffice. Know you are a busy man.

Your Loving Father

KKK

PS Trust Iffianachukwana is as robust as ever. I do worry about her. Don't want to lose her. Make sure she is looked after, son. Oh hush. I know, I know, your father is such an old softie.

PPS Shhh, don't tell your mother!

———

Dear Son,

It is with some consternation that I am forced to enquire as to what, exactly, is happening on my plantation. Djenaba sailed into Doklanda from New Ambossa yesterday, whereupon he immediately hurtled by carriage through the city to inform me that his position as book-keeper had become untenable working under your office. Indeed, so untenable he was afraid to write me of the current 'situation' until he had departed the island, for fear of unpredictable behaviour from yourself. What, pray, is happening on my estate? I enquired, after I had calmed him down with one of my finest Codiba cigars. Thus refreshed he was able to inform me that you appear to have lost your way, somewhat. Rum for breakfast, lunch and supper? Surely not, I replied. Ten of my workforce deceased in one month alone? How come? Gambling at table, with my profits? 'Tis not true! I protested.

Nonso is neither a drinker nor a gambler, I avowed, determined to protect the reputation of my eldest son. A disciplinarian? Of course, but not to the detriment of the business. The Katamba men are honourable and decent and the lad has always been mindful of my maxim – Punish to deter or reprimand, but take life only as a final solution.

I am loath to admit, however, that Djenaba was entirely convincing.

Dear son, I await your reassurance without delay.

Your Concerned Father

- - -

Nonso,

Took the liberty of writing to Chief Tembi over at Worthy Park Estate with a request that he personally ride over to tell you that your father is awaiting a reply from his correspondence. This, he assures me, he carried out to the letter, and you, apparently, assured him you would respond forthwith.

Yet nothing.

Whatever you are up to, it's not too late to make amends. Show some respect and get in touch, otherwise I will have to take drastic action. My small stock of patience is fast running out.

Father

- - -

Boy,

You always were a sullen little tyke, weren't you? Now is not the time for sulking or hiding away.

I have not been to the island for three years. Methinks it's time for a little visit, don't you?

Congratulations are in order, by the way. Emblazoned across the front page of yeterday's Morning News *was a cartoon of:*

NONSO KATAMBA ELDEST SON OF CHIEF KAGA KONATA KATAMBA I

You were lampooned as the most despicable kind of planter-vulgarian – inebriated, gambling, unrefined, lecherous and stupid.

That you have shamed me thus.

Be aware that Bamwoze and I shall be arriving in four weeks on the Demerara Dream. Have the master bedroom prepared and be prepared to face your maker – me.

Bwana was only days away. What was I going to do?

First I had to clear up the office, checking every darned piece of paper trashed about the place in case it contained important information. When I came across a pile of paper thrown into a corner scrunched into balls, all of them scrawled with the mantra I HATE DADDY! I HATE MUMMY! I HATE BAMZY-WOO!, I almost fell about laughing. *Like, get over it, Nonso, you tosser*, toppled out of my mouth just before I saw the man himself appear in the doorway like a propped-up corpse: sober, ashen, a silver satin wrappa which was slung so low over his almost childbearing hips, tiny coils of black pubes showed.

An excess of expensive aftershave flooded the room, drowning its mustiness. I recognized its unmistakable mix, favoured by Londolo's rich young gadabouts, I recognised as cedarwood, musk and the acid surprise of grapefruit.

'Amused, are we?'

Nonso had lost his fast, edgy, city-boy voice and adopted the droll, languorous mumble of the planters, as if the act of speaking was simply *too, too* tedious.

I shook my head as vigorously as a child caught out in a lie.

'Is our naughty little runaway going to let her master in on the joke?'

I didn't move an inch. Burning up. Not brave. Shit-shit-shit-shit-shit-shiiiiiit!

But instead of the eruption of anger I expected, he sounded resigned.

'It seems not. No one lets me in on anything. No one cares about that silly chap called Nonso who has so much *potential* he's been left to rot away in this godforsaken hell-hole with the savage bush nipping at his ankles and the workers biding their time before they come for him in his sleep with a machete to chop him up and barbecue him as choice tenderloin pieces.'

We, or rather he, fell into silence. A silence noisy with the buzz of bees sucking at the pollen of the bougainvillea at the window and the *ack! ack!* of parakeets in the trees outside. A silence so palpable the very walls seemed to be whispering. A silence that is never comfortable for a slave, when her master has stopped talking, yet continues to eyeball his possession.

But it wasn't threatening with Nonso. It was almost as if he was trying to connect, or reconnect, to something.

He lumbered towards me, tilted my chin up with the palm of his hands and forced me to confront his dung-like eyes – the only part of his chubby, boyish face which showed signs of growing into adulthood. Although they hadn't matured, exactly, but diseased.

'Oh, *please*, don't be petrified of Nonso the *Monster* or what-ever they call me. How else am I going to control a workforce of six hundred on my lonesome own-some? I have feelings too, you know, it's just that I can't show them or I'll be taken advantage of by the masses. Forgive my earlier abruptness, it wasn't me but the drink. Isn't that what I'm supposed to say?

'Anyway, fear not because I'm sure I suckled at your breast and you sucked the snot out of my nose with your mouth or some equally vile nanny-type thing when I was an infant and my mother was too busy shopping for diamond-studded nose-rings or platinum lip-plates or gold lamé headscarves to bother looking after her first-born. Besides, until you did a runner the family thought of you with some affection, you'll be *fascinated* to hear. Efficient, plain, dreary.'

Then an unexpected compassion came into his voice, which was creepy.

'Rest assured, I am not going to harm you, Omorenomwara. You have not felt the sting of the whiplash since you've been here, have you? Mnn?'

My eyes watered but I wasn't sure if it was safe to shift them down.

'As it happens, I would have made use of you up here earlier. Why waste such expertise? It's just that the pompous old S.O.B. was emphatic that you should, in his words, "be made to undertake an honest day's work in the fields".

'I spared you that for a while, did I not? Then my grunt Rotimi goes and gets his favourite whore up the duff and comes grovelling to me about lightening her work load.'

He leaned closer.

'Why not think of me as your invisible benefactor. Mnn?'

Was he going to kiss me?

Letting go of my chin, he brushed his fingers down my throat, stopping short of my clavicle.

Then he swept an affected, world-weary arm over at the room.

'Look at the mess Djenaba left this room in. But what do

you do when your book-keeper is an arsehole? Oh well, to the business at hand. *Your* job is to make *my* losses appear as profit. Understood? We call it creative accounting, don't we? When the pompous old git enters the plantation on his fiery steed, you will go back to the fields. Fear not, if you do a satisfactory job, as I am sure you will, as soon as he's gone your new place of work will be this office. Bam*weasel* won't mind once I get him on my side. Easy enough when I let him install in the compound whatever tasty half-breed bitch he takes on as mistress.

'As for our losses, I have to sell off some of the stock, which is my only available option. A discreet planter from the Amarikas is already lined up, as it happens. There's always a market for healthy young males of the *species*, who won't be noticed as missing by Kaga the Omnipotent when he does his round of inspection.

'Naturally, the dutiful son will lay on the mother of all welcome-home parties. Everyone will attend – neighbours, dignitaries and all the workers, who will look ecstatically happy because Rotters will make damned sure of it. Festivities will last for three days and three nights with the slaughter and roasting of many heifers and hogs, endless barrels of rum, tobacco and plenty of grub. There will be much merry dancing to the fiddle and bagpipes and much jovial singing of the usual round of imbecilic native songs, like, oh you know the one – *She be comin round de mountin, she be drivin six white horsey, she be wearin red pyjamas, she will hav to sleep wid granma* – or somesuch piffle.

'As for those depressing *I wanna go home* spirituals, they will be *banned*, I say. Banned!

'After three days of drunken hedonism, all those mealy-mouthed gossips and green-eyed planters will have to swallow their malicious tongues and concede that business is booming on the biggest, the baddest and the best plantation on the island. Yay!'

Nonso punched his fist in victory and let out a whoop, baring a set of teeth as yet undamaged by rum. Not a single one was chipped, stained, rotten or missing. I'd not seen that in a long time. They were strong, white, beautiful.

'In the meantime, here's the list of those who will disappear.'

He pulled out a scroll which had been rammed down the back of his wrappa, probably lodged in his crack. Lovely.

'Make them unborn or dead by disease or missing by escape some time ago or he'll get it in his head to chase after them. Whatever. However. Just make them go away. And do it yesterday. My client will collect the boys from a prearranged location the day after the father arrives so they must be hidden when he gets here. King Shaka will see to that. He docks in approximately two days. We must not delay.

'Hail Yemonja. I need a fucking drink!'

His crocodile-skin sandals scuffled down the passageway with the walk of an old man on his last legs, not a young Ambossan male in his first years of manhood.

He called out for service, barely raising his voice, yet a flurry of female feet squeaked over the floorboards as if they had read his mind.

Yao, son of Ye Memé = C£300
Dingiswayo, son of Ye Memé = C£500

I pushed my back against the clammy mud wall and slid down.

A shock started in my guts and charged around my body as if lightning had struck and was desperate for the exit point it could not locate.

It kept charging through me.

On and on until I opened my eyes and released it.

Hours later I'd tidied up the office and got going on the accounts ledgers. First of all, I had to help Yao and Dingiswayo, or I'd never live with myself. Secondly, I had to work out how to stitch Nonso up, without paying a price. Unused to spending my days cooped up inside, I longed for some air but I hadn't been given permission to go anywhere. Eventually recklessness propelled me down the corridor towards the room which branched off to the left. I found myself in the immense oasis of a sunlit drawing room which, to my surprise, was just like the Ghika residence I'd lived in all those years ago.

Some planters kept their homes minimalist – bamboo, wood, silver, reed, linen. Others were stuffed with objects to silence (they hoped) their toffee-nosed critics who declared them devoid of refinement and culture. Still others needed to fill up the lonely empty spaces of living on a remote island, neighbours few and far between and always fearful, like Nonso, that the seething masses were on the brink of insurrection.

They couldn't afford self-examination so they fortified themselves with things.

Furniture as therapy. Objects as friends. Furnishings as arsenal.

How novel.

In Nonso's showroom a vermilion armoire decorated with golden butterflies stood next to a rosewood cabinet which in turn nudged shoulders with another cabinet inlaid with tortoiseshell marquetry. Next to this hung a six-foot teak mask of the god Shangira, and next to that a red-lacquered cupboard whose doors were painted with oversized camels amid palm trees and pyramids.

A key had been left in the cupboard door, so in my reckless mood I opened it and found myself on a trip into Nonso's mind.

Self-help books were stacked on shelves, loads of them:

They F**k You Up – How to Survive Family Life.

Healing Your Inner Child.

How to Start a Conversation & Make Friends.

Dealing with People You Can't Stand.

How to Motivate Your Workforce.

Hidden away at the bottom, spines turned inwards: *Inheritance Tax for Dummies* and *Curing VD the Natural Way.*

Not a single book had a creased spine.

I had to laugh.

Scattered around the room were several 'thrones' – swan-shaped armrests and seats upholstered in damask embroidered with gold and silver thread; and there was a divan in the shape of an elongated tiger with a giraffe's pelt thrown over it.

Ormolu mirrors with carved bellflowers, scrolls and swags stretched from ceiling to floor, yet the woman I saw in them was so dark I barely recognised her. Where her complexion once had been flawless, now it was webbed with fine lines. Her oval jawline had slackened and her thinning, shoulder-length hair was bleached white-blonde or, perish the thought, had it begun to grey? She had bulked up too, with hefty, scarred shoulders and arms which looked like they could deliver a mean right hook. Her breasts remained lifeless, stretch-marked sacks.

Above all, the unhurried, otherworldly eyes that looked back at me were no longer a crisp morning blue, mocking, ready to quip, but spoke of a sun-frazzled landscape of hills and fields and mud and hoes and infinite skies.

God! I looked so rough and so *rural* . . .

Tearing myself away, I wandered through the room, sliding my hands over the cool, sensual curves of statuettes made from bronze, jade, ivory, and life-sized sculptures of men, women and children, as well as tiny figurines of the gods – all in pure gold.

A real lovebird hung in a cage.

A low, rectangular coffee table with ball-and-claw foot pads displayed several glossy coffee table books, all of which had been well thumbed:

Planter Chic – Master of Taste.

Beyond the Colonial – 100 Inspired Ideas for Your Home.

The Three Stages of the Evolution of Man: A Visual Guide.

I stepped onto rugs from the Chinas and the Indias so delicate and silken I wanted to roll myself up in them, and when I craned my neck upwards it was to look into the dome of a ceiling depicting a sun bursting through a cloudy sky.

Unable to resist, I found myself drawn to the open panelled doors which led out onto the lawns, where I could see a little girl playing on the grass, a tubby little Ambossan girl wearing a pretty turquoise beaded flap. She had velvety dark-chocolate skin and lovely pinchable cheeks. Her hair was done up in plaited hoops into which yellow ribbons had been sewn, and she was pretending to breastfeed one of those Aphrikan Queen dolls.

A perfect child.

Just like Little Miracle.

Then she looked up and shot me such a filthy scowl it extinguished all her loveliness.

'Who are you?' she demanded.

(Boy, those kids learned fast, especially with Bwana in their genes.)

I took a step back inside the drawing room.

'Miss Omo! What yu doin here?'

King Shaka appeared at my side and waved at the girl.

'Greetin, Missa Dalila. Carry on wid yu playin, chile. Everyting all rite here. Dis Omorenomwara, come to wurk in de house, dats all.'

At the sight of King Shaka she looked relieved and waved back with a beatific smile, a little brown angel again.

He pulled me inside the room, closed the door, grabbed my arm so hard it pinched, and pressed his lips to my earlobes, his breath steamy, garlicky.

'Dat one Massa Nonso yungez. Steer clear of his pikney becorze dem mek trubel fe dose slave dem nyot like. Nastee likkle vermin tell any ole lie to git yu arse wipped. Massa Nonso too forkin weak to control dem an so stoopid he beleeve every damn ting dey say. As fe der mudder? Madama Salmé? She no betta. Spend all day in bed bawlin becorze she huzban forcin hisself on most of de slave gyal. She tek it out on viktim instead of de purpatrata. Nuff gyal got licks from Madama Salmé wid bunch of hickory-sticks she have speshally seasan in de fire.'

Had I heard right? Uncle Tom dissing his masters? Surely not?

I followed him out of the room, down the vanilla-scented corridors again, through the various yards at the back of the compound where skilled craftsmen were going about their daily work at a much more leisurely pace than we field and factory workers. A carpenter filed down the legs of a wooden bench, a woman dipped cloth in a boiling vat of indigo, her forearms stained dark blue, a baker plaited dough while his assistant fired up the clay oven.

'Spect yu want fe eat. Food betta up here, git leftova. Nonso hav five pikney an one wife but cook must prepare feast fe 5,000 every day so Nonso feel like him big chief wid monee to burn. Skwandara, dat's what he iz.'

We entered a cool, shaded area where food was bubbling away in a copper pot over a fire. Several of the domestic slaves were gathered.

King Shaka brought me a bowl of pepper-pot and turtle soup and led me to a spot underneath a breadfruit tree.

'Why are you telling me all this?' I asked, still trying to work him out.

'Becorze yu in de lion den now, honee.'

He lay down on the mat, untied the headband from around his forehead, dropped it over his face, crossed his arms to cradle his head, and folded his legs at the ankle.

'One more ting,' he said, blowing air through the cloth. 'Don't eva repeet anyting mi say. Yu heer?'

He was soon snuffling like a contented horse.

I looked around at the others: three men were sucking the meat off a plateful of fried chicken legs, several people were sleeping, opposite me two youngish women, maids probably, sat cross-legged on mats listening to a big hootchie-mama character holding court in the shade of a cherry tree in full blossom.

She was so pale it was obvious she didn't work in the fields.

Her thighs and buttocks spilled over from a tiny three-legged stool which just about managed to keep from toppling.

Her wrappa and headscarf were of a creamy, frothy taffeta.

Her face, arms and breasts were nipped with swirls of decorative cicatrices.

Her jewellery was all gold – Nefertiti earrings, chunky nose rings, a flowered neck pendant, coiling snake armbands and anklets, bangles, precious-stone finger rings, and her talons were painted with pastel-blue glitter polish.

What slave went around dripping in gold?

She had noticed me and was, I felt, speaking loudly for my benefit.

'Wonder what mi Bwana bring fe mi dis time? Furz ting he do is com see his Miss Iffie. Him cyant resist. Like ritooal. Last time I did aks fe fashanabal lace fabrik from Londolo, but spect to git gole jewallree too. Gole, gole, gole, him always bring mi gole, neva dat silva rubbish.'

What a ridiculous, obnoxious cow, I thought. It had to be that Iffianachukwana.

Young Olunfunlayaro entered the cooking area heading straight for me, grinning as she approached.

'Mi did heer!' she said in her light, excitable voice, dropping next to me, hugging her knees.

'Ye Memé well-vexed parantly dat yu neva did tell her who yu waz. Everybawdee talking about *yu*, Miss Omo.'

Before I could defend myself, the super-hootchie interrupted us with a booming voice, clearly perturbed that Olunfunlayaro had distracted her target audience.

'An mite one aks who dat dere? What straynja com hitha to we uptown communitee? Frend or foe, declare thyself, becorze we heer yu iz a comman-a-gardan *feeld* wurkaaaarr!!!!'

She gathered up her shaking stomach and held it in her hands as she and her fellow coven-members exploded with coarse laughter.

Olunfunlayaro leapt up.

'Com, mi hintroduce yu to Miss Iffie. Don't pay her no neva mind. Bark wurz dan bite. She alrite. Show off, dat's all. An bored. All she do iz natta, natta, natta.'

We walked over to the cherry blossom, watched silently by the acolytes who appraised me from top to toe with spiteful looks.

But not Miss Iffie, whose expression changed from downright smug to outright shock as I got closer.

'Mi cyant beleeve it!' she exclaimed, her voice hoarse, clasping her chest as if she'd been stabbed in the heart.

'Mi reellee cyant beleeve it!' she repeated, all traces of blood fast disappearing from her face, eyes filling up.

It was those eyes that did it for me, not azure, as she'd once fancied, but a colour we had no word for then – lapis lazuli.

They hadn't changed at all.

She tried to jump up but stumbled, the young women reached out to stop her fall.

By the time we were face to face, she'd regained her balance.

And then we were in each other's arms.

Crying into each other's necks.

Her squashy wet-pillow of a belly convulsed against my hard abdominal muscles.

I stepped back to stop her weight crashing both of us to the ground.

Mi cyant beleeve it.

Mi reellee cyant beleeve it.

Neither could I.

Doris, mi likkle sista!

Sharon, my big sister.

Who'd have thought it.

Sharon Scagglethorpe.

Last known address:

Apple Tree Cottage, Montague Estate, England.

Wade in the Water

Madge Scagglethorpe was dragged into the forest by the kidnappers who besieged our home, never to be seen again.

Jack Scagglethorpe died of dysentery in the hold of the first slaver Bwana had captained, the *Hope & Glory*.

Because Eliza Scagglethorpe refused to eat, the sailors threw her over the side as a warning to others.

Alice Scagglethorpe died within a year of toiling in the cane fields of Worthy Park Estate.

Sharon was hand-picked by Bwana to be his mistress, installed in her own hut, had babies and fattened up, which pleased him.

She begged for her baby sister Alice to be brought to live with her, but Bwana didn't believe Europanes had real emotions or family ties.

The first swell of my grief lasted hours in Sharon's warm, flabby, maternal embrace.

The images kept replaying themselves:

Madge raped to death.

My father dying in his own excrement.

My mother, drowning.

Little Alice's suffering, all alone in the world.

My one surviving sister loving, or so it seemed, the man responsible for all of the above.

I cried until my lungs felt as brittle as dried tobacco leaves.

*

We sat outside Sharon's white-stucco home with red tiles and latticed windows, talking so late into the night that when rays of blue light shone like a flare from behind the mountains we were still going strong.

Her isolated, compact little house faced away from the Great House and towards enclosed fields where horses roamed with athletic freedom.

Her three mulatto sons stayed up too.

The eldest, Kolladao, was a notoriously tough overseer who'd never been in charge of my gang, thankfully. I could see the brute in him, the ego which needed to be stoked by the subservience of others.

I'm sure Ndewele was relieved that he'd never stripped and whipped his auntie (Christ, I was an aunt all of a sudden). He was as dreamy as his mother once was.

Ako was the truculent young man I'd seen at the warehouse when I first arrived. Too young to be promoted to junior management, he seemed to simmer with ignored-younger-son syndrome.

When the air began to chill, the boys brought us quilted blankets which Sharon had sewn.

When we got thirsty, they fetched a pot of tea and poured it into dainty clay cups, hand-painted with the roses of our homeland by Sharon.

When we felt peckish, they returned with trays of *ole-kuntree* desserts she'd made – *hedgehog puddin, molasses rolee polee, gingabred man, banbree kake*.

The two older boys, in their roles as overseer and slave driver, were among the most feared and loathed people on the plantation. Yet towards me in my new role as their mother's sister, they were polite, almost deferential.

It was very unsettling.

Kolladao was keen to make an impression on his aunt (which made me laugh).

'Mi mudda iz a diffrant purson wid yu here,' he said.

And it was true, because whatever vulgar, horrid character my sister had become, with me the facade slipped and the sister I'd once known peeked through.

The Sharon who longed to be called Sabine.

The Sharon who used to wear a garland of buttercups in her hair.

The Sharon who stood in the doorway waiting to be rescued.

(What a pity her knight in shining armour turned out to be Bwana.)

My nephews, sitting against tip stools, were hearing about their long-dead aunts and grandparents for the first time because whatever tale Sharon had spun before, I could tell from their reaction it wasn't this one.

Kolladao appeared incredulous at first, then he muttered something about looking to the future and letting sleeping dogs lie.

Ako took this new information into himself and kept it there, for his own private examination.

Ndewele looked curious at first, then those pretty violet eyes of his glazed over, as if it was all too much. But by the end of the night they were blazing coals.

Me and Sharon sat shoulder-to-shoulder in those candlelit hours, wrapped up in quilts on her front lawn.

Our legs spread straight out in front of us like we were on our shared bed in the cottage again, wriggling our toes.

My feet were bruised, scarred, crusty, burnt, battered, my toenails blackened or broken off.

Hers were smooth, creamed, plump, unblemished, her long,

manicured toenails polished with blue glitter.

I struggled for words, overwhelmed at the task of painting for her the pictures of my intervening years, unsure that I could. Should I pick out the main events or start at the beginning?

Sharon, on the other hand, couldn't get the words out fast enough and referred to our childhood as if it were yesterday.

'Member yu waz always singing dat song to git at mi? How it go? *Lavanda bloo, diddy diddy/Lavanda green/When he is king, diddy diddy/Yu won't be kween.* Lemme tell yu, Doris, it reallee did piss me off! You waz always windin mi up and getting away wid it.'

Arrested development, I think they call it.

I had put my childhood in its rightful place, as history to be revisited but not relived.

When I began to tell her about my punishment at the hands of Bwana, she winced and changed the subject.

'Lawd! Member Percy?' she said, pinching my thigh.

She told me that Percy had been enslaved too.

Percy?

Even though he was a slave trader himself.

Are you kidding?

'Dem call him Adongo an mek him wurk like a donkee at Wordee Park. De odder slaves despise him when dey find out who he iz. Ran off twice, end up krippel when ovaseer chop off him two foot. Non-a de odder slaves kould afford to feed him, or wanted to, so him starve an die.'

The mighty so fallen, it was hard to imagine.

BEFORE –
Name: Lord Perceval Montague
Abode: Montague Manor, England
Occupation: Feudal landlord

239

AFTER —

Name: Adongo
Abode: Hovel, Worthy Park Estate, New Ambossa
Occupation: Field slave or (colloq) *Feeld wiggarrrr!*

When morning finally made its exhibitionist entrance in
all its blazing, hazy, twittering glory, my nephews brought
their mum and auntie breakfast of thick red sazda porridge
with peanut sauce. Ako barely touched his before scooting
off to the warehouse, as if he couldn't wait to be rid of us.
Kolladao and Ndewele, clearly fascinated by me as their
reinvented aunt, set off at a more reluctant pace for the stables
to saddle up.

Watching those boys disappear up the dirt pathway, dressed
in clean calico loincloths, trailing whips in the gravel, I saw they
had inherited my father's gangly frame, his stoop and dogged
walk. Something in their genes or the way Sharon once moved
must have transferred – before she submerged herself.

With a different twist of fate those boys would have been
growing cabbages on windswept moors by now, men of integrity, serfs who would rant about the working man having his
day. They wouldn't be carrying whips to work knowing that,
in order to keep their jobs, at least one person was going to
feel its licks before the sun set.

Sharon turned to me, looking as tired as I felt.

'Betta go work, Doris, or Nonso git mad or madda. He iz
one crazee man dese days. Bwana nyot so bad. Bwana haz
morals but dat Nonso just a hanimal.'

I coughed and almost choked.

'Sure,' I replied, clearing my throat. 'I'd better go fiddle the
accounts to save Nonso's sorry arse.'

Except that was lowermost on my mind.

I took a deep breath and decided to say what was uppermost, aware that wherever my sister's loyalties lay, she would never betray me.

I told her about Yao and Dingiswayo and their mother, Ye Memé, who had taken me under her wing when I first arrived and saved my life; and about Ma Marjani too, both good women and good friends to me.

I told her about the imminent sale of the boys to the Amarikas and how it would break their mothers' hearts.

I told her that King Shaka would be instructed to keep the boys out of sight when Bwana arrived.

I told her that by the end of the first day of festivities everyone would be so rat-arsed I could sneak off.

I asked her, without stopping for breath, if she could, or would, help me escape with the boys?

Sharon was silent for so long that when I eventually dared look at her, I saw tears streaming down her cheeks.

'So dis iz how it go? Mi find yu onlee to loose yu, mi sista?'

I wiped her face dry, which only made her cry more. Now I was the big sister and she was the big baby.

I gathered her hands in the palms of mine.

Yes, this is how it goes.

'Wid yu, Doris, fe de furz time since I waz a-kaptcha it feel like mi git Sharon bak. I had to kill her becorze nobuddee wanted to know dat gyal. Bwana call mi Iffianachukwana an dat waz who I had to be. Sharon ded. Sharon famlee ded. Sharon home ded. Sharon kuntree ded. All I had to do waz mek shure Miss Iffie stay alive.'

That's all we ever did.

'Mi cyant complane,' she added, sniffing. 'I hav a gud life in dis place. I got it easee, parativly speakin. Yu had it harda dan me an if mi sista want fe free, she must be free. Cyant deny her dat.'

I helped her rise to her feet, slowly. She stopped midway and rubbed her knees.

Then, she stood upright, without leaning on the canes, and arched her back.

A surprise, she was taller than me, and quite imposing.

She would have been magnificent, once.

Sharon blew her nose with her thumb and spun into action.

'No use cryin in dis life. Cryin nyot help anybuddee. Mi neva cry cept today, Doris. Troolee, neva. Mi iz one bad-ass knuckle-hed. Best way, Sista.

'Now lissan carefully. We hav to move like milatree oper-ashun so yu don't git kaptcha. I been here longa dan anyone so I know de ropes.'

King Shaka had helped others escape, which was less shocking to hear than if I'd been told a day earlier. He and Sharon were good friends, she said, crossing her fingers – 'Like dis!'

He would hide Yao and Dingiswayo in one of the mountain caves.

I would tell Ye Memé and Ma Marjani the plan, and get their approval.

I'd been thinking of Qwashee too, wondering if my man was ready for a little freedom.

'Okee-dokee,' she nodded. 'Den yu must aks him, but onlee if yu trust him wid yu life.'

'Ndewele mite be ready too,' she threw in, looking up at the sky.

I was horrified. He might be my nephew but he was also a slave driver.

She leapt to his defence.

'Yu tink say mi bwoys hav-a choice? What choice? Dem slaves too, like all a-we. If he don't grab dis chance, he will live a-regret it. Ndewele always dreamin about bein free. De odders? Well, Kolladao like bein in charge, tek afta his poopa. Born leeder, dat one. Ako? Who knows what goes on in dat bwoy's head becorze him neva open up.

'Doris, yu mite tink mi iz a selfish ole sow livin it up, but dis will show yu mi iz a betta purson dan yu tink. Why? Becorze mi lov Ndewele so much. Yu tink say I want him a-go? No ways! Mi know I *hav* to let him go. Big diffrance. It time fe dat bwoy to eskape afore he turn out like one-a his brudders.'

What about the danger for those left behind?

'Bwana neva suspec his Iffie. King Shaka always cova his trak so he be all rite. Ma Marjani one-a de best wurkers on dis plantayshun so dey shud leave she alone. Az fe dat Ye Memé? Nonso fava dat one fe some reason nobuddee can work out becorze she iz so damned facety an stand up to him. Mebbe he admire her deep down. Oh! Don't be surprize about what I know, Doris. I hear *everyting* – about yu too, de new arrival wid de scar-up bak dem call Miss Omo, onlee mi didn't know yu waz mi sista.

'King Shaka will git message to Magik who always tek rekommendashun from him, so long az he onlee aks once in a bloo moon. Yu heard a-him? Leader of Maroon Guerrilla Armee, used to be carpenta at dis place.'

That floored me. Of course, she would have known him.

I had, I replied, and always wondered if he was the man who'd been my lover back in Londolo.

'What his name in dose days?' she asked.

'Ndumbo,' I replied.

Her eyes lit up.

'An his home-kuntree name?'

'Frank.'

'Guess what, Doris. Same one, dearie, same one. What a gorjas man if eva I did see one. Him neva did speak much but I'm de kinda purson who prod an pry until peepal open up.

I almost passed out.

'Magik's men will come down to meet yu halfway, probablee. Mebbe yu luky an Magik hisself will come all de way for his ole sweetheart.

'Lissan hard, Sista. Trik to eskapin dis place is to avoid de forest becorze it like trap an dose hounds will sniff yu out. Yu hav to hed fe de riva when de festival iz in full swing an de gards slak becorze dem don't suspect anybuddee be tryin to eskape. Moment yu start a-walk, scatta peppa to confuze de dogs. Den, hed fe de riva an keep to it. Wade in de wata, Doris, member to wade in de water, becorze dat way dose bludhownds neva pik up de scent an yu larfin all de way to dat place call Freedom Kuntree.

'Whatever happen, Doris, member to wade in de wata.'

Adrenaline made me feel as if I'd slept a full night.

The first thing I did when I got into work, the *office*, was to sort out Nonso's accounts. Where money had been withdrawn and was unaccounted for, I entered it under a new heading – Gambling Debts.

That should do the trick.

I did follow one of his instructions to the letter. I made Yao and Dingiswayo disappear from the records.

Then I printed up a fake account sheet to show Nonso, although King Shaka told me that our boss was in such a panic about Bwana's visit he'd spent all night hitting the bottle again. He'd spend all day sleeping it off, I replied, confident that surrogate mummy was taking care of business.

Nonso needed me, the woman who had looked after him as a child, and in his fugged-up state he had no choice but to trust me.

Once I'd stitched the pair of them up, I realised I had to take the milky-white sap of the oleander plant with me when I hit the high road, because if my neat little plan went awry, nobody would get a chance to roast *me* over a fire, alive or not, thank you very much.

King Shaka was in and out of the office all day like a man on a mission. In between running errands for Massa Rotimi who was co-ordinating the welcome-home party, he'd been sorting out my Great Escape.

Magik's men had been contacted via talking bagpipes and responded. We were set to go at the end of the morrow.

Yao and Dingiswayo were to be taken to the mountain cave that night by King Shaka.

We agreed that when I finished in the office, I'd go down to the quarter to tell Ye Memé and Ma Marjani our plans, which I was dreading.

I'd then ask Qwashee if he wanted to come too.

(I hoped the Frank–Qwashee conundrum would sort itself out.)

I left the fake accounts information for Nonso on the desk, should he wake up and remember what he'd asked me to do before he drank himself into oblivion again.

It was pitch black when I made the trip back down the logwood drive. I held a candle before me, flicking off a plague of irksome midges, and found myself entangled in the luminous blue threads of glow-worms which hung from the trees to catch their prey. As I stepped on twigs it felt like I was crushing tiny bird bones. I prayed I'd avoid an encounter with the snakes and poisonous spiders which crept freely around the grounds in the absence of human sound.

I was leaving Nonso's palatial quarters for the spartan world of the slaves' quarter and as I got nearer I could hear laughter and song: *Don't sit unda de appal tree/ Wid anyone else but mi/ Anyone else but mi/ anyone else but me.*

People were staying up late, enjoying the prospect of a three-day holiday.

They'd be so happy.

When I entered that intense, noisy, throbbing, overcrowded society it was as a changed woman.

In less than two days the inconceivable had happened.

I had found a sister.

I had become an aunt thrice over.

I was making my second bid for freedom.

I had carried out a serious act of sabotage and I would soon meet the man I'd once truly loved.

Above all, I had discovered the fate of my family.

There would be no family reunion around the fire, no toasting muffins over it, no sing-song and bashing of pans.

Now that it was gone, I realised how much I was embedded in the past.

I had to let it go because there was no future in it.

But to let go of hope? After so long?

I was tearing up inside but I had to hold myself together.

For myself and the boys.

Until we were free.

Then, and only then, would I allow myself to grieve.

I found Ye Memé and Ma Marjani waiting for me, both in their dirty work-a-day wrappas, sitting with King Shaka behind some bushes some distance from the silk cotton tree which was noisy with revellers. As soon as I sat down, he slipped away to wait in the shadows.

This was my call.

After even the shortest time in the airy upper echelons of plantation society, my field worker friends suddenly seemed so downtrodden, so grungy, so deeply unpampered.

The quarter looked so ramshackle too, so damned *poor*.

'Hark! Look what de cat drag in!' was Ye Memé's cut-eye greeting to me before she produced the loudest, most disgusted, most vulgar, most extended tchups ever directed at a human being.

I thought she was going to land one on me and was prepared to duck.

Instead she went to stand up as if to make a dramatic departure, changed her mind, sat herself back down again and with much arm-waving proceeded to get it off her chest.

'Yu iz one ungrateful woman, Miss Omo. Yu iz a lyar an a deceeva. Mi did tek gud-gud care of yu an mek yu mi speshal frend when all dis time yu been keepin big-big sekret. What!? Yu wurk in Bwana house as hiz pursonal hassistance bak dere ova de wata an neva did tell mi? How yu tink dat mek mi feel to hear from odder peepal when I should be de furz to know? Yu iz one snake in-a de grass, laydee!'

It was so good to see her again, in spite of her tirade. I knew that as soon as she let off steam, the valve would be just as quickly turned down and her rage would fizzle out. I had grown to love her and Ma so much. But I *was* afraid of what I had to tell them.

The bottom line was that they were about to lose their sons.

As best I could, I tried to explain myself to my two friends. How I didn't want to be singled out as different. How I never thought anyone would find out about my past because I was consigned to field work for ever. I even told them that I didn't think they were interested in my life back in Londolo, because whenever I spoke of the capital city, they changed the subject. This had made me feel insignificant, I said, laying it on a bit thick. Worthless. Unaccepted.

The women, so used to occupying the moral high ground, were taken aback that they could be at fault here. While they were in this doubting state, I broke the news about Yao and Dingiswayo's imminent sale overseas and my plan to thwart it.

Ye Memé seemed helpless in the moments that followed. My friend, who was so powerful at times she almost appeared superhuman, could do absolutely nothing to alter the fact that two more of her children were going to be taken away for ever.

Watching her break down was awful. Ye Memé, the strongest woman I had ever known, lost it. She screwed up her face and emitted a silent scream. She threw herself onto the ground, thumped it with her fists. She clawed at the soil and grabbed fistfuls and stuffed them into her mouth, spitting them out when they choked her.

Ma Marjani put a hand over her mouth and tried to restrain her. King Shaka and I joined in until she became subdued.

All four of us then wept.

King Shaka too, who, some sixty years after he had been kidnapped, still thought about his family back in Margate every day.

The revellers under the tree hadn't heard a thing.

Finally she sat up and spoke, looking as vulnerable as any adult could.

'Mi betta go say gudbye to mi sons. Miss Omo, yu tell Mista Magik to com fe mi an de rest of mi pikney when dey iz olda. Mi nyot stay here no more if mi can help it. Dis iz too much fe a woman a-tek. Iz time fe Ye Memé to find some freedom. Ma, yu comin?'

'No! Mi stayin,' came the adamant, injured reply.

Ma's whole world was falling apart.

'Ma Marjani ain't climbin no mountanes or gettin tortcha if kaptcha. An mi tink it de best ting a-happen fe Dingiswayo, by de way. We lose dat bwoy but freedom mek a betta man out-a him, away from dose wotless gang boys he admire an aspire.'

She paused, muttering, 'If him reach . . .'

I stood to go, never more energised, never more exhausted.

When Qwashee opened his door, wading out of the stupor of sleep, the irritation which flickered across his features was quickly superseded by relief. When he saw me he hugged me warmly but when I told him my plan he held me at arm's length.

He then revealed a backbone I wasn't, up to that point, quite sure he even possessed.

'Yu want me fe up stiks an go off on wild-goose chase? Yu expect me to mek instant desishun to risk mi life? Yu know how lawng it tek mi to aks yu to come a-courtin? Mi ponda it fe ova a year, dat's how lawng. Mi need time to mull it ova but yu don't give me time. Iz dat reasonabal?'

Nothing about our lives is reasonable, Qwashee.

We spent that night as if it were our last.

Ripe, red pinches stained the glutes of his thin, hard thighs.

Crab-claw scratches ran down his bony back.

I sucked the blood out of his neck.

'Yu iz one pashanate woman dis nite,' he whispered.

'No – furious,' I grunted, leaving tooth marks on his shoulders.

★

My last morning on the plantation arrived and Qwashee still hadn't made up his mind.

I left him before he awoke, knowing that the boys were my priority.

Wotless man!

The whole quarter was awake before dawn, as normal.

Instead of the usual mass exodus up the hill, however, people pottered around their huts, the air bristling with expectation. After a late night people were in conservation mode, saving their spirits for the drinking, dancing and loving-up which would last the next three glorious days.

Ye Memé didn't emerge all morning.

I took care of Lolli, while Ma Marjani looked after Inaani, Akiki and Cabion.

By early afternoon a messenger ran in announcing that Bwana would shortly enter the gates of the estate:

Boss-man comin! Git in line! Boss-man comin! Git in line!

I was playing hopscotch with Lolli, one of my steps equalling two of hers. I tried to match her shrill giggles as if I too was having the greatest fun in the whole wide world.

I dreaded to think what was going to happen to her when her bones stretched lengthways and female curves began to round off her vertical planes.

Would she even have that long?

Ye Memé staggered out of the darkness of the hut into the glare, rubbing her eyes.

While Ma lined the children up I snatched Lolli from where we were playing and put her down outside the hut. I held her tight against my legs, my arms clasped over her chest.

My peripheral vision registered Qwashee watching me.

Everyone wore Sunday-best, which visitors to the plantation

always found quaint. They kept readjusting their garments: realigning the waists of ruffled white skirts, smoothing down calico breeches, retying elaborate headscarves, wiping sweat off foreheads and upper lips.

The singing must have begun at the gates. We picked it up and amplified it – just as the chariot of the gods appeared over the hill:

> Yu iz we sunshine
> We onlee sunshine.
> Yu mek we happee
> When skies iz grey.
> You neva know, Bwana
> How much we loves yu.
> Please don't tek we sunshine away.

Bwana was in a kind of gold-plated, open-top carriage more suited to the flashy metropolis than the outback. He wore a leopard-skin cape and feathered headdress. A heavy gold chain with a massive gold pendant in the shape of a ram's head hung between his not inconsiderable breasts.

At his side was Bamwoze, who looked amused.

Sitting in the seat opposite was Nonso, who didn't.

Walking in front were two Ambossan men who conducted a head count of the workforce.

The carriage moved at a trot to where I stood.

My arms tightened around Lolli.

Bamwoze was initially surprised when he saw his former nanny. This soon gave way to a patronising shake of his head which read, *You certainly ballsed it up, didn't you?*

Nonso flashed me a look intended to reaffirm a contract he imagined we had agreed upon.

Bwana, who would have been expecting to see me, was

nonetheless taken aback. He arrested a gasp just in time to keep his composure. Maybe it was that I looked so different? Or he suddenly recalled my flogging? Did he feel guilt? Sympathy? Doubt?

The chink in his armour encouraged me to look up at him with the kind of kamikaze boldness I'd last displayed when I'd had my final face-off with Little Miracle. While appearing to sing the welcoming song, I mouthed something so vile that even if Bwana couldn't lip-read, he'd still get the message.

It worked. He looked embarrassed. Take that, bastard! He switched his attention onto Ye Memé, who stood at my side singing her heart out. He bestowed a flustered proprietorial nod of recognition upon my friend as the wheels of his carriage continued to roll on around a corner.

At which point there was a communal sigh of relief, people fanned themselves with their hands or sank to their knees to take five.

Not me, though. I wasn't unduly sticky or hot, nor did I have the shakes.

I couldn't afford to.

Then the festivities began.

Barrels of rum and beer were rolled down the lanes and carts of food arrived. There was so much of everything: conch soup with coco bread, rice with red kidney beans, chiken-a-palm-wine, mash-up sweet potato, Welsh rarebit, *gizzada* tarts filled with shredded coconut, *duckanoo* dessert.

Once people had stretched their guts to full capacity they began to work off the calories. They swayed hips and stamped feet, clapped hands and shook rattles, banged drums and played fiddles. They blew into raspy flutes made from reeds, and bagpipes made from leather, and trumpets made from metal tubes, and mouth organs made from wood. They thumbed the fingers of the *mbira* and ran sticks up and down the serrated grooves of washboards and started up line dances and *ole-kuntree* dances and supple-hipped Ambossan dances.

Ye Memé kicked up her heels and drank more rum than anyone more quickly than anyone and spun herself into such a sweaty, wild-eyed frenzy of flapping white cotton that she soon collapsed onto the ground.

Two men carried her inside.

I went to say goodbye.

She was out for the count.

I kissed her cheek and told her I'd *mek damn shure Magik come a-callin fe yu an yu pikney when dey iz olda.*

Up at the Great House a more sedate party would be in full swing. The local slave owners and island dignitaries had been arriving in their carriages all afternoon.

I could just imagine it: tinkling goblets, dainty finger food before the evening sit-down feast, the delicate chords of a quartet of koras, a humming chorus, a Bedouin-style pavilion, discreet two-faced chit-chat among the ladies, competitive ribaldry among the men, flirtatious gestures between those already betrothed or married to another.

Bwana would have no choice but to play host to his most *esteemed* guests.

The audit would have to wait until the festivities were over.

Nonso would be crapping himself.

Lolli stuffed herself with so many *gizzadas* she vomited.

I picked her up and carried her inside.

My fragile sunflower of a child was so light, damp and limp in my arms.

I laid her down to sleep next to her mother and kissed my little darling goodbye.

When I left that hut for the last time, I caught Ma leading the other kids on a rumba through the quarter.

Before they turned a corner, she turned her head and saluted.

I saluted right back.

And then there was just me.

I sat sober and quiet outside the hut in the dark, away from the lamplight and noise of the party-goers.

I sat on the plain, solid, practical bench which was all Frank's handiwork.

I ran my hands over its smooth, worn, splinterless surface as if it were a lover.

Qwashee was nowhere to be seen.

Damn you, Qwashee. Damn you!

After an age of waiting, King Shaka ambled past.

I slipped away unnoticed by the party-goers, provisions strapped to a cloth on my back as if I were carrying an infant.

Tucked into my skirt was a leather pouch containing oleander sap.

I followed King Shaka at a distance up the deserted pathways which ran by the river and fields, keeping to the bushes, aiming for the edge of the estate.

The old man went so fast I struggled to keep up. With each step he shed years. The utter determination in his walk gave me confidence.

It was chillier beyond the quarter, away from the heat of buildings and bodies. I looked forward to the cooler climate of the mountains and for the first time wondered what kind of life I'd have up there.

If I made it.

If *we* made it.

We passed the shrine which normally rocked with the frenzied outpourings of its congregation.

It was now a tomb-like catacomb.

I walked as if I was invisible.

Aware that any heavy breath or clumsy step might alert one of the few guards not given time off.

Thank God the moon was a no-show that night.

King Shaka reached the perimeter fence, two planks of which he easily uprooted. Once we'd passed through, he set the planks back down again.

We were now beyond the borders of the plantation.

I was officially a runaway, an absconder, someone to be made an example of.

I walked side by side with King Shaka, who had not yet said a word.

Some distance in, he collected a sack from under a bush and scooped out a handful of ground red chilli pepper which he began to scatter behind us, handing me some to do the same.

It stung my hands, but I wasn't complaining.

On and on we went, keeping close to foliage, to trees, sometimes leaving the river before picking it up again.

Eventually we came to a low range of foothills where, hidden behind some bracken, was a cave.

King Shaka crawled inside and I followed.

He pulled the bracken back behind him.

I could hear breathing, sense the warmth of human bodies.

Yao rushed into my arms and I held his trembling young body.

Dingiswayo came over to sit at my feet. I patted his head.

King Shaka lit a candle.

Both boys were shaken, although Dingiswayo kept his head down.

I had thought about their rescue but not their losses – family, home, the known.

To be honest, I hadn't thought *any* of it through.

When Dingiswayo tried to restrain a whimper, I gathered him close to me too. He tried to pull away but I was insistent.

I held one boy under each arm.

Soon we heard the sound of bracken brushing against the ground.

Ndewele crept in on his knees, looking more alive than ever he had.

Terrified, the boys scuttled to the back of the cave.

It was Ndewele, the slave driver.

He reassured them that everything would be fine. They must think of him as a big brother from now on.

He would take care of them.

I felt grateful.

I told them he was my sister's child.

I wondered if I could love him – my nephew.

Next came another man who was so light on his feet we barely heard him before he ducked into the cave. It was Qwashee.

I muffled a laugh and slapped him playfully on his backside.

He grinned bashfully, whispering, 'Yu tink say dis man cyant mek up his mind?'

King Shaka addressed us all:

'Ndewele has instrukshun on where Maroon will meet yu. It tek two nite and a day, so pray to de gahds nobuddy notice yu missin an if so, dey keep schtum. Mebbe Bwana notice

Ndewele gone but him have so much a-do wid sortin out Nonso, mebbe he let it slip.

'Furzlee, yu must be careful of de man-trap, nyot just Massa nastiness but Maroon clevaness, what dey call "five finga wiss". It a vine stretched ova a hole in de ground wid stakes comin right up so yu git impaled.

'Secundlee, all-a yu have to bush-up. Outside yu find leaves an branches wid string attach so yu can git disguise.

'Now – tek dis.'

He handed us each a bundle of large, heavy leaves which I didn't recognise.

'One leaf store enuf rain wata to drink fe one day. Yu will need it when de route divert from de riva.

'An dis too.'

He dumped the sack of pepper onto the floor of the cave.

'Lastlee, if yu git kaptcha?'

He seemed to shout the following words without actually raising his voice:

'KEEP – YU – DAMNED – MOWTS – SHUT!'

At that, he crawled back out of the cave.

And was gone.

Stunned, we sat there a few moments.

A tight family unit now, relying on each other for survival.

I expected Ndewele or Qwashee to take control, then realised it was I who should assume leadership. Ndewele knew the route and Qwashee was a strong male, but I had made this happen, for myself, for the boys, for the friends I'd left behind.

I felt so calm, so level-headed, so powerful.

We left the cave, bushed-up as directed, and headed for the river.

Ndewele asked, with surprising deference, if he should walk in front to test the best way over the riverbed.

I nodded.

He kept to the shallow edge, careful with each step.

Dingiswayo followed him, trying on Ndewele's manly walk for size.

I gripped Yao's clammy hands, remembering how Garanwyn had once gripped mine.

Qwashee brought up the rear, carrying the sack of pepper.

When I stepped into the river, soft sludge seeped through my toes and the rush of cold water invigorated my hot, dirty feet.

It was coming all the way down from Freedom Country.

Postscript

Nonso was banished from the plantation by his father and died a few years later at the Port of Mo Bassa from syphilis. He left behind one estranged wife and five legitimate children.

Bamwoze turned the plantation into the most prosperous in West Japan, and the most fortified. When emancipation arrived fifty years later, he was renowned worldwide as the most venerable Chief Katamba II.

Bwana died peacefully in Londolo, surrounded by various wives, children and grandchildren. In the last issue of *The Flame* he wrote that he'd had a good life, but only because, *Dear Reader, I was willing to roll up my sleeves and work bloody hard*.

King Shaka was implicated in Yao's and Dingiswayo's escape but blamed Ndewele, in whom he'd confided their whereabouts. Sharon corroborated his story.
    She got away with it. He didn't.

King Shaka escaped physical punishment but was put out to pasture. He was forced to subsist on the goodwill of the slaves' quarter – which was bountiful.

Sharon remained Bwana's favourite until her heart finally gave up the ghost – eight months after she lost her son and her sister.

Ye Memé was subjected to the thumbscrews. When this didn't break her she was flayed with a thorny switch until her back was a mess of bloodied flesh. When she still refused to talk, Massa Rotimi sawed off her tongue.

Frank was not the quiet man I had once known. He was an angry man, a warrior man, a married man. He took care of the love of his youth, but was never again my companion.

In the Maroon camp, Qwashee wasn't fierce enough to stake his claim – to land, to rank, to the woman he loved. He took to palm wine, until palm wine took him.

Lolli had her first child at thirteen and died giving birth to her seventh at twenty-three.

Ma Marjani raised the ones who survived.

Dingiswayo went down as the most fearless Maroon guerrilla leader in history. Many times he tried, and many times he failed, to rescue his family enslaved in the valley.

The Maroons never trusted Ndewele. I was his only advocate. He took off for the port, hoping to pass as free. If he succeeded, we never found out.

Yao grew up a kind man, a thinking man, a free man. He taught his kids to read and write. After emancipation, his eldest son, Dingiswayo II, became the first whyte school-teacher on the island of New Ambossa.

As for my three lost children – they never found me.

*

When freedom came, an elderly man called Pa Yao and a very old woman called Miss Doris trekked down from the mountains to Home Sweet Home.

The pathways were exactly the same, even the red gingers, purple bougainvillea and the golden heliconia.

Sleeping in a hammock slung between the sprawling branches of the silk cotton tree was a shrunken old woman with sucked-in cheeks.

Her bones were still those of a Viking.

When she opened her eyes and saw us – she was speechless.

In the twenty-first century, Bwana's descendants still own the sugar estate and are among the grandest and wealthiest families in the United Kingdom of Great Ambossa, where they all reside.

The cane workers, many of whom are descended from the original slaves, are paid.

Acknowledgements

I would like to remember and thank my wonderful agent Kate Jones at ICM who sadly passed away a few months before this book was published; and to thank my new agent Karolina Sutton and the team at ICM/Curtis Brown for getting this book on the road.

As always, big up to my editor Simon Prosser for casting his expert eye over my drafts, and to Lesley Bryce for doing likewise; and to everyone else at Hamish Hamilton/Penguin especially Juliette Mitchell, Anna Ridley, Anna Kelly, Jayde Lynch, Donna Poppy, Debbie Hatfield, and, before she left, Francesca Main. To my early reader, Jacob Ross and to my later reader Jason Todd – *tank yu*. To Arts Council England (London) for an award to write, especially Charles Beckett. And for reading, encouraging, teasing and always supporting me with my writing, my life and everything – a big hug for my partner, David.